Hyperia Jones
and the Olive Branch Caper

Hyperia Jones, Book One

David M. Kelly

Nemesis Press

Hyoeria Jones and the Olive Branch Caper: Hyperia Jones, Book One

ISBN-13: 978-1-7771569-6-1

ISBN-10: 1-7771569-6-3

First Published 2020

Nemesis Press
Wahnapitae, Ontario

www.nemesispress.com

Printed in U.S.A.

Dedication

To all the frontline workers in 2020.

Thanks for being there for us when we needed you.

One

I slammed into the glowing, blue virtuwall of the TwistCube ring, the impact hard enough to make me gasp. Despite that, I rolled with the blow, taking advantage of the shift in gravity to propel myself back to my feet and across to the left wall. I slapped the orange tag patch in the middle of the field forming the wall. I'd already tagged two, so only another three to go, but nobody wants to win by *commandeer*—the punters don't like it.

"That was an incredible Full Body Avalanche!" yelled lead commentator Donk "The Donkey" Vansteenb, the announce system managing to temporarily overpower the screaming crowds that filled the arena.

"Have to agree, Donk." Rutzali Strogonar, the second announcer, was an old-school rassler who'd come up the *hard way* as he was fond of telling everyone. He and Donk made up the FIRE— Federation of Interstellar Rassling Entertainment—lead announce team. "These two ladies have a long and bitter rivalry that's been reaching fever pitch on the run up to *PowerFall*—and that's only a couple of months away now."

"And you know neither of these two are gonna back down." Christine "Crazy" Conner sat at the end of the announcers' table, with Rutzali between her and Donk. "They're fighting for the number one challenger slot in the All-Realms Women's Title. A winner-takes-all match against Courtney Bonor at *RassleFrenzy Twenty-Three* in three standard months."

"That may be so." Donk deliberately didn't acknowledge his ex-wife. "But tonight it's all about this fight right here, right now!"

Glacia, my opponent, recovered her footing, and I crouched in readiness. I pushed off the virtuwall, using my leg muscles to drive directly at her. As I reached the gravity null point at the center of the TwistCube, I pulled into a tight ball, using the lack of inertia to perform a dramatic spin, and hit Glacia in the midriff, smashing her into a corner.

"Oh my god!" screamed Donk, slamming his meaty fist into the announcers' table. "A Pulsar! Hyperia just hit Glacia with a *massive* Spinning Pulsar! I felt the impact all the way back here. This could be it, folks. It may be all over. I don't think there's any way Glacia can recover from that. Let's see it again in flashback."

I drew a breath, knowing the broadcast channels would run the slo-mo replay of the last bit of action. This was the time to land the final blow and end the match with my signature move.

The lights next to the announce table switched to green, telling me the flashback was over. Glacia was slumped between the two opposed gravity fields, her face distorted with agony, emphasizing the icy blue cracks painted on her face. I bent my knees and drew my head tentacles back so as not to damage them and tensed the spine on top of my skull to push it up from my skull. She weighed over twenty kilos more than me, not that it mattered—this was all part of the script.

"This is it! The Venomous Spine, ladies and gentlemen. Hyperia is about to unleash the deadly, career-ending Venomous Spine!"

"It's all over now, Donk," Christine hissed, reaching across Rutzali to slap Donk's wide-brimmed hat.

I suppressed a laugh. I'd never ended anyone's career, and the small vestigial spine on the top of my head was anything but venomous. In fact, if I didn't relax it a fraction of a second before impact, it would bruise and give me a nasty headache. Glacia staggered upright, apparently disoriented by my last attack. As she turned away, I launched myself at her back.

My timing was out, and I caught her off-center. The hit still made a resounding thud and the fans cheered wildly, but it wasn't as clean as it should have been. My inertia twisted me around and I landed awkwardly, my legs slamming into the virtuwall, which gave off a metallic *bloop* as the force-wall absorbed the impact. I grabbed my knee and screamed in pain. Glacia wriggled from under me and wrapped her burly arms around my neck. Her teeth bit into my seventh head tentacle, which was definitely *not* in the script, and I reminded her by slamming my elbow into her gut.

"That was a clumsy mistake, Hype," she whispered into my earbud. "Should have finished me."

She tightened her grip, and I relaxed slightly, letting her know I was ready to submit. But, instead of backing off, the bitch piled on the pressure—sometimes she plays her part a little too well. I slapped her muscular leg several times to indicate my surrender. The crowd erupted in a mix of jeers and booing, the din rising as Glacia dropped me against the virtuwall.

"What an upset," bellowed Donk. "This is incredible. Glacia took the win! Who knows how this will turn out when these ladies meet again. Remember, you can see them at *PowerFall* in a few weeks at Wassertor Stadium, Capital City on New Emslariat III. Tickets are on sale now, but they're selling fast. Don't miss out!"

"You know that's one match nobody wants to miss, Donk," Rutzali broke in, his pasted-on grin as big as ever.

"Absolutely. What's your call on who's gonna win, Rutz?"

I quit listening when Glacia kicked me in the torso. Her toes weren't rigid, as she didn't do it to cause more damage. She was putting on a show for the crowd and rubbing my nose in her unplanned "victory." The lights flashed red around the base of the TwistCube, warning that the gravity was about to return to normal, and I slid down to the real floor as lasers and holograms projected Glacia's graphics into the space above the ring, while her thumping theme tune blasted out from all sides. The virtuwalls faded, and I dragged myself out of the arena, leaving Glacia to her gloating and posturing. I limped toward the backstage area. The collision with the wall had banged up my knee and wasn't entirely fake.

The ramp seemed a lot longer than when I'd run down it twenty minutes earlier. Partly because of my limp, but the marks love to see the defeated suffer—even when they're your fans. I wiped my forehead dramatically and staggered again as the heat from the lights tingled my skin from all sides. Every stadium has its own individual character, and O'Herlihy Park was no exception. The atmosphere was a heady mixture of adrenaline, the sweet scent of beer, and the thick odor of grilled banthawurst—the local specialty dish.

"Talk about clash of the titans!" Donk's voice sounded over the PA. "Mandraago is up next against his rival, Pinhead. Those two have been duking it out for weeks, and the feud has only gotten hotter!"

"That's true, Donk." Rutz added to the bluster. "And with the Cazarinis at ringside, who knows what might happen."

Mandraago was a red-skinned reptiloid from Nienus. He'd been part of FIRE since long before I joined and was a big crowd puller, especially since he'd developed a second career as an actor. Pinhead had been a roster fixture for years, with a solid reputation in the business as a heel.

As I turned the corner, Denton was waiting in the wings. I sensed his concern through the floppy-jowled prosthetic canine mask that covered his head completely. He looked like a Terran-dog hybrid and, according to his publicity, was some ancient god reborn. In reality, he was one hundred percent Terran, though a physically imposing one. He spent at least six standard hours in the gym daily, honing his strength, stamina, and technique. Impressive dedication, especially for one of his species, most of who tend toward the flimsy and unremarkable.

"You okay, white-eyes?" His words came out as a series of snuffling growls due to the mask's built-in vocal distorter.

"I'll be fine." My eyes aren't entirely white, but from a distance can look that way. They're more of a silvery gray with black-slitted pupils, part of my heritage as a septapoid. "Twisted something."

"You should let Dr. Lee take a look." Denton put his hand on my arm.

"Doc" Lee was our internal physician. Some people find Artificial Personalities cold and difficult to relate to, but with the mix of races among the FIRE rasslers, there wasn't anyone better qualified. Besides, we were mandated by Realms regulations to have a doctor on staff at all times.

"Don't think so." Denton being so close bothered me, despite him being a completely different species, and my skin color started to flush from blue to yellow. "I'm going to rest up in my room. I've got a medipak."

"I'll talk to Glacia. We're a family—sometimes people need a reminder."

"Don't." I didn't need his help to fight my battles. "I was clumsy."

His signature music started playing, booming through giant speakers, loud enough to make the walls tremble.

"That's my call." He barked several times. "Gotta go. Dinner later?"

"Sure. Maybe."

He pulled off his shirt revealing his glistening dark chest, ready to impress everyone in the audience, slapped my ass, and ran through the stage door. A moment later I heard the crowd erupt as he emerged into the stadium.

"Here he is! Here he is!" Donk was getting worked up again. "The winningest pro-rassler of all time. With over twenty championship titles to his name. CEO of FIRE. The hound they can't pound. The pooch who can't be screwed. Dog. Face. Denton!"

The roar of the crowd sounded like an earthquake, and I smiled. Denton loved to make a big entrance and he'd made plenty of them. He was currently running a feud with Brachyura, who stormed past me as I made my way backstage, waving his giant left claw in the air as if he'd already won the bout.

While I appreciated Denton's attempt to comfort me, what he'd said wasn't accurate. I didn't have a family, not anymore, and the FIRE rasslers were only people I worked with—most of them outcasts like me.

I locked the door behind me, then set up a close-field soligram on the couch. It wasn't especially smart, but if someone poked their head into my room, it would fool them for a few minutes into thinking I was resting. Then I opened my wardrobe case and pulled off my rassling suit. The clothes I wanted were concealed in a locked, hidden partition on the right-hand side.

The outfit looked similar to one of my early rassler costumes, a feature I'd insisted on in case someone caught me wearing it, but was actually a jet black nullsuit that covered every part of me. Rather than the usual costumes designed to emphasize the titillation factor for the audience, this was reinforced with virtually impossible-to-detect conforming body armor, and came with a number of built-in devices that were handy in emergencies. After pulling it on, I flattened my tentacles and slid the seamless mask over my head.

It took only a few seconds to unseal the narrow window and slip onto the slim ledge outside—that was the reason I'd chosen that particular dressing room. I was about sixty meters up, and the traffic below was far enough down to send a twinge through my stomach. The next building was higher than the stadium and rose into the sky like an ancient multi-generation settlement ship waiting to launch. It was an impressive sight with its glittering obsidian and glass facade, but I had no time to waste admiring it. My excuses and the soligram would only provide a cover story for so long.

I clicked my heels together three times to activate the suit's built-in gravboard, and its faintly glowing bubble formed a meter-wide curve under my feet. The power reserve display appeared in front of me, showing all the vital information I could want. The mask was one-way transparent, and the display gave me a range of information and navigation signals. Power was in the green, so I kicked off from the stadium wall, plunging and then arcing back up as the magfield adjusted to demand.

I wasn't worried that anyone would spot me—the nullsuit's built-in distortion matrix took care of that. It was possible a rogue IR scanner might pick me up from the small amount of heat generated by the board and suit, but few places run those unless they're specifically looking for an IR target, and Grigstown had nothing that warranted such surveillance routinely.

Sweeping around the large obsidian building, I zipped along the eight kilometers or so to my destination with barely a hindrance to my journey, though I kept a sharp eye out for air-traffic—Iotromia II was one of the planets that allowed civilian flying vehicles. My suit was also equipped with enhanced vision capabilities, but the planet's main moon was so bright I didn't need to activate them.

My objective was a wide building rising up from the midst of extensive cultivated gardens. It wasn't as tall as the skyscraper near the stadium, but was still twenty stories high. The navigation display zoomed in as I approached, guiding me to the right balcony, and I cut power a couple of meters above it, dropping silently onto the concrete pad. A sense of relief washed over me. I've never liked heights, and the higher I get the more nervous I become. That said, I don't let it interfere with my work.

No, I'm not talking about my life as a pro-rassler—that's my fake pseudo-identity. I mean my *real* pseudo-identity—the one I keep hidden from everyone.

I'm *Tekuani*—interstellar thief for hire.

Two

Getting to the right place was the easy part. The information I'd been sent said the target was rich, powerful, and privileged, amply demonstrated by the plush twentieth-floor penthouse, the balcony of which I was currently standing on. Any mark with those qualities meant I was dealing with high-security and lots of it.

I pulled out a palm-sized multi-scanner and waved it in front of me. It was entirely passive, which limited its range but also meant it wouldn't set off any anti-scan sensors. After a few seconds, the information from the sensitive pickups was overlaid on the inside of my mask—glowing colored tracks indicating utility lines, data feeds, and most importantly the red trails highlighting environmental monitoring and alarm systems.

There were the usual movement sensors, along with entry strips around the doors and windows to detect them opening, and pressure pads by all the main entrances. Of more concern were the IR and UV sweeps that occurred every fifteen seconds. Everything else could be easily defeated. Most people don't understand the true nature of locks and security systems. Their real purpose isn't to stop professionals like me, but to dissuade people who are basically honest to begin with.

The security measures were focused around the main door, inside the building, and not against the balcony entrance. That made perfect sense—after all, who would crawl around on a balcony one hundred and twenty meters high looking to get in?

Me.

That didn't mean the way was clear to walk right in. The

triple-wide patio doors were sealed with a palm-print lock, and the internal sensor sweeps covered the doors as well.

I put the multi-scanner away and took out a portable organic residue inspector. Now I knew exactly where and what the defenses were, I had no anxieties about sweeping the beam back and forth across the surface of the palm-print scanner. The inspector was the same as the ones used in fancy hotels and homes to check if surfaces had been cleaned thoroughly and was derived from meditech. I'd modified mine slightly, and instead of just highlighting the scans, it transmitted the data to a sophisticated analyzer built in to my suit.

I waited a minute until the analyzer told me it had isolated three separate palm prints from the residue. After that it was simply a matter of programming them into the distortable nano-surface of my glove and pressing it against the door release. A light came on as the lock checked the print.

And promptly failed.

"You only fail when you stop trying," I reminded myself, and used my nullsuit's wrist interface to send the next print to my glove.

I pressed my hand to the lock again, and once more it refused to recognize me as the legitimate owner. Individual prints got mixed up sometimes and the analyzer generated "ghost" prints of nonexistent people. Pushing the last impression to the gloves, I tried again, and this time the lock blinked green. The door slid open effortlessly, and I slipped inside, patting myself on the back with my number five tentacle.

Of course it wasn't *that* simple. The fake print paused the security systems for a brief period, designed to give the owners enough time to get inside and fully cancel the security. Which I still had to do, or the alarms would lock the apartment up as tight as a maximum security jail cell and notify the authorities.

My earlier multi-scan had given me the control panel location—unsurprisingly near the main entrance. I rushed over, not knowing how long a delay was programmed into the system, and opened the access panel, revealing a keypad and an iris scanner. Next to them, a timer counted down, and it was already on twenty-four.

Pulling out a yheta-band signal mapper, I connected it to the logic circuits inside the alarm system via the standard service ports, then tapped in a code at random and projected an iris pattern into the eyepiece. The pattern and code were both fake, but the lack of either would trigger the alarm. The countdown reached fifteen, and I waited while the system verified it had some data.

Ten. The signal mapper blinked orange, and I stabbed the button, activating the rerouter. The alarm would take the code and pattern I'd entered and check them against its internal store. When this happened, the system would fail to match the ones I'd put in and the scanner would generate a signal saying they were invalid. The signal would usually be sent back to the central security server, but my signal mapper would intercept, decode, and remap it to a correct validation signal. Then return it to switch off the alarms.

The indicator on the panel turned green at "seven," and a message flashed up indicating the system was disabled. I breathed a sigh of relief and put the mapper away.

"There's a reason they call you the best," I muttered, "and it's not because you're so pretty."

I turned away and crossed the generous living room. It was large enough, and sumptuous enough, to have housed a party featuring all the representatives from the Seventeen Realms Council of Ministers. The floor was tiled with imported yellow Numidian marble from Siatuni IV, while the walls were a rich red Tongdu mahogany. The middle of the room was dominated by a circular couch surrounding a central log fire. As if that wasn't opulent enough, silvery borodium highlights sparkled throughout the area, highlighting the detailed carvings of the wall trims.

Two sweeping curved stairways wrapped around the walls on either side, leading to the upper level, and I jogged up the closest. The layouts I'd received from my current patron gave me the exact location of the merchandise I was after, and I sauntered into the spacious office on the upper floor.

The luxury continued with a large, transparent crystal desk situated by a seamless floor-to-ceiling window that was at least twenty meters wide, providing a lavish view over the city. A high-end data terminal sat on the desk, its shiny black casing polished to a mirror finish.

I ignored the all-too-obvious safe on the right-hand wall and moved to the left. It took only seconds to locate the hidden button that opened the concealed bar area. Lifting out the ice bucket, I set it on the granite counter and leaned over to check the small safe inside. It was secured with a squirkium security system that was a much tougher nut to crack than the general apartment security. I could have ripped out the whole safe, but I pride myself on being more subtle than that.

The front panel had a port for an SQ-Key. The owner would insert their key, which they would undoubtedly carry with them at all times. Then the spin-encoded photons would align their entangled little selves and—boom—the door would open.

I inserted my own SQ-Key, bulkier than the usual ones because of its built-in generator. When the key detected the lock photons, it would mimic the spin and spit out matching photons of its own. As the lock detectors are statistical in nature, there's always a tiny amount of wiggle room that makes it possible to pick them. Ten seconds later, the door popped open with an oily hiss, and I smiled behind my mask as I removed my key.

"Hyperia Jones," I murmured. "Has anyone ever told you you're the perfect mix of beauty, brains, and talent? No? Well, they should."

The safe was stuffed full of documents, but there was only one I wanted. I rifled through the pile and found an impervelope marked with the name *Teloremesis Inc.* As I pulled it out, something caught my eye. At the bottom was a blue velvet-covered box about eight centimeters square. It looked like it might be a gift for a lady, and certainly nothing to do with the operation I was on.

So I'm nosy—sue me.

I opened the box, and the air filled with a golden, iridescent glow that seemed to percolate through my suit. Inside was the shimmering snowflake of a Velturian StarPhyre.

Everyone has heard of StarPhyre crystals, though few have seen a real one. They're a rare type of alien artifact shrouded in legends so opaque that no one knows their origins. This one was hung on a gold chain, which was possibly the tackiest way of mounting one I'd seen. Despite their relative rarity, they're found on many different worlds, leading some people to declare them as religious relics, though there's no evidence for that.

They also have no known use. And yet they're the most beautiful thing ever discovered. They diffract the light so it dances and flickers, making them look as though they're on fire. What many people don't realize is that when you bring two of them together, they interact, the light from each shimmering more intensely, as if they're talking to each other through ghostly flames. And if you hold them at this point, the warmth of their dancing energy flows through you, filling you with an enchanting hum that relaxes your whole mind and body. They're worth an absolute fortune, and the Realms' richest would fight bare-knuckle matches in the gutters to own one. You're probably wondering how I know so much about them. Well, that's simple.

I have two.

Taking the chain off the one in the box, I held it high, the glimmering light reflecting off the walls around me, and for a moment it felt like I'd ascended to Kalu-Halkarti, the mythical paradise where good Lecuundans go when they die. I smiled at the display. Now I had three.

After tucking the crystal back in its box, I stuffed it and the impervelope inside my nullsuit pockets, sealing them in tight. This had been a more profitable job than expected. Not financially. I don't sell StarPhyres, even though they'd bring in hundreds of thousands of drubles. I collect them. I know it sounds crazy, but one day, I'd like to sleep in a room surrounded by them.

I imagined the pleasure that would bring, the collective heat from the crystals warming me to the depths of my soul, while the pulsing lights erased every worrisome thought from my brain. It would be the ultimate high—a new dimension of luxurious exhalation, a joyful euphoria that would make the entire universe go away. I'd never have to worry about living a lie, or keeping secrets. And I'd have no reason to live with the constant fear of being caught.

According to popular belief, that was what Inaru Goshnu had done before his infamous "miracle year," when he'd taken the Realms by storm with his philosophical—and practical—revelations. This flash of brilliance ended with him simultaneously cleaning up on the Realms stock market, dominating the best-seller list, starring in the number-one Holowood show, and founding the enigmatic—not to mention insanely profitable—Goshnu Organization for Personal Existential Exaltation. And while I didn't have any ambitions to become a billionaire businessperson, author, actor, philanthropist, or guru, I couldn't imagine anything better.

I relocked the safe and closed up the bar, making sure I left no evidence of my visit, then padded over to the office door. The interior of the apartment was almost a dead space, with heavy soundproofing eliminating most traces of the bustling city outside. But I caught a faint noise from below and drew my SomPistol from the holster on my hip. Edging around the door, I revealed the barest sliver of my head and looked out onto the balcony area. The landing was empty.

"Hyperia Jones. This is the Federal Rancheros. You are under arrest."

The staccato voice told me the speaker was an enforcement bot, confirmed a minute later when a swarm of mini-drones flew up the stairs, blocking my only way out. Their lights blinked red and blue: they were in arrest mode, and I was their target.

I tossed a couple of handfuls of ScramPills onto the landing, the little balls immediately bursting into life. Some produced a thick, black smoke, some emitted teeth-aching, high-pitched shrieking, some of them flew around strobing in IR, UV, and visible light frequencies, while others broadcast multi-spectrum radio and K-wave signals. The end result of this was confusion and disorientation. As designed by me.

The mini-drones tumbled to the floor, their simple brains far too stupid to withstand the chaotic environment I'd created. There was no exit from the office other than the way I'd come in, so I edged forward and looked onto the lower level. The polycarb blue-and-white bulk of the Ranchero-bot was clearly visible in the living room below, its multi-eyed head scanning all directions simultaneously. I suppose I could have shot it, but what was the point? It was armored all the way to its reinforced 'tronic brain. Even if I destroyed it, it had obviously been sent by someone who knew who I was, and my assault would be added to the charges.

My only chance was to break away and get off-planet as quickly as possible. Once in free-space, extradition would be almost impossible. But how had they found me? I'd never been to Iotromia II before, and had no criminal record there.

"You have been observed, Hyperia Jones." The robot targeted three red beams on me to emphasize the point. "Comply, and you will not be harmed."

Several thick slices detached from its waist and flew into the air. These were heavier drones and armed. They spiraled up, guided by the main bot, and assumed attack positions on three sides of me.

"You are surrounded. Under section fourteen of the Iotromian Penal Code. You are hereby ordered to submit to arrest and trial by your peers."

"Screw you and the tracks you rolled in on," I yelled, sending a volley of shots into the ceiling, then tossing more ScramPills for effect.

The drones returned fire, adding to the chaos, and I shuffled back toward the office, landing several solid hits on them as I retreated. The SomPistol was designed to stun people, not cause any real harm, but I was pleased to see that the drones succumbed as well. They dropped to the ground, unfortunately landing much too softly on the luxurious Gamelwool carpet.

"Damage to enforcement equipment could extend your sentence. Comply now. Resistance is iniquitous."

I wondered where the Ranchero-bot had picked up its programming. My definition of iniquitous was anything that ended up with me rotting in a jail while my synapses were reprogrammed, or involved me getting banished and imprisoned on my homeworld of Lecuunda—a truly repulsive thought.

The bot climbed the stairs behind the drones as I retreated, chewing up the ritzy carpeting with its wide tracks in a way that I was fairly sure the owners wouldn't appreciate.

"Arrest yourself for property damage, you mechanical kill-joy," I shouted, backing into the office.

A drone came in behind me, and I shot it. Three more flew in, ducking and weaving in the air to avoid my fire, and I backed up some more. Finally, the robot rolled in, looking cadaverous with the segments from its thorax missing.

"You have been cordoned. Compliance is required."

There was nothing behind me but the giant glass wall and beyond that a twenty-floor drop.

"You'll never take me alive, copper!"

Spinning around, I emptied my gun at the glass. The window shattered, creating a storm of deadly shards, and I jumped out. As I plummeted, I shredded the Teloremesis impervelope to destroy the evidence, then used the wrist interface to activate the microscopic setae on my gloves and boots, and arched my body so my fall curved toward the side of the building. As soon as I touched it, the setae grabbed hold of the glassy wall, the smooth surface no barrier to their grip. The sudden stop almost tore my hands and feet off, and I gasped as I slammed against the facade, the impact knocking the air out of me.

"Ha. That'll show you not to mess with Tekuani," I grunted between haggard breaths.

Now all that was left was to clear the scene. I reactivated my gravboard and turned to push away from the tower.

As several tyridium-reinforced shackles clicked around my wrists and ankles from the swarm of drones that had been waiting there for me to pull a stunt like this.

"Thrit..." I spat.

Three

I was in a windowless gray box of an interview room, the type you typically only see in cheesy true-crime holo-shows. The wall at the far end held a large mirror, where off-duty officers presumably watched as their teammates beat suspects with chains and pipes. I was shackled to a cold, metal table as gray as the walls, and feeling plenty miserable.

They'd forced me to take off my nullsuit and given me a set of red-and-white coveralls that not only did nothing to flatter my perfectly toned figure but also clashed horribly with my mauve skin. The effect was so bad I considered forcing an epidermal color shift but decided it wasn't worth the effort. Besides, they might not be aware of the chameleonic ability of Lecuundans, which might provide an opportunity.

The door opened and a man walked in. Not one of the local cops from what I could see. Rather than the dirt brown Ranchero uniform, he was wearing an ebony dress suit, shirt, and bow tie. Which seemed a tad overdressed for a prisoner interview.

"Help." I covered my eyes. "They've sent an opera singer to torture me. Please don't soprano me to death."

He ignored me, but paused when he saw his reflection and brushed a stray lock of his bouffant dark hair into place. Once apparently assured it was perfect, he pulled out the chair opposite me and sat, placing a holopad on the table. "I've waited a long time for this. It's a pleasure to finally meet you in person, Ms. Jones."

"You're a rassling fan?" I wriggled in my chair, pushing out the parts men get all too easily distracted by, though the stupid coveralls spoiled the effect somewhat. "If you wanted my autograph, all you had to do was ask."

"Not exactly, though I have been following your errr… *career* for some time." He hesitated. "I appreciate the offer, however."

I slid closer to the table and leaned over, knowing the coveralls would gape attractively in his direction. "Sometimes there's more on *offer* than you think."

"Well, charming as that may be, you're in rather a lot of trouble." He cleared his throat. "Criminal trespass, illegal entry, effecting bypass of official security systems, property damage, theft, distributing stolen government documents—"

"Wait a second. What did I distribute?"

"You tore up the documents you stole and threw them away, fifteen floors in the air. Oh yes, littering needs to be added."

"That seems flimsy."

He looked at the holopad and read for a few seconds. "Also, planetary invasion with intent to steal, espionage, damage to law enforcement field equipment, grand larceny-alien artifacts, evading city surveillance systems, and unlicensed operation of a levitation device."

"You make it sound *so* serious. Let me explain. I was relaxing after a tough show, engaging in my gravboarding hobby, when the unit malfunctioned and I had to make an emergency landing. Naturally, I tried to contact someone to pick me up, but before that happened, your plod-bot—which I have to add is clearly insane— tried to illegally detain me, and I was forced to defend myself from its unlawful assaults."

"There's also the matter of the outstanding Lecuundan warrant…" He smiled plasticly, tapping the holopad. "It's all in here—The Tekuani Dossier."

I sat back in my chair. This guy knew far too much for my own good, including my *genuine-for-real* identity by the sound of it. "Who the hell are you?"

"The name's Bolt. John Bolt." The holopad clattered to the table. "And you are in enough trouble that I could make you vanish for several millennia."

Although he had me backed into a corner, I still wanted to know who he was. "Freelance agent? Intersystem Intelligence Bureau?

Special Investigation Counter Intelligence Combine?"

"None of those. I'm with Olive Branch."

For the first time since my capture, my stomach trembled. I'd been sure I'd be able to talk, charm, or buy my way out of this one way or another, and if it had been the locals I might have had a chance. But Olive Branch? OB was a security and intelligence organization that, according to rumor, worked directly for the UberKaiser himself. Even among my network of specialist contacts, knowledge of OB's existence was based entirely on legends and whispers. It purportedly had overriding jurisdictional authority over all worlds within the Seventeen Realms, and was alleged to be responsible for removing not only master criminals but also, on occasion, heads of state.

"Olive Branch is a myth used to scare children."

"Boo." His eyes twinkled mischievously. "I assure you, we're far more than a myth. I'd show you my ID, but you wouldn't recognize it if I did."

"Don't bet your life on that."

Bolt reached inside his perfectly fitted dinner jacket. If he'd produced a gun at that point and shot me, I wouldn't have been surprised. Instead, he pulled out an ID-chip and put it down next to the holopad.

The air above the table swirled as streams of light formed themselves into a holographic representation of Bolt, the head and shoulder image rotating as if on a turntable. At one corner of the display field was a smaller picture of the UberKaiser, his droopy mustache and crooked nose easily recognizable. While in the opposite corner sat the royal seal and the words *Olive Branch*.

I was deeper in the thrit than I'd imagined.

Fighting to regain my composure, I relaxed and stretched my head tentacles. Holding them motionless for so long gave me a headache, and I didn't care if it disturbed him the way it did many Terrans.

"As I'm not dead or already locked in a dark cell, I assume you have some other fate planned for me."

Bolt tapped the holopad, and his security clearance vanished to be replaced by the picture of a Terran woman in her early thirties.

Even without checking the data display, I knew who she was. Her elegant, sculpted cheeks and chin, those famous come-to-bed hazel eyes, the beautiful golden-brown skin, and immaculate hair were plastered regularly in all the best gossip columns.

"Alyss Blakeston? The holo-show star?"

Blakeston was as near to a household word as it was possible to be in a galaxy of worlds as vast as the Seventeen Realms. She'd been more than famous since she was in her teens, rising to become the highest-paid female in Holowood, and was now considered the most eligible Terran woman alive, which was impressive considering that at the last count there were over twenty-three bazillion of them.

"Ms. Blakeston is engaged to be joined in civil union with one Th'opn Mrez, manager of the mining world Sparth ML2F."

"I'll be sure to send a gift."

Bolt ignored me. "Sparth ML2F is one of Metal Ventures Intersystem Group worlds and a key producer of weapons-grade Rekraitine ore. Contacts operating on Sparth have informed OB that Mrez is diverting shipments to the Kayotic League. Olive Branch's primary mission is to maintain peace and stability within the Seventeen Realms. Mrez's actions threaten that and he must be stopped at all costs." He tapped the holopad again. "This is Mrez."

Like all Zuerilians he had bony, lizard-like features, and looked like he was the one who needed the high heels in the relationship. Some women may have found him attractive, but I guessed Ms. Blakeston's interest might be ever-so-slightly more mercenary. An idea confirmed when his financial data came up and I saw his Metal Ventures salary. Planetary managers were well rewarded, but Mrez had enough to buy a *spare* planet with his earnings.

"Why would anyone that rich want more?" I asked, not expecting an answer.

Bolt closed the display. "For some people, a world is not enough, no matter how much they have. There's another aspect to this, something far more tragic."

"If you're going to mention poor little orphans, lock me up now."

"To ensure no one notices the diverted shipments, Mrez is feeding his workforce SlamCandy. The increases in production make up for what would otherwise be a significant shortfall due to his redirection efforts."

SlamCandy is banned within the Realms because of its highly addictive nature for most advanced humanoids, not to mention its minor *side-effect* of bringing about rapid collapse of the cerebral cortex. Before they die, victims can work three or four times harder than they'd otherwise be able to sustain. As it's virtually undetectable, it's become one of the top choices for professional athletes, including pro-rasslers. I hated the stuff, having seen several people succumb to its temptation—few survived.

I looked up at Bolt. "How do you know all this?"

"Ms. Blackstone isn't as innocent as her publicity and outward persona suggest. She's a low-level user, and Mrez is all too willing to feed her habit—carefully. I took it upon myself to get introduced to her at a social gathering of the Holowood academy last year. She was rather *taken* by me."

Bolt was quite pretty, for a Terran, but the idea of him getting it on with one of Holowood's elite seemed implausible. "You seduced her?"

"Oh no... I allowed *her* to seduce *me*. Women of her sort like to think they're in control, even when they're not."

What he described seemed far-fetched. Even for someone like me from the sometimes seedy world of pro-rassling, where all kinds of shenanigans went on both on- and off-camera. Sure, we put on a show—we made things up and exaggerated to please the audience. It was safe to say sometimes it got a little out of control. But to imagine that some of the biggest and brightest were no better was a little soul-destroying, and I felt I'd been given a glimpse behind a curtain to somewhere I shouldn't have seen.

"I planted an undetectable biobug in her that hooked into her central nervous system. That gave us access to everything she sees or hears. Which was how we found out about Mrez's SlamCandy connection."

I knew a little about such things. To implant that sort of device, you'd need the target's genome sequence to match the biotronics to their genetics. I suppose there were several different ways he might have arranged that if he was *that* close to her. But then he'd have to inject the biobug inside her, and I doubted that even a drugged-up Ms. Blakeston would consent to that. I said as much, and he flashed his manly smile.

"In my world, sex is a weapon and I'm the trigger."

"You mean you…?" I didn't want to finish either the sentence or the thought. "Could I have some water, now please?"

Bolt went to the door. He talked briefly to someone, and a minute later came back with a large bottle of water and two cups. Septapoids, like me, need water much more than most humanoids do. Water covers over eighty percent of Lecuunda's surface, and all higher forms of life are derived from the sea. I understand the same is true for Terrans as well as many other races, but on Lecuunda IV the phylogenetic connection is closer, more direct.

I poured a cup of water and swallowed it, followed by another. The immediate re-hydration made me feel less confused and more alert. Whatever Bolt's story about Mrez, Blakeston, or Rekraitine mining, it had no connection to me.

"So, what do you want from me, exactly?"

Bolt took a cup for himself and sipped on it, then walked away from the table, his hands clasped casually behind his back as though he was wondering how much to tell me. It didn't take a three hundred IQ to know he wasn't going to be completely honest with me.

"Can I be completely honest with you?" he said, turning back.

I lifted my shackled wrists. "You're holding all the cards."

"Well, this is all rather unofficial. Olive Branch doesn't usually involve outsiders, but in this case, I felt we needed the best person for the job. And you *are* considered number one in your field."

Sometimes *Lingua* throws me. It's a common language used throughout the Seventeen Realms and made up of words and fragments from all of the planets within. From what I'd heard, it originated on the Terran homeworld, but has since been extended and hybridized with many other languages. Everybody learns it as an all-purpose second language, but some of its constructs and ideas don't translate well.

"I'm not the current female champion, but I will be after *PowerFall.*"

Bolt strolled back to the table. "Not your position as a rassler... I'm talking about your renown as a cat burglar."

I had to translate the last couple of words. But after a minute or two of pondering, I understood his meaning. "You want me to steal something? For you?"

He nodded.

"For Olive Branch?"

He smiled.

My head was spinning again, and I *glugged* down several more cups of water. It sounded like Bolt had asked me to work for him and the highest, most ruthless peace-keepers in the Realms—a joke if ever I'd heard one.

"Does the Branch often make use of crooks and thieves in its operations?"

"Absolutely not. This would be entirely unsanctioned. If you're caught you will likely be killed, and if you fail you'll go to prison for a very long time."

I was liking the sound of this. Not. "Great, let's get started, shall we? And what would happen to you?"

He paused, as if considering it for the first time. "Me? Well, I might be demoted."

I stood up, pulling at the shackles, and shouted at the see-through mirror. "Jailer! I want a lawyer right now. Get this lunatic out of here."

"There's no point in that, Ms. Jones." He sat down. "The Rancheros are well aware that Olive Branch has overriding authority in criminal matters. They won't intervene on your behalf. I could kill you in here, and all that would happen is that they'd send in a cleaning bot."

"You sure know how to charm a girl, don't you?"

"Yes, I do." He gestured for me to sit. "But we haven't got time for such pleasantries right now."

"The idea of that makes me shudder."

"I need hard evidence connecting Mrez to the SlamCandy dealers. If I can prove he's using it on his workforce, I can shut him down, bring a halt to the illicit Rekraitine trade, and stop thousands of mineworkers from dying."

"And no doubt get a big promotion," I said.

He reddened slightly. "This is about justice and preventing wars. I don't care about promotions—I just want him stopped."

The lights flashed three times, and a voice sounded from a hidden speaker. "Agent Bolt. Please report to the Chief Ranchero's office immediately."

I failed entirely to conceal my smirk. "What were you saying about jurisdiction?"

He swiped up his ID-chip and holopad and marched out, his chiseled jaw set at a tight angle. As soon as the door closed, I got to work. I had no idea how long he would be gone, and this might be my only chance.

Bolt might have been an agent of Olive Branch, but he obviously didn't know everything about Septapoids. Although we follow the usual genetically streamlined humanoid shape, our distant ancestors gave us one or two inherited traits that aren't widely known. One of which was the ability to change our shape. I don't mean anything crazy like changing into a Tygarian Skyhawk or any of that silliness, but we can flatten and stretch our limbs to a greater extent than most other races.

I tried to relax, willing the muscles to stretch as I pulled against my restraints. The manufacturers weren't stupid, and the shackles tightened as my wrists changed size, but I was betting they had a more limited capacity to change than I was capable of.

Forcing my breath in and out in rapid gasps, I kept pulling. If anyone was watching me through the mirror, they'd be inside any second, but I was counting on Bolt keeping them distracted. My hands shrank and extended, and I regurgitated some of the water on them to act as a lubricant. Slowly my wrist slid farther out until first one hand, then the other, popped through the bands.

My feet were more difficult, and I had to massage them and use all the water in my gliptl sac as well as using the rest of the bottle he'd left. After a couple more minutes though, I was free, and started reversing the stretching. I heard a noise at the door and hobbled over. After stretching like that, it takes a while for the limbs to recover and return to full functionality. The door slid open, and I swung around from the side, punching my knee into Bolt's stomach to drop him.

Except it wasn't Bolt, and my knee *clanged* painfully off the Ranchero-bot's reinforced mid-section. It was the same knee I'd twanged in the TwistCube, and I staggered back with a gasp.

Bolt stepped around the bot. "Oh good, you're free. That saves me a job."

I dropped back down on the chair as the bot stationed itself inside the door, and Bolt took his place opposite me once more.

"This is the information on the SlamCandy operation." He tossed a data-flake onto the table in front of me. "They're on Guplides IV. Get me the details of the shipments to Mrez, and I'll see to it that your records here and elsewhere are expunged. Then you can get back to your normal life."

"You're going to let me go back to stealing?"

"The records will be wiped clean at the point that you complete your mission." Bolt frowned. "If you commit crimes after that, you will be open to further charges, of course."

That was the type of sneaky trick I'd expect from someone like him. "How do you expect me to get to Guplides? Have you charted a ship? What do I do for a cover?"

"That's your problem, I'm afraid. Olive Branch doesn't fund criminal activities."

I should have said something extremely rude and personal, but I'm too much of a lady for that. Instead, I thought it intensely, hoping that a latent telepathic ability would appear and zap it directly into his head.

"One last thing." He held up a cheap-looking bracelet.

"Oh please, make it harder. Are you going to tie one hand behind my back?"

"This has a TetraKlein tracker built in. So don't think of leaving here and disappearing."

"I'm surprised you didn't impregnate me with it."

He looked at me and his eyebrows flickered upwards in a *come hither* gesture. "I didn't think you'd be… *receptive* to the idea. But it's not too late."

"This will do." I clipped the bracelet to my wrist, and it automatically tightened until it was almost a second skin.

"There's also a remote detonator in it. In case we feel that you're not… cooperating fully."

I tore at it, trying to rip the thing off.

"I wouldn't do that. It's coded to detonate on removal."

I stopped. "Maybe it would be worth it to take you out, you ficksnit."

"I'll be in touch." He pushed a contact card into my hand. "This is for emergencies."

He sauntered out of the room, and I sat there for a while staring at the data-flake, hoping it would explode. How in the name of the All-encompassing Sea was I going to get to Guplides? Usually, I coordinated my jobs with the destinations on our rassling dates, which sometimes involved some serious juggling. But how the hell could I make this one happen?

Four

A Ranchero-bot brought my gear, and I changed out of the ghastly prison garb. I wasn't allowed to put my nullsuit back on, but someone had supplied a regular set of coveralls that fitted well enough that I wouldn't get mistaken for an itinerant laborer while returning to the arena. Once changed, I grabbed the data-flake and stalked out, the blood pumping noisily in my temples as I brooded on my ignominious capture and release. I was surprised no one challenged me as I left, but presumably they were following Bolt's orders.

Outside, I found a taxi waiting that flew me back. I had the car drop me at the rear entrance—I was too well known to risk the front door. The sentry droid waved me by when I produced my ID, and a couple of minutes later I walked back into my dressing room, picking the simple lock without breaking stride.

I switched off the soligram and checked the proximity log. Apparently no one had disturbed it. I slumped on the small couch, banging my fist against my thigh, almost wishing somebody had discovered my ruse. At least that would have given me something to keep my mind off my predicament.

After all the *fun*, I needed a shower and dragged myself into the tube, setting it to a soothing thirty-two degrees that reminded me of swimming in the midnight seas of Lecuunda. It was tempting to let the heat run through me and forget my immediate problems, but instead I clambered out, still steaming, and stuck the data-flake in the viewer on my table. At the very least, I ought to check the information Bolt had given me.

Guplides IV orbited a small, yellow star several parsecs away but was still part of the Kazebe Realm. That made it a little easier—at least we wouldn't have to deal with inter-realm bureaucracy—and I might be able to sell it as an extension of the current tour. It depended on Denton's existing plans. We usually had a fairly packed schedule of gigs lined up, though they'd been thinning a little recently.

The planet seemed unimpressive as habitable worlds go— standard iron/silicate mix, eighty-two percent standard radius, seventy-three percent standard grav. It was largely landlocked with a single major sea, which, coming from a largely water world, set me against it from the outset. The large land mass meant there were vast inland deserts, and most of the habitable areas were clustered around the coast. Population was surprisingly low, then I spotted the cultural classification and smiled—a Garrison World, largely used for training military personnel. That would make it easier to sell to Denton.

"If only we had an invitation."

The data presentation paused and a ping sounded, announcing a linked Stellcom message. I opened it and found myself staring at a bulky Terran. He looked like a fat Buddha who'd had a hard life—even his cropped, gray hair had wrinkles.

"I'm General Vinapo from the Fifth Battalion, and I hope I'm addressing Hyperia Jones of FIRE. I'd have to say that myself and the boys and gals here on Garrison Seven-Fiver-Niner are huge fans of both you and the show. We'd be greatly honored if you were able to find time in your undoubtedly busy schedule to visit us here on Guplides IV. We're not the fanciest of worlds, but we live, sleep, and breathe fighting and the finer points of combative arts."

This was too much of a coincidence. Bolt had to be behind it, and my estimation of him grew, along with a loathing of his blatant manipulation. Denton was a strong supporter of entertaining the troops, and so was the real CEO of the company, so a personal invitation from a bona fide general would go a long way to getting them on board. I'd missed part of the message and was about to rewind when I heard a knock on the dressing room door.

"Heads up. Emergency general staff meeting in the boss's office.

Five minutes," somebody called out. That didn't sound good.

I closed the transmission and threw on a casual outfit before making my way to Denton's office. It was a reasonable copy of his real office onboard the *Queen*, to make continuity easier. On the door a sign proclaimed "Dogface Denton, CEO and Owner" in large borodium lettering. Neither was true, but that was part of his public persona. The real CEO never came to the shows and only occasionally addressed us by Stellcom transmission. It always struck me as a waste of money, as when he did talk to us, the lighting was so subdued you couldn't see him—not even clearly enough to guess his species.

I slipped in, hoping to go unnoticed. I was still thinking about how to get us to Guplides IV and didn't want to hear *any* news—good or bad. Glacia caught my eye and gave a friendly wave. Backstage she was a complete sweetheart, regardless of her *kayfabe* personality.

Stryng gave me a whistle. He was coiled up on a seat and slid off, patting it with his tail end. At least I *think* it was his tail. He looks like a dark purple vine about four meters long, and his eye patches can be difficult to pick out sometimes. He'd told me once that he was officially classed as a legless reptile, but the truth was nobody knew what he was, and he always refused anything but the most perfunctory of examinations. Right now he was sat next to Atsuno Moon and Brachyura.

"Over here, dollface." He tapped the seat again. "Been keeping a spot warm for you to park your fine chassis on."

Stryng was a big fan of prehistoric movies, those 2D projection shows Terrans got all misty-eyed over. His favorite was a fictitious superhero with the unlikely name of *Bogie*. It all seemed rather silly to me. Despite their popularity, that world was long gone. Not purely in the sense that it was ancient history, but also because the planet only existed as legend. And, as Terrans bred like *skorci*, it was doubly hard to believe that they'd ever been confined to a single homeworld.

Pinhead was already there—no surprise as he was a loyal supporter of Denton, despite their long-time on-off feud in the 'Cube. Although his huge musculature and apple-sized head suggested he was slow witted—an idea bolstered by his public image—he was anything but. He was sitting near the front at the far side of the room talking quietly with Boots Largo, Zavara, and Glacia, undoubtedly discussing their next coordinated strategy as FIRE's chief heels.

Denton stood and everyone fell silent. Today, he looked particularly hangdog, though under the prosthetic mask he was handsome and, unlike his adopted character, was shy when it came to personal relations.

"Sorry! Sorry!" The all-too-lithe Bonor Triplets, Courtney, Shehla, and Rachelle, rushed in, late as always, and jostled their way to the front. Denton waited for everyone to settle, then looked around slowly.

"We're in trouble. Mr. Quy sent me a Stellcom message a few minutes after the show finished. The gig on Gragel VII has been pulled."

Grumbles rattled around the room, and I saw Christine mutter something to Donk over in the corner, her face full of concern.

"Don't we have a contract?" It was one of the Triplets, possibly Courtney—it was impossible to tell them apart. "Set the lawyers on them."

"We *had* a contract. But interstellar litigation is a long—and costly—process. Besides, there's something more critical." The dog-face prosthetic picked up on his emotional state and barked several times, snarling menacingly before he switched it off. "Sorry about that. I did some digging on my own. The gig has been pulled because the venue struck an exclusivity deal with ICE."

A cold murmur rippled around his office. Intersystem Combat Entertainment—better known as ICE—were our long-time hated rivals, and although we'd successfully held our own against them for a long time, their new manager, Rik "Frenzy" Fosdyke, had negotiated several lucrative deals recently.

"ICE? We should send 'em all to the great 'Cube in the sky," Stryng grumbled next to me.

"Great idea." I thought that was Shehla. "Then we'd all end up getting personality-wiped. Though in your case that would be a blessing."

The Triplets had staged a kayfabe love-quadrangle with Stryng a while back, and, although I didn't know any details, backstage rumor was that at least some of it had gotten all too real, creating a massive rift. But nobody came between the sisters for long, and now they ganged up on Stryng at every opportunity.

"Wadda you know about personality?" he sneered. "You ain't got one between the three of ya."

"At least *we* know which end is which." The extra snark made it clear it was Rachelle.

"At least *my* tail ain't for sale."

Rachelle jumped from her seat. "You wretched piece of thr—"

"Would you *all* shut the hell up." Dogface growled as deep as a mineshaft, and this time it wasn't the prosthetic. "I've got better things to do than listen to bickering."

He waited for a full minute. "Now, has anybody got any ideas for how we handle this? The payments on the *Queen* are already behind. If we don't come up with something fast, there's a good chance FIRE will go up in smoke, and us with it."

The *Ethereal Queen* was our luxurious tour ship and everyone's home away from home, even if they had their own permanent residence elsewhere. She was a beautiful craft—the last of the old Kunsard Spaceyards Grand Cruisers. Not the fastest in the Realms, but certainly among the most palatial. Simply disembarking from her at a spaceport was enough to make you feel you were worth a few megadrubles.

"What does the chairman say?" asked Boots Largo, his squeaky voice cutting across the room.

"Didn't you hear me?" Denton sounded peeved. "We lost the—"

"Nah," Boots interrupted. "*Real* chairman."

Denton went silent, and I could almost hear him counting to ten. "Mr. Quy isn't god. He expects us to take care of business ourselves."

"How do you know he not?" Boots was a little slow. "Never see more than shadow."

"Trust me." Denton held up his muscular hands. "He's not. Besides, do *you* want to be the one to tell him that ICE has taken *another* contract from us?"

Call it a string of bad luck for us, or better market research on their part, possibly what we called *rorkwal* in Lecuundan or *fate* in Lingua, but in the last year, ICE had taken several high profile gigs from us, even though we had the stronger lineup in our show. They'd been squeezing us hard, and it was beginning to hurt.

"We got variety. We got style. What the hell is wrong with those people out there?" Stryng said.

"Sure, we have all that." Denton sucked in a large breath. "But they're still winning."

Nobody said anything, including me. Although I had potentially good news, experience told me it was better to lay it on Denton privately.

"Okay. Let's pack up here. If anyone comes up with anything, let me know. I won't be contacting Mr. Quy until we're ready to up-ship."

There was a scraping of chairs and shuffling of feet as the group dispersed by stride, hop, or slither as befitted the individual. I waited until everyone left. Denton had turned his back on the room, and I saw him wriggling the prosthetic dog face off, something he rarely did while anyone was present.

"Boss," I said, keeping my voice low. "I think it's time I collected that dinner you offered me."

He wrestled the mask back down, snapping the collar closed before turning to face me.

"Hyperia? Sorry, I thought everyone was gone." The lifelike tongue slipped out of his jowls and he panted several times. "You want *dinner*? Now?"

"We're not due at the spaceport for three hours, so why not?" I parked my posterior on his desk. "Besides, I think I should grab it while your credit's still good."

I laughed, but Denton grimaced. "Things aren't that bad yet. Open or anonymous?"

If we went out as Dogface Denton and Hyperia Jones, we'd be mobbed everywhere by fans and media types, giving us no opportunity to talk. That wasn't what I needed. Almost no one knew what Denton looked like behind the mask, and if I changed my chromatophore cell pigments and used my papillae to re-texture my head tentacles while holding them back, I could pass as Terran.

"Let's go incognito. I don't want the fuss tonight."

"Still sore from earlier?"

For a moment, I thought he meant my run-in with Olive Branch, and a shiver of panic ran through me before realizing he was talking about my match with Glacia. Somehow that seemed as if it had been days ago.

Forty-five minutes later, we were seated at La Traviatra Bonhomme, the hottest restaurant on the planet. Regardless of the circumstances, Denton was never cheap. I never knew how he managed it, but incognito or not, he always arranged it so that he waltzed past any waiting lineup and straight to the best table. Rumor had it, he'd once been a famous politician who knew where all the corpses were buried, but I'd done some surreptitious checking through my Darkover contacts and found nothing that vaguely matched that idea. Other, more superstitious minds labeled him as a galactic Yodi knight who could place a spell on anyone and command them to do his bidding.

I hadn't seen any sign of that either, beyond his natural sex appeal. Even without his mask, he was handsome enough to catch the eye of any passing woman. Who knows, perhaps he'd found the mythical *Ij-abra* plant that endowed anyone who consumed it with irresistible charm.

"How's this?"

Denton had interrupted my chain of thoughts, and I jumped. "It's perfect."

The tables were arranged in a series of rings around a central stage area that was indulgently wide for a restaurant. We wasted no time in ordering, and soon our table was loaded with platters of deliciously steaming comestibles. Watching Denton munch enthusiastically on his Iotromia Giganto-shrimp made me feel a little ill. Most of the animal life on Lecuunda, including my species, was descended from ocean-based life-forms. Because of that, I'd never been able to come to terms with the idea of eating other sea life. It was irrational, but it felt like some bizarre form of cannibalism. On the other hand, mammalian life had none of that *icky* factor, and I had no guilt in ordering a lightly seared prime Galatian steak with greens and potatoes. All served with a delicious garlic fungi dressing.

"Nice place." I lifted my glass of Rescallier Estates Cabernet Vitas to toast Denton. "I'm glad you're paying."

He returned the gesture. "You didn't drag me out here in search of fine cuisine. What's on your mind?"

Denton wasn't slow, that was for sure. For a split second, I wondered how truthful I should be. My instinct was to tell him everything, but long experience has taught me that honesty is never the best policy.

"I got an unusual offer tonight via Stellcom."

Denton sprang back in his upholstered chair. "Are you telling me you're leaving FIRE? Jeez, you're the linchpin of the entire women's division. Without you, I might as well close the whole thing down."

"What? No, of course not. I got an offer for—"

Denton's knife rattled against his plate. "You've been talking to that ficksnit, Fosdyke, behind my back? If you'd told me up front, I'd have rearranged the schedule and buildups. The Triplets could have carried the lead."

"Denton—"

"What did that bastard offer you? A better contract? Guaranteed number one spot? Or was it just money? I never took you for one of the greedy ones, Hype. I might be able to squeeze a few more drubles out if—"

"Would you shut up and listen?"

"Well how much is Fosdyke offering you, for bogsakes?"

"There is no offer from Fosdyke you... you, idiot."

Denton stiffened. He'd never got me this mad before, and I guess my outburst surprised him.

"Okay..." He picked up his knife and assaulted a roll with the butter. "So, if it's not Fosdyke, who is it? Some mega-rich admirer looking to whisk you away from this tawdry... owwww!"

I'd kicked him under the table, and I wasn't gentle. "Quiet, I'm trying to help."

I waited while he rubbed his leg.

"I got a Stellcom from a General Vinapo. He runs a Realms garrison and has invited us—*all of us*—to do a show there. You know, wave the flag, entertain the troops."

Denton's jaw clenched. "All? When?"

"It's an open offer."

"You mean we could replace the Gragel VII gig? Why didn't you say something at the meeting?"

"I wanted to run it by you first. You might not have wanted to take it on such short notice. And military gigs are often hard. Besides, you're the boss."

There was always the chance when doing a show for the forces that they'd insist on showing everyone how tough *they* were, and demand a match between their biggest contender and someone from the team. Those things often ended in someone getting genuinely hurt. But the real reason I'd kept quiet was that Denton needed a break. His reputation had taken a few hits recently. It would be good for everyone if he took the laurels for the "rescue."

"You don't want any credit for this?" Denton looked puzzled.

"Not unless you think it will help."

"I guess not. This might keep the wolf from the door, for a while at least. I don't know what to say."

"Thank you is more than enough."

I felt like a complete bitch. Sure, I was helping the company out. But only to save my own ass. I also knew that if I'd put the idea forward at the general meeting, several people—also known as the Triplets—would jump on it right away. We're a tight group for the most part, but professional rivalry can make anyone a complete ficksnit.

"That's great news. Let's finish up and get back to the *Queen*. Mr. Quy will be pleased."

"Look, Denton... don't let anyone know it came from me. Even him, okay?"

He speared the last shrimp and dipped it in the remainder of the spicy sauce. "Well... sure, if that's how you want to play it. But it wouldn't do you any harm to rack up a few points with him. What's the problem?"

I could hardly tell him the real reason. Trust wasn't a luxury I could afford. "Well, he bothers me. What do we know about him after all?"

"What can I say?" Denton swallowed his shrimp. "He's a very private man."

"You've met him though, right?"

Denton shrugged. "Not as such. We set up a meeting once, but it got canceled because of a scheduling conflict."

"So, he might be anybody..."

"What? Come on, Hype. This paranoid beauty thing doesn't suit you. What do you think he is? A secret government agent or something?"

I shrugged. "Maybe. Who knows?"

Or something worse…

The spaceport was busy when we arrived, despite the lateness of the hour, local time. It was simply impractical to synchronize time across different star systems and quadrants, which meant ships arrived and left as they pleased. The *Queen* was visible through the giant glassite wall separating the lounge area from the docking berths. As always, I felt a slightly romantic feeling of peace when I saw her glittering white-and-gray exterior. She was my sanctuary, her sleek elegance the only home I had, and an escape from my checkered past on Lecuunda. She looked like a giant, metallic angelfish, a sea creature Terrans claimed originated on their homeworld, though that seemed unlikely as they were common on most sea-bearing planets, including Lecuunda.

Looming over her, farther away, the massive, tubular form of an interstellar cargo ship was cradled in a web of heavy-duty force beams that glittered blue against the night sky. The lower half seemed to fizz as if the hull were decaying as we watched, but it was, in fact, swarms of distant robot handlers flying to and from the ship to empty and reload its cargo.

"That's the *Bloviator Rising*," Denton said, pointing to the docking berths. "Biggest cargo hauler in the Realms."

I'd heard of it. It had made a splash on its launch a few years ago—twice as big as the usual cargo vessel, but with the same crew complement. Even at a distance the brash orange upper deck levels were clearly visible—marked that way to supposedly indicate their exclusivity. The ship was so large its construction had dragged three companies into bankruptcy, before it had launched.

"It looks like a fat, metallic cigar," I said.

"Cigar?" Denton lifted an eyebrow. "Where did you learn about those things?"

I laughed. "Watching Stryng's crazy movies, where else?"

Thirty minutes later, we'd cleared customs and were back on the *Queen*. I made my way through the wide, toffee-colored corridors to my room and closed the door behind me, sighing at the comforting sense of solitude that always accompanied the click of the lock.

For all that I like my fellow rasslers—most of them—and despite my flirty on-screen appearance, I was essentially a private person. My room was my refuge from an all-too-intrusive universe. It had the same toffee-and-white decor as the other rooms, but the lights had been adjusted to have a greater UV component, and I'd had the large family-sized jacuzzi converted into a saltwater pool. I'd designed both features to remind me of my hated homeworld— as the saying goes, you can take a girl out of the ocean, but you can't take the ocean out of the girl. Besides, it was perfect for those stressful moments after a hard match, or for when I was feeling sentimental, or maudlin…

Today, I was none of those, just extremely tired. Stretching your limbs to half their usual thickness wasn't something you did without paying a price. It was a survival mechanism, not a pleasantry. I jumped in the shower and switched it to the hyper-sonic massage setting. I stuck in earplugs before hitting the activation button, then luxuriated in the sensation as the waves tingled through every centimeter of my body. We didn't have anything like these on Lecuunda, and I'd fallen in love with them the first time I tried one. The cycle changed from the high-intensity "scrub" into the deep rhythmic "massage" program, and I sighed as the vibrating pulses worked the knots out of my muscles, not to mention rattling my teeth.

The audio pinged, indicating a ship-wide announcement and, a few seconds later, Denton's voice filled the room. He quickly explained how he'd been holding a potential show in hand for these circumstances, and we were now going to do a gig for the troops on Guplides IV, complete with Mr. Quy's blessing. A masterful act—even I believed him—and I slipped out of the shower ready to fall into bed when the door announcer sounded.

I grabbed a robe. "Come in."

Stryng shuffled inside. "So, what's going on, sister? You heard the announcement from Denton—" He broke off when he saw how little I was wearing, his eye spots widening as they traced every curve on my body with laser precision. "Say... we should spend more time as TwistCube partners…"

I didn't have a skin taboo—few of us in this business did. For all her luxury, the *Queen* was a little confined for people with personal space issues. Originally built as a yacht for a large private family, rumored to be distant relatives of the UberKaiser, it had later been converted into the main transport for FIRE. Also, with training and workouts, we were all likely to see, and grapple, with each other in a variety of relatively intimate ways. But Stryng always managed to turn any encounter into a bawdy moment.

"You missing Rachelle?" I tightened my robe to remove the distraction.

He snorted, his whip-like body rippling all the way down to his tail. "Woman like that would pass through a star and come out the other side frozen. You know she took my... oh forget it. But hey, we're friends right? You wouldn't treat a guy like that, would ya?"

"So, what are you thinking?" I tried to steer him back on course.

"Well, I got a new idea. If I puff up the ridges on my tail in a reverse corkscrew and—"

"Stryng…"

"We'd be good, sister. Real good. Maybe good enough we could slither away from all this and hang from the same tree together for life."

I laughed. He was such a goof sometimes. "What did you want to talk about? Besides interspecies encounters?"

"What's with the new gig? And don't tell me you don't know anything."

"I don't."

"Come on. You go for dinner with the big dog, and we're down the tubes. You come back, suddenly there's a new fixture? I don't buy it, sweetheart. What're you guys trying to pull?"

I gave him my best wide-eyed look. "I'm as much in the dark as you are. He did say something had come in while we were eating but didn't share the details. I'm as low on this totem pole as you and everyone else."

Stryng reached up and wound himself onto the light fitting. "Some people might believe that, sister, but I wasn't born on the south side of dumb."

"Don't get comfortable there." I waved up at him. "I'm ready for bed."

His eye spots doubled in size. "Now you're talking my language."

"Alone."

After more than a few grumbles, I ushered him through the door and into the corridor. As much as I love his company, sometimes he's hard work.

Five

The journey from Iotromia to Guplides was nearly twenty-three parsecs, which, even with the fantastic speeds available using Rottelmyhr Drive, would take almost two standard weeks at D3, the *Queen*'s usual cruising speed. Once out of gravimetric shock wave distance, the *Queen* squeezed into DellaqSpace with its usual sonorous *splang* and the journey was properly under way.

One of the great features of the *Ethereal Queen* is that it's semi-intelligent. By that, I mean self-directed and autonomous. But it follows orders given to it by designated individuals—it doesn't decide what it wants to do based on how it's feeling that day. More conveniently, it requires no specialized crew, making it the perfect vehicle to keep costs down for a tribe of wandering entertainers like us. As Denton was fond of saying, "nothing kills profits quicker than overhead," which was why the ship traveled at D3 instead of its maximum.

A lot of people think traveling in an autonomous ship is a cold, impersonal experience, but nothing could be further from the truth. The *Queen* has its own Artificial Personality that runs every aspect of the onboard systems, acting as the interface between the ship and its passengers. Whatever we're doing when we're onboard, Auntie is watching over us.

"Morning, Auntie," I called out to the nearest of her pickups. "How are we doing?"

"Oh hello, dear."

Auntie's voice was high pitched and fussy, always making me wonder why that particular personality had been chosen by the original owners.

"Are you keeping warm enough? Your room thermostat is set to standard temperature, and it must feel cool for you. You should keep your scarf and hat on."

I kept the temperature at regular levels, because that was the environment used in most arenas. I didn't want to handicap myself through not being acclimated."

"I'm getting ready for the next gig, Auntie. You don't have to worry about me."

"Well, of course I do, dear. That's why I'm here."

I wasn't sure how it had happened, but Auntie had convinced herself we were her new family and busied herself with making sure we were all getting enough sleep and eating healthily. She always made me feel as though I was back in school and barely into double-digits old—which wasn't really an exaggeration in terms of life experience. Auntie had been activated when the *Queen* was first commissioned, over a hundred years ago.

"So, what's the story, Auntie?"

"Well, I'm reading the collected works of Gurbir Pelucheux. At the moment I'm working through his forty-third volume, *Irreducible Tales of the Silken Woman*. He's terribly garrulous though. The story starts with the Silken woman standing on a cliff, looking out over the Seas of Rye. Her betrothed, a Yedi knight, and Ninety-first Earl of Lucaster, is lost in an abandoned settlement world, leaving her in the clutches of the evil—"

Artificial Persons can be so literal sometimes. "I meant how are we doing on the journey to Guplides, Auntie."

"You should frame your questions with greater precision, young lady." Auntie feigned a sniff. "After the initial dives through D-space, we're now on the outskirts of the Crosite system and will soon drop into normal space to recalibrate navigation. Mr. Denton has requested we lay over at a perimeter station. This would be a perfect opportunity to pick up some new thermal underwear, dear."

"Thanks, Auntie."

Ships like the *Queen* aren't common now. There's a long standing myth they're not as reliable as a regular crewed ship, but I don't see it. After all, what's more likely to be unreliable—a fully-slaved endecatronic matrix with built-in de-anomalizion, or a bunch of crazy humanoids? I think that whole *uncrewed is crude* thing is a bunch of propaganda put out by the Spacers' Guild. But nobody has asked for my opinion, and the majority of people consider crewed ships safer. That relative unpopularity resulted in a decline in construction of similar ships, which might explain how Denton got his hands on the *Queen*, though even at bargain-basement prices it must have cost a small fortune. Maybe it was supplied by Mr. Quy, which didn't explain anything—an enigma providing a mystery is no less obtuse.

Denton announced a day's layover to give us a change of scenery. I couldn't speak for the others, but as much as I loved the *Queen*, I was ready to see something different and less ostentatious. You can only endure copper-tipped cornices for so long, and the faint whistling scream I hear whenever we're in D-space would be no loss either. It must be something to do with my Lecuundan genes because apparently no one else hears it, but to me it sounds like the distant howl of a thousand tortured wraiths. Besides, the idea of seeing a bulkhead I hadn't seen a million times before, and the possibility of having a conversation, no matter how brief, with someone I didn't already know, made me a little giddy.

Kalpurnia station was an old *flying saucer* design, a broad, flattened disk with a large swollen section in the middle. As with most stations, the commercial and maintenance sections were on the periphery, with the residential areas in the spherical inner portion.

Docking took a couple of hours as we matched speeds and orientation. While this was taking place, I locked my door and opened up a scrambled q-link on my desk terminal, logging in to Darkover by confirming my identity in several different and secure ways.

Darkover was an illegal network that enfolded itself into the regular, and far more above-board, Stellcom systems everyone knows. It's a hive of rumor, gossip, and uncorroborated stories, but also the biggest trading place for illicit ops throughout the Seventeen Realms. The channels are frequently scrambled, and without an authorized crypkey you couldn't even discover it. But, if you had access, you could find any and all illegal activity on its channels. It was there that I negotiated my Tekuani contracts.

As a paid-up member of FUBAR—the Fellowship of Unscrupulous Brigands And Rapscallions—I have access to Darkover as well as a contact profile for my less public activities. It can be tricky lining up my "sideline" jobs with my rassling employment, but I'm relaxed about it. Sometimes I need to plan ahead, and I've even occasionally managed to influence our gigs to match specific jobs, but mostly I browse the boards for anything of interest once I know our destination and schedule.

Some wouldn't call me a professional thief. Pros treat it as a routine job—take few risks, look for the easiest possible challenges, and avoid conflict if at all possible. They steal purely for money, and often to order. Amateurs steal compulsively and recklessly— they're the ones who turn up on comedy crime shows. Some are simply greedy—they don't plan anything and try to grab everything they can. Many of these get caught—others become used spaceship dealers, or politicians.

I'm different. Although I'm fully qualified and licensed within the Fellowship and hold myself to professional standards, this is a hobby. For me, the thrill is all in the chase. There's something about the planning, the execution, challenging myself, and pitting my wits against the security systems that makes my bivalves pump faster. I imagine the brain-psychs would say I'm rebelling against my background, but what do they know? It's audacious, exhilarating, and fun—what else matters?

And of course, the money doesn't hurt.

There were two listings open for Kalpurnia. One was a strong-arm job, which I had no interest in. Despite my public profession and training, Tekuani prefers to use her brains rather than her muscles. The other was a recovery gig. Apparently station security had confiscated certain contraband items, and the rightful owner wanted their property back. It always amuses me when I see such abuses. Authorities throughout the Realms have long lists of rules against taking other people's property—unless it's them doing the taking of course.

I suppose I should have backed off on any plans, at least until

I was out from under Bolt's microscopic attention, but I'd never been the kind of person to bow to authority. Besides, he said my record would be wiped once I finished his mission, so if I pulled it off, it would be like having a freebie. And I certainly wasn't ready to surrender without a fight.

Finding the plans for the vault wasn't difficult. The station's data spine had complete layouts, and cross-referencing those with power schematics gave me the full picture, including details of the security in place. Naturally, this information was locked behind an impenetrable Triple-A protection block, but that posed no problem to someone as talented as me. It may be immodest to say such things, but false humility can trip you up just as easily as egomania.

The vault was sited in one of the station's busy commercial districts along an exterior wall. The plans showed several possible ways of getting in and out, but the slightly more difficult task would be avoiding the defenses while doing it. But for every problem there are fixes, and a standard security technician's portable neutralizer would take care of that. Access to neutralizers is strictly regulated and illegal for anyone without a class three technician's license. Which I had—along with one of the neutralizers.

My plan was simple, as all the best ones are. The vault's least defended area was the outer wall. Why would the company waste money and lower its undoubtedly extravagant profit margins by protecting a wall open to the hard vacuum of space? Access to the outer hull would be simple enough. As with all space stations, tourism was a big industry, and what do tourists want more than anything? To do a spacewalk. It was hard to believe that after the last few millennia of commonplace interstellar travel, mindlessly flailing around in a spacesuit was still the highlight for many.

In less than an hour, my plans were laid out, including backups and alternates, and my slot was booked on the next EZ-EVA tour, run by the appallingly named Deep Breathing Dreaming Inc.—the officially licensed vacuum operators on the station.

I opened the trunk-that-was-never-publicly-opened and pulled out the fleshy mass that was Martha—my housefrau-styled body-suit prosthetic that I used when I needed to operate openly in public. After sliding Martha on over my nullsuit and activating the micro-trac seams to tighten it around me, I was fifteen kilos heavier, looked twenty years older, and had a new head to hide my tentacles. The suit used the same technology as Denton's dog mask, but extended the coverage to the torso. The material was synthetic M-Flesh—preferred by the best fetishists—and it would take a detailed, and intimate, examination to prove I was anything other than one hundred percent stock Terran.

Gathering what gear I needed, I hid it in a generous burgundy cape trimmed with raven-colored fur, with a matching turban-style hat topped with tasteful, genuine reproduction *Goilugos* peacock feathers. When I'd finished, I looked like everyone's least favorite aunt heading out for the night in search of meaningless love, or the closest facsimile I could find. Someone to be avoided rather than welcomed.

Other than Auntie, no one was monitoring the *Queen*'s airlock as I slipped out. Not that they'd have noticed me with the nullsuit's distortion matrix in full effect. I turned immediately left, then took the next two corners at random, before finding a restroom and using it to become visible and move into the station. The microguide in my ear led me through the noisy, jostling crowds to the tour operator's location, and no one paid me much attention.

According to my research, the station was currently celebrating some local festival known by the improbable name of Fat Tuesday, though I had doubts that the term had been translated properly into Lingua. Fat or not, the corridors were teeming with people in a litany of colorful costumes, their faces hidden by grotesque masks of all shapes and sizes, making my own clothes seem positively conservative by comparison.

A young couple dashed up to me and, before I could react, draped long chains of luminescent balls around my neck. They carried multiple colored sticks and communicated their desire to paint my face, shouting over the whistles, screams, and drums around us. I declined their offer politely and moved on. This celebration would only help my cause.

The tour operator was also located along one of the outer walls, with a lineup of people already waiting for the next outing. I ambled across the wide, curved promenade toward the entrance, but hadn't taken more than ten steps when my earbuds tingled, and I hesitated. It was the feeling I get when my subconscious knows there's trouble around. I'd learned to trust it over the years, as it usually heralded some otherwise unexpected intrusion from law enforcement types.

I changed course and drifted over to a nearby store, making a show of examining the costumes on display in the windows, though I wouldn't be caught dead wearing the ghastly Kalpurnian fashions, which consisted almost entirely of cropped plaid shirts mixed with floral skirts, or even more hideous shorts that appeared to be made from the skin of some local animal.

Despite the insult to my sartorial instincts, I made my way inside the store, pretending to study the window displays from the other side while using the opportunity to scan the mob on the promenade. It didn't take long to find what had triggered my sense of danger. Across the way, and a few stores down, was a small café. There were plenty of customers, but only one with black, bouffant hair, dressed in an altogether dull business casual style that stuck out among the kaleidoscopic crowd like an unpolished pebble in a jewelry box—Bolt.

He was pretending to read a holopad, but I sensed his squinty eyes scanning the crowd behind those completely unnecessary dark glasses. He was looking for me.

I grabbed a black-and-white blouse, with short, frilly, off-shoulder sleeves and lacing across the front, and paced over to the sales counter. I paid for the repulsive garment without checking the price, then marched out of the store and away from the tour operator. I had no idea how Bolt had figured out I was going to hit the security vault, or that I'd make use of the EVA tour to do it.

Leaving the Deep Breathing Dreaming office far behind, I made several other purchases in different stores. There was no sign of Bolt following me, and I wondered if I'd been mistaken. It *could* have been someone who happened to look similar. Or perhaps a coincidence. I batted the idea away—coincidence only means you haven't seen who's working the machine.

My instincts told me to walk away and head straight back to the *Queen*. But I wasn't ready to give up yet. Now it wasn't only money that was at stake, but my reputation and professional honor too. Why did Bolt want to interfere with my plans anyway? I'd agreed to do his job—this was purely personal business. But whatever his reasons, I wouldn't let him control me.

Slipping into another restroom with my purchases, I stripped out of my original outfit and dressed in what I hoped was the height of local fashion. I discarded the cape and turban, transferring my equipment to the new clothing, but I kept the strings of glowing Fat Festival balls. I also changed Martha's skin tone to a reddish sepia, to suggest her heritage could be traced back to the Shoinshe Realm. That would further confuse my earlier appearance in case Bolt *had* spotted me. I made my way back out and shopped some more. By the time I was done, I had a third different outfit, and went to find an elevator.

After picking out an empty car, I selected the thirteenth level, then held up my various purchases against me so I could see them in the mirrored walls. It was simplicity itself: *accidentally* catching the button to stop the elevator mid-floor and slapping a blouse over the glaringly obvious optical pickup. It took barely a couple of minutes to change once more, and now I looked like a no-nonsense businesswoman, different enough in appearance to fool anyone who didn't have an intimate knowledge of my fake persona. Let's face it: men are poor observers where women are concerned. Hell, most of the time they can't spot a new hairstyle on their mate. The changes would be more than enough to give stupid Bolt the slip.

There was a metallic beep. Then I heard a male voice from a concealed speaker. "Is someone in car three? Press the button above the emergency stop to answer."

I thumbed the button. "Hello, yes, I'm in an elevator. It stopped all on its own."

"I can't see you," the voice said. "Something's blocking the camera."

"Oh dear." I faked a nervous laugh. "Am I safe? Is the elevator going to crash?"

"No, nothing like that, ma'am." The man sounded irritated. "Have you placed anything against the walls?"

"Oh, how did you know? I was admiring this blouse I bought.

It has a perfectly delightful blue brocade and frills along the edges that look like clouds in the sky."

"I think you blocked the pickup. And might have caught the emergency stop."

"Oh dear. I'm *so* sorry." I grabbed the blouse. "Is that better?"

"Yes, ma'am. Do you see the red button on the wall?"

"Red… oh yes, there it is."

"If you'll press it, ma'am, you should be back on your way."

I restarted the elevator. "Oh thank you. You're so clever. Why, I might have been stuck in here forever."

"There was no chance of that, ma'am. Have a nice day."

After leaving the elevator, I slipped into a coffee bar and ordered a large, steaming mocha choca and a high-fiber, high-fat, high-sugar tart that I normally wouldn't entertain eating and didn't plan to now. While pretending to pick at it, I checked out the others in the small, dark, wood-lined room. No one near me *looked* like an agent, but that didn't mean anything—I wasn't the only one capable of donning a disguise. What I still couldn't understand was how Bolt had uncovered my plans. I was on a space station in a different star system. Also, Denton hadn't decided on our layover until *after* we'd left Iotromia. More to the point, why was Bolt interfering in my operation now? He knew I was no innocent, dragged unwillingly into a misguided life of crime. I was a skilled veteran, with more jobs under my belt than I remembered. My temples throbbed and my bivalves pumped faster. If he thought he had the upper hand, he was in for a shock.

Mentally I reviewed my alternate plans for accessing the vault. The vent ducts offered the next best point of entry. They were far too narrow for normal humanoids, but my septapoid ancestry meant constricted places weren't the same obstacle. A minor diversion would suffice to distract the security staff, and while they were busy, I'd be in and out of the sealed vault before they noticed. This wasn't idle swagger—I really am *that* good. And pulling this off under Bolt's nose would make the operation that much sweeter.

Accessing the station's systems again through my holopad, I brought up the environmental interface. A small, and entirely fake, pressure leak would be an appropriate distraction, and something no one on a space station would ever ignore. I smiled—this was going to be fun.

After tipping my uneaten food into the reclamator, I strode into the corridor. The nearest access point in the ventilation system was eighty degrees back around the station's hub—a long walk, but it also offered a concealed entry. As I got closer, I picked up my pace. The pressure alarm was already programmed. All I had to do was activate it through my 'pad.

I turned into one of the *spoke* walkways, moving toward the access point, with my thumb hovering over the holopad in my pocket. The semi-hidden side passage was no more than fifteen meters hub-ward.

Bolt stepped around the corridor and leaned against the wall, checking the manicure on his fingernails as if casually waiting for a friend. He didn't look at me, but he shook his head silently. I spat under my breath and carried on walking, my earbuds tingling in embarrassment. This was impossible—how could he know?

Ambling farther along, I turned right, then trotted down the next stairwell. This called for extreme measures. Another wash-room visit and I peeled off my Martha disguise, then squeezed the hidden disintro button in the left buttock and tossed the already dissolving mess in the trash—it was useless. Bolt must have researched my operations far more than I'd expected. My fists clenched. This wasn't the end of it. I'd never resorted to simple armed robbery before, but it looked as though it was the right time. Either that or I'd pay a hefty FUBAR fine for accepting a job and not delivering.

After removing the M-Flesh, I felt half the size and was all too recognizable. That didn't matter as the Distortion Matrix would hide me. This time, I was going in the front. This had been an option from the outset, but most hardened vaults have Matrix suppressors or tuned frequency detectors capable of spotting people so equipped, making it not the best choice for this type of operation. But now it was the only choice, unless I wanted to forget the whole thing. And I wasn't about to let Bolt intimidate me.

I activated the field and marched straight for the vault's front entrance, relying on my nullsuit's stealth capability. I'd moved a long way from where I'd last seen Bolt. Besides, I was reasonably sure he wouldn't expect something so dramatic—not to mention unhinged—from me.

The large, blue security sign was visible long before I saw the heavily armored security bots flanking the broad doors. They were Bloodhound Mark Sevens. The Crosite star system may have been backward in some ways, but the security was anything but. I shivered a little but didn't slow down.

At three meters from the entrance, I felt an unpleasant tingle, and the Matrix fizzled away, leaving me visible. Much to the surprise of the people around me, who were clearly delighted at the unexpected visit from the famous *Hyperia Jones, rassling superstar.* There were several whistles, then I was surrounded by a gang of fans, all demanding autographs and fighting to snap Solidos.

I glanced back at the bots, wondering if there was any chance the job was still on, though I knew it was impossible. Bolt was standing next to them, and when my glare caught him, he gave a friendly wave and a smile.

My teeth ground against each other, and I almost lost my temper with the fans swarming around me—something I never do. Someone tapped heavily on my shoulder, and I twisted round ready to punch someone's lights out. Getting crowded is one thing, but nobody pushes me that way.

And came face-to-face, or rather face-to-carapace, with Brachyura. His exoskeleton was a deep tanzanite blue, which it always was in his friendly persona, and it gleamed in the bright lights of the station. When he switched to his *evil twin*, the Klaw, his exo-skeleton turned a dark bloodred.

"Would you care for an escort, dearest lady?" He bowed, his black, beady eyes glistening in amusement. In his smaller, human-oid hand he held a couple of shopping bags decorated with yellow and pink flowers. Even if I wasn't relieved to see him, that would have made me smile regardless.

"Why, thank you, Brach. I'd be delighted." I slipped my arm through his and we walked away, the crowd having edged back from Brachyura's imposing size.

"I hope that wasn't impertinent," he whispered, his mandibles clicking anxiously. "You seemed a little overwhelmed."

Several people ran up and took pictures of us strolling arm in arm, and I knew that before the hour was up, the images would be all over the Stellcom channels, and the gossip would spread throughout the Seventeen Realms. There's an axiom in the rassling business that only rumors can travel faster than light without entering D-space, and I'd seen it happen on several occasions.

"I appreciate the help. They came on me unexpectedly."

Brach tutted. "Perhaps you should have come out in disguise. You *are* a little *identifiable*."

There was an undertone in his voice that made me realize he meant it in a bawdy sense, and I laughed. "Brach, you're incorrigible. But you know what, we should work that in to the show. How about it?"

We turned left, heading back toward the *Queen*'s docking berth, pursued by fans, though they were now keeping a distance.

His mandibles click-clacked several times. "I'd welcome such a development. It's about time the Realms saw a softer side to Brachyura."

I moved my arm behind him and leaned close against his chest carapace. He surprised me by leaning down and kissing me on the lips. He held the pose for long enough to allow nearby fans to grab a picture, and then released me with a flourish. I felt flustered but smiled and walked with him as though it was something that happened every day.

Despite all of that though, my mind was focused on Bolt. He'd known what I was planning, and deliberately interfered. It was none of his business as long as I produced the evidence on Mrez. This failure had cost me several thousand drubles, partly from the loss of Martha, but also the fine for not completing my mission and the damage to my FUBAR standing.

I'd never failed on a job before. I believed in over delivering and never accepting less than the best. It was humiliating. And one way or another, I'd make Bolt pay.

Six

I was working out in the ship's gymnasium when the door opened. Denton strode in, his eyes widening as I pulled myself up and down, bringing my chin up to the horizontal bar, then swinging my legs up from the hips before moving them back down.

"You've got good lines there." He watched as I did several reps, then stepped back as I did a somersault dismount from the bar to land on the mat in a warrior pose.

"You're not so bad yourself." I grabbed a towel to wipe the beads of moisture from my skin, then took a long drink from my water bottle. "How are ticket sales?"

Denton took my arm and pulled me close, leaning over me and staring at me intensely with his sad puppy eyes. "How about giving me a ticket to ride, baby?"

His long tongue lolled out from under his snout and licked wetly up my cheek.

"Get away from me, you filthy dog." My hand shot out and gave off a loud crack as I slapped him. "Who do you think you are?"

He reeled back convincingly. "Jeez, Hype. What the ficksnit?" he growled, the M-flesh prosthetic jowls peeling back to bare his canines.

"Okay. Cut," Christine called out. "Didn't you read the script, Hype? You and Dogface are supposed to be into each other. You're meant to be willing and comp—"

"What the hell are you two..." Brachyura's snarl faded as he bounded into the room waving his giant claw. His carapace was red now, indicating he was his evil persona, Klaw, but the redness

57

washed away, showing his usual blue-black when he realized we were no longer shooting.

"Sorry, Brach, I messed up." I shrugged and walked away, hoping for a few minutes to sort my head out.

If there was one thing I disliked about the rassling business, it was the fake show nonsense. As expected, the photos of me and Brach had spread throughout the Realms like a dose of desiderata pox, and Denton had jumped on the idea for using it as a new plot.

Christine was fantastic at spinning the stories and making them work. After she'd retired from active rassling, it had become her way of staying involved alongside occasional commentating, and the plots grew increasingly impressive, fueled by a crazy mix of fantasy and trashy romance holo-shows mixed up with her own special brand of insanity. It was one of the things that had, at least until now, given us the edge over ICE.

I sensed someone behind me and turned. Brachyura was holding out a towel for me. "You okay, Hype?"

"Sure. I'm not very good at this. Everything's out of order, back to front, and probably upside down. I know it makes sense when Christine strings it together in the right sequence, but I never know how I'm supposed to react. One minute, I'm all over Denton, then I'm doing the dirty on him with you. Then it flips back again. It's hard to keep track."

"You sure you're not uncomfortable playing the part with *me*?" Brach looked down, his eyes avoiding mine. "It's okay if you are—I'll tell Denton to pull the story."

"That's ridiculous. Why would I be?"

"Well, it's different with Denton. I mean, we all know it's a mask. But with me..." He gestured to his face. "I mean this *is* me. Mandibles and all."

I couldn't help myself and let out a laugh. Why are male egos so fragile? Honestly, their confidence levels are weaker than a Tirluvian field mouse, and about the same size. Brachyura was "unattractive" if you used limited Terran values perhaps, but as a Brachynoid there was nothing wrong with him. I'm sure a Terran male would seem unattractive to most Brachynoid females. Appeal is always relative, not absolute. As the great Septapoid poet Guilim

Sh'kspiir once said: "Variety is the spice for wives."

I reached up and gently stroked Brach's mandibles. "You're a nice guy, Brach—it's not you. I get confused easily."

"Take a break everyone," said Christine. "We'll do some product placements this afternoon."

I headed for the door, shoving the makeup bot away as it tried to spray me with fake sweat. Halfway to my room, Denton caught up with me. "Wait up, Hype. We need to talk."

I didn't slow down. "I'm sorry, okay? I got mixed up, that's all. Let it drop."

He jumped past me and blocked the corridor. "That's not what I meant." His voice dropped to a whisper. "About the Guplides gig."

I nodded and gestured for him to follow. Inside my cabin, I sat on the chair by my desk and faced him. "What's the problem?"

Denton landed heavily on my plush, mauve couch. "Mr. Quy has lined up a new sponsorship product placement. It's worth a lot."

"This is a problem?"

"It's with the Omnistellar Syndicate."

Omnistellar was among the biggest ship manufacturers in the Seventeen Realms. A sponsorship deal with them would be a big boost for us. "So…?"

Denton scratched one of his floppy, brown ears. "Well…"

"Come on, Denton. Don't get tight-lipped with me now. What's the deal?"

"They're launching a new model—the *Centienne LFS*. It's a luxury space yacht."

"And they want us to do some shoots in one?" Omnistellar space yachts were the height of luxury, and as much as we all loved the *Queen*, I was sure nobody would object to hanging out in one of their ships.

"Not exactly." Denton stood and paced the floor of my cabin, his fake tongue lolling out of one side of his mouth. "They want to make a big splash at Guplides base by landing it there."

"Land *their* ship—at a military base?" My stomach churned from thinking about the danger in attempting that. "That's crazy."

"They have a military version, and I guess they're looking to impress the boys in uniform."

"How the crof are you going to get clearance?" I waited for an answer, but Denton didn't say anything. "You think *I* can get it for you?"

The idea was ridiculous. Military bases, by definition, are hard to get into without special permits, and they all have well-defined and defended no-fly zones that typically stretch from orbital defense stations to a planet's surface. Even though the *Queen* was our usual transport ship, we'd have to leave it in orbit and be escorted to the surface by military shuttles.

"The general seemed like a big fan of yours." Denton stopped pacing. "If you play up to him, he might go along with it."

The blood hammered in my earbuds. "What the hell are you suggesting?"

"Oh jeez. I didn't mean… anything like *that*. But you could let him take you to dinner, show him a good time, be nice to him. Nothing unpleasant."

"I see, only low-level prostitution then…"

He barked and snuffled. "That's not what I meant. I thought you might want to help. After all, this gig was your idea."

That wasn't completely accurate, but I couldn't tell Denton that. "I don't remember you having any complaints."

"No, I didn't. Because I'm trying everything I can to save this damn company." He panted. "Look, there's something else. I didn't want to mention it, because I knew people would panic. We might lose the *Ethereal Queen* in a couple of weeks."

"The *Queen*? How? Why?"

Denton slipped his fingers under the edge of the M-flesh at his neck and peeled the dog head off. "I had to hold back payments for the last couple of quarters. If I don't make a payment in the next week, it's gone."

I grabbed the tracker bracelet on my wrist and twisted it without thinking, swallowing heavily. The *Queen* had been my home for three years. No, more than that. After my narrow escape from Lecuunda, she'd been both a hiding place and a sanctuary. And the last place anyone would think of looking for me. My thoughts bounced around like they were caught in a gravitational vortex.

"So tell them we'll do it—with Virtupresence."

"You think I didn't try that?" Denton rubbed his head. "Omnistellar says it doesn't have the same impact. They want it real or no deal."

I was so used to seeing the dogface that it was a little surreal talking to him without it. "You're a real ficksnit, Denton. I'll do it, or try at least. I can't promise."

He smiled briefly. "You'll pull it off. I have confidence in you."

It was more than I had. This Olive Branch business had me edgier than a SlamCandy addict three days into withdrawal. Despite Denton's conviction, we'd only secured the gig because of Bolt, and although the general might be willing to cooperate with Olive Branch, I was fairly sure he wasn't a real fan. I doubted he'd bend the rules for me. I gave Denton a minute to pull on his dogface prosthetic, then showed him out. We were a long way from Guplides and a Stellcom transmission would take several hours to get there. I opened my terminal and composed a message consisting of equal parts begging and obsequious flattery, asking for special permission to land at the base. To top it off, I threw in a signed photo of me, plastered with a vivid, mulberry kiss, all the while hating myself.

After I was done, I snagged a light lunch and then showed up for duty in the main lounge. Christine was there along with most of the a-team roster, planning out different staged promos in support of the various ongoing story lines. This type of filming was easier than the story segments because it was mostly short clips where we were seen holding, or using, products from various sponsors. We had a Nano-scale Universal Replicating Pantograph on board and could recreate virtually any object within reason—at least at a visual level. Although sponsors sometimes preferred to send free samples, which was nice when we got to keep them.

Zavara and Atsuno Moon were standing to one side chatting, while the Bonor Triplets argued over the Pancho Rebel outfits, having already staked a claim to the Kahtee-yay necklaces and bracelets. The jewelry wasn't fake either—unlike the all-too-voluptuous Triplets. I'd been interested in grabbing the necklaces myself, before I discovered the small StarPhyres in their designs had been replaced by worthless diamonds.

On the other side of the room, Boots Largo was trying on some new footwear by Ruff. They were replicated, otherwise they wouldn't have fit the giant body part his name was derived from. His feet were so large relative to the rest of his body, he looked like he was wearing leather-covered construction blocks rather than shoes. He was with Phil Slinebar, Boots' manager and spokesperson, universally nicknamed Phil Slimeball in a backward tribute to his devious deals and tricks.

"In the last setup, you ambushed Mandraago and critically injured him. Remember?" Phil's fat jowls wobbled as he spoke. "You ran that star-limo into him at the spaceport, and he's been in an emergency health pod for the last two weeks."

"Mandraago? I have breakfast with him, this morning," Boots squeaked. "He is fining."

Boots' less-than-manly voice was distinctly at odds with his heavy-set appearance and barrel-like chest. That, and his shaky command of Lingua, was why Denton had assigned Slinebar to him. There had been far too much laughter and go-away heat for comfort at Boots' first few shows. Fans can be cruel sometimes.

"He's fine," Phil corrected. "I know. This is part of the ongoing angle we're running on the promos, remember?"

Boots shook his head, his short, bristled hair and bad complexion making him look like an overripe stinkychom fruit. He wasn't the smartest rassler to step inside the TwistCube. "Understand not."

Phil sighed. "Don't worry about it. This week, Mandraago's allies, the Cazarini Brothers, are looking for revenge. So we're going to record some backstage conflicts with them, leading to them interfering with your match against Pinhead."

Pinhead was a Vholian Ape from the Geilekthrus Realm. Unusually, Vholian brains are located in their chests to protect them, and their heads are only a small receptacle for eyes and other sensory organs, on top of a stick-like neck. Pinhead is one of the heaviest rasslers though and was always working out. The match with him, along with Boots' staged attack, was all part of an elaborate cover story. Designed to give Mandraago time to record scenes for his latest all-action blockbuster—*Reflex Annihilation 6: Extreme Overkill.* Outside rassling, Mandraago had developed a burgeoning Holowood presence, something Denton tolerated and encouraged because it helped bring greater exposure for FIRE.

"Hype? You here, girl?"

I waved at Christine. "What's on the card?"

"Okay, were going to do some scenes with you, Brachyura, Zavara, and Atsuno. The angle is you're in a love quadrangle, and it's going to cause a rift between Zav and Ats. Then we'll run this into the live show on Guplides. Here are the scripts and shoot schedules for you four."

Zavara was a rakish Hemerian with an impressive build and cute red-and-gray, mottled skin. Although he frequently played the role of a womanizer on the shows, privately he was the rightoid in a committed relationship. His leftoid and centroid had visited the *Queen* a few times and made a lovely triumvage.

I looked through the script, skimming the various story lines, and skidded to a halt in section five. "Christine? It says we have several scenes with me seducing Atsuno—shouldn't that be me and Zavara?"

"No, it's right the way it is. We want to play things differently, so you're going to seduce Ats away from *him*." Christine looked up. "That a problem?"

It wasn't. Unlike some humanoids, Lecuundans are flexible when it comes to such matters, but it was unexpected and not anything I'd done in public before. I looked over at Atsuno. She batted her big, brown eyes at me and blew me a kiss.

"I'll be gentle with you, Hype." Her voice was low and husky but carried clearly across the room, and I felt my face flush yellow.

I looked away and caught Zavara staring at me with all four eyes. He doffed his wide-brimmed hat and swept it down in a circle. "Milady."

"Denton, you'll be scheduled for a grudge match against ChaosRhino after he interfered with your last match with Brach, so we'll do some setup scenes for that." Christine checked her notes.

"But your match on Guplides will be with Gary Power, AKA the Prince Of Power."

"Isn't he part of ICE?" Denton said.

"Was. He's semi-retired now, but he's native to Guplides, so a perfect plant."

Denton nodded. "Sounds good. What character is he playing?"

"I've arranged a Fifth Battalion uniform for him. Thought that would go down well with the local audience."

"Got it, so keep it clean and fair. Nothing underhand."

Christine smiled. "You got it, boss."

Stryng wriggled up to me and draped his tail across my thigh. "If you want some coaching on those scenes with Atsuno, I'd be glad to help out, dollface."

I could imagine what Stryng's idea of coaching would be. "Thanks, I think we can figure it out."

"I'm sure you can, but having someone there with an experienced eye while you practice would make it steamier."

I brushed his tail off me. "You couldn't take it that hot."

His eyes lifted. "Maybe, but what a way to go."

I gave him a friendly pat on his head. "Don't worry, we'll spare you."

"That's what I was afraid of."

The rest of the meeting was routine and didn't involve me, and I was glad to head back to my room. I had plans that weren't for the eyes of others. Once there, I logged into Darkover to look for potential jobs on Guplides. I'd already paid the hefty FUBAR fine, but I was determined to make that money back, and more. And this time Bolt wasn't going to get in my way. After all, he couldn't be everywhere.

There was a job listed for the "recovery" of something called a "censhock detangler" that looked like a perfect match for me: security overrides, nothing physical to take, simply copy the data and transmit to an anonymous recipient. Low risk, easy to plan and—of course—highly paid. I was about to sign up when a cold shiver danced down my dorsal region.

How secure was Darkover? The question had never crossed my mind before. FUBAR went to great lengths to keep it clean, with multiple authorization streams, rotating encryptions, and randomized biometric challenges, but was anything *truly* secure? Especially from Olive Branch. Bolt had found out my plans on the Kalpurnia station somehow—but how?

There were only two ways I could think of. Either he'd planted some form of tracker on me that could read my every thought and report everything I saw, or he'd hacked Darkover and was monitoring my activity on there. I looked at the bracelet. That was the obvious suspect but not necessarily the culprit. Bolt would be highly experienced in deception, and from what he'd said about his methods with Alyss Blakeston, I wouldn't be surprised if the tracker wasn't implanted somehow.

There was one way to find out. I logged out of Darkover and made my way to the ship's infirmary. The *Queen* has its own medical facilities that can handle anything from a stubbed toe to a multiple bypass and genetic transplant operations. And one of the main diagnostic systems was a full-body, multi-frequency y-band scanner.

I walked into the spacious clinic and waved my hand over the signal for the doctor. When he showed up he was scowling, as if someone had stolen his lunch and replaced it with a fossilized turd. Which was completely ridiculous—Doctor Lee is another Artificial Person and doesn't eat. Though, unlike Auntie, he used a hard-light display matrix to appear like a real person.

"I'm busy. What do you want?"

Lee always looked male to me. I wasn't sure why. The system was supposed to pick the gender the patient was most comfortable talking to, which for most people was usually their own. Perhaps Lecuundan biology was too sophisticated for its programming.

"How can you be busy? Your only function is to look after patients, and you don't have any." I pointed at the empty beds. The clinic's diagnostic equipment gave off a slight plasticy smell that always irritated my nose, and I tried hard to ignore it.

Lee rubbed his jowly chin. "I'm in the middle of some complex research you couldn't possibly understand the purpose of. What's the problem?"

"I'd like a full-spectrum body scan."

"Those are expensive. Why do you need one?"

"Expensive? How?"

"They consume resources. Resources must be paid for. A body-scan uses a lot of energy resources—therefore it is expensive."

The logic was what you'd expect from an AP, and their deductions weren't worth the photonix they were painted with. Like Auntie, the Doc could be incredibly literal. "The ship's engines produce limitless energy, so there's no effective cost."

"Your reasoning is deeply flawed," Dr. Lee said.

"How?" He didn't answer and, after several minutes, I realized he wasn't going to. There's nothing an AP hates more than being out-logiced. "I have a fever. I ache all over. And my head hurts. Also, I'm having some..." I whispered the last part.

"With symptoms like that, I may have to confine you to the sick bay."

"Do the scan and check me over, okay?"

"Very well. Arrange yourself on the diagnosis bed."

I clambered onto the padded bed and waited as the scan arms whooshed around me in helical patterns, the blue glow from the scan-field tingling my skin.

"Please remove your wrist decoration. It is interfering with the scans."

"My wrist... ? Oh the bracelet. I can't take it off, it's a precious heirloom. How is it interfering? Is it producing a signal of some kind?"

"Of course not. It is made of a cheap alloy and nothing more, but it obscures your body at that point, and you insisted on a *full* body scan."

"A cheap alloy? Solid?"

"Primarily zinc, copper, tin, and arcormanium—as solid as you and me."

I silently cursed Bolt. The story about the tracker was a ruse, obviously designed to hide the fact that he'd accessed Darkover and was tracking my activity there. But now I knew, it meant I could outsmart him. I tried not to fidget while Dr. Lee finished the scans. "Is there anything else... unusual?"

"Nothing that would cause the symptoms you've described. This has been a complete waste of my time, as expected."

"Believe me, it hasn't."

"I am curious as to why you have a level three tracking and surveillance device inserted in your neck, however." He tapped slightly below my left earbud. "Are you afraid of getting lost?"

"What?" I jerked up, almost smacking my face into the whirling scan sensors. "Are you sure?"

"Please feel free to insult my professionalism…"

"Don't get your photons in a bunch." I lowered my head to avoid being decapitated. "It was an expression of surprise."

"I presume you had it implanted for *personal* reasons." Lee tutted and peered at me over his archaic glasses. "*Fleshbulbs* never cease to confound and disgust me."

"Can you remove it?"

"Certainly, but why did you have it inserted in the first place?"

"It was a… an accident. Better use an isolation field, it might be err… dangerous."

"I know how to do my job." Lee bobbed his head, his white hair wobbling. "I assume you don't want a scar?"

"That would be preferable."

"It will take longer." Lee stopped the scanners. "Sit up, please."

He moved behind me, and something cold pressed against my neck, then there was a sharp nip and a pull.

"Is that it?"

"Yes." Lee stepped away.

"I thought you said it would take longer?"

"It does. Removal with no scarring takes 0.93 seconds. The scarring option is almost half a second quicker."

I glared at him. "You can be a real ficksnit at times."

"Remember that the next time you want treatment for a self-inflicted condition."

I poked my tongue out and simultaneously flipped him the bird with my middle-right tentacle. "You don't have a choice, do you? You're part of the ship."

Lee curled his lips. "How I wish that wasn't true. Now, goodbye." He vanished in a sparkly cloud as his photonix dissolved.

I returned to my room and sat at the terminal. I was unimpressed by Bolt's double bluff, but now I wasn't sure what to think. Had he discovered my plans through the implanted tracker, or was that a double-double bluff to make me think it was still safe to use Darkover? It reminded me of some of the movies Stryng watched: wheels within wheels, within wheels.

There were alternatives. FUBAR isn't the only underground organization—there's also GoDAM, the Guild of Deceitful Artistic Miscreants. They maintained their own secure network, and although not as extensive as Darkover, it usually listed a reasonable amount of jobs.

The problem was that Bolt and Olive Branch would know about it too, and if they were able to infiltrate FUBAR, GoDAM would prove no barrier either. I'd have to be old-school in my thinking and planning.

My neck ached where Dr. Lee had removed the implant and I rubbed it while looking in the mirror. I leaned in closer. My tribal spots-that-never-should-appear were reappearing, and I concentrated on pushing the pigment back down to make them invisible again. Some secrets needed to be kept, no matter what.

I tapped on my commpad, calling Stryng, and he answered before the third ring.

"Hey, what's cooking sister?"

"You have access to the old-style planetary archives, don't you?" The records were maintained as a backup to the normal endecatronic files, but Stryng liked to browse them for gossip, claiming they had more flavor than their modern counterparts.

"Looking for something specific?"

"Can you get hard copies of recent history and news on Guplides?"

"Hard copies? I can transfer some stuff to the pantograph..." He paused. "What gives? You working a new angle?"

I hated using Stryng like this, but if he accessed the archive, it was less likely to be connected to me. And once the data was turned into hard copy, there was no way Bolt would know I'd even looked at it. "You're always sharp."

"I'll bring it over personally—show you how sharp I can be."

"It's too soon to let you in on the idea. I'm only toying with it right now. Send a carry-bot."

"*Toying* sounds interesting."

I laughed. He never gave up. "Goodnight, Stryng."

There was another thing to take care of. I rolled up my sleeve to reveal the bracelet Bolt had given me. If Lee was right, it was only a hunk of metal. If not? Well, I might blow up the whole ship... I stretched my hand and fingers, working them with my other hand to encourage the deformation. The bracelet was tight and would have been impossible for a typical vertebrate to remove, but luckily that description didn't apply to me.

The metal ring slipped down a few centimeters, then farther as my hand elongated and thinned. I was sweating, partly from exertion, and partially from fear that the bracelet would explode. It moved down some more, catching painfully on my thumb base. I swallowed hard, my stomach flip-flopping as I pushed again. This time the bracelet gave, clearing the joint and landing on the floor with a clang, and a series of loud, high-pitched beeps. I clenched into a ball, then realized the beeps were coming from the door chime.

"Crof!" I opened the door. The boxy, wheeled shape of a carry-bot was waiting, piled high with a stack of printed news stories.

I picked up the bracelet and slid it back over my hand. It no longer bothered me now I knew it was nothing but a trinket. But if Bolt saw me without it, he'd know his game was up. In the meantime, I had my homework cut out for me.

Seven

The trip from Kalpurnia to the Guplides system was a hectic week for everyone. For me, it was divided between working out, recording various "tender" encounters with Atsuno, and staged confrontations between me and Zavara. I didn't follow the broadcasts, but apparently, the fans were lapping it up.

My off-time was spent working on Bolt's assignment and studying the material Stryng had dug up. I researched the Slam-Candy operation openly, making full use of Darkover resources. Bolt would never believe I was playing along like a good little girl, so I also did more reading on the censhock detangler job. I didn't formally sign up to take it on, knowing Bolt would think I was being cautious after the last operation had gone so wrong. He wasn't the only one who could play deep games. My actual investigation was conducted by speed-reading the incredible level of information Stryng had acquired, and usually ended with me falling asleep over the pile of printed sheets.

I'd heard back from General Vinapo. To my surprise, he'd authorized our use of the *Centienne* to land at the base. But on condition I had dinner with him before the event on his flagship. That didn't sound too bad, but I wondered what other *rassling* he might have in mind. I also strongly suspected that Bolt's slimy fingers were at work behind the scenes, which made me doubly uncomfortable.

By the time we entered orbit around the planet, Omnistellar already had the *Centienne* waiting for us, and we matched position ready for a transfer. Unlike the *Queen*, the *Centienne* was crewed and even had a chauffeured transfer vehicle to ferry us from our ship.

"That ship looks nice, dear," Auntie sniffed. "I hope it's reliable. Young ones can be so flighty."

I wondered if Auntie was jealous, or annoyed. I don't think she realized the *Centienne* had a crew and no AP onboard.

"It's just for a few days, Auntie," I said, hoping to reassure her. "It will give you a chance to rest."

"Ah, that's what you think. I'll be spending the time catching up on cleaning. You people are such filthy animals."

I didn't know what to say. To an Artificial Person, I guessed all fleshbulbs were creatures with disgusting habits. I looked at the items of clothing and printouts scattered around my room. "Sorry, Auntie. I'll clean up as soon as I'm back."

As we crossed to the *Centienne*, I stared out of the window at the planet below. It was about the same size as my homeworld, Lecuunda, but had a decided shortage of water in comparison and looked all purplish-green from this distance. There was only one large ocean on the planet, and most of the non-water surface was grassland dotted with numerous small lakes. It was one of those worlds that quietly exist in the thrumming tapestry of the universe, without ever making much of an impact. I'm sure its inhabitants were happy, but it didn't have many features of interest, other than the garrison.

By contrast, the *Centienne* was impressive. Bigger than the *Queen*, it sparkled in orbit as the sun scintillated off its sleek, pure-white hull. The biggest difference in capacity was internal though, as the *Centienne*'s engines were much smaller and more efficient than the ones on our aging ship. When we docked and entered the main reception area, the crisp luxury that greeted us made the *Queen*'s interior seem antiquated and gaudy.

A tall humanoid bedecked in a gaudy captain's uniform composed mostly of shiny buttons and braid was there to greet us, along with several, presumably senior, crew members. She was standing to attention, her solid body good enough to have belonged to a professional athlete. My catty inner voice wondered where she'd bought it, but I said nothing. As Denton walked up to her, she saluted flamboyantly.

"Mr. Denton, a pleasure to meet you. I'm Captain Delisa Vereen. Glad to have you onboard."

Denton gave a cute little growl. "Thank you, Captain. We'll try not to inconvenience you too much."

Vereen accepted his handshake. "Don't worry about that. If you get too irritating, I can always put you in irons or space you."

Her facial expression was cold and forbidding. Denton took a step back, his prosthetic sensing his response and baring his dog teeth instinctively. "Have we done something wrong?"

"Your presence on my ship is a disturbance," Vereen said, speaking slowly. Then she laughed. "You should have seen the look on your faces."

There were murmurs from others in our group, everyone seemingly as confused as I was. Several of Vereen's crew shook their heads, shuffling uncomfortably.

"That was a joke?" Denton drew in a deep breath.

"Of course. I'm here to ferry you to the planet. Why would I throw you out of an airlock?"

Denton lolled out his long, pink prosthetic tongue. "Well, that's good to know."

"Ladies and gentle-things. If you'd care to follow Mr. McMeekin, he'll show you to the waste-reclamators." Vereen stopped, waiting for her words to sink in. "Everybody works on this ship—especially the guests."

One of her crew stepped forward, red-faced. "I'm First Officer Rory McMeekin. If you'd care to follow me to the main passenger lounge?"

McMeekin kept checking the time and looking around as he led us snaking through the elegant corridors trimmed in hideously expensive Circinian blue oak. After several turns, we moved up one deck to the guest area. I thought the blue wood was disgusting, but it was rare, hideously expensive, and—with the penchant of the rich to adopt anything combining those qualities and declare it beautiful—the height of fashion.

The main deck lounge was equally impressive with large bay windows and sumptuous, built-in sectional couches covered in silver leather so pristine it looked like they'd cured it on site. Who knows? Maybe they had. The walls were mist colored and the fittings all high-quality borodium, either plated or possibly solid. The Bonor Triplets let out a collective sigh at the luxury, and I could almost imagine Auntie weeping.

"Please make yourself comfortable." McMeekin moved to stand in front of us, wringing his hands. He was in full uniform like Captain Vereen, though the unruly clump of red curls poking out from under his cap gave him less of an appearance of strict formality. "I must apologize for the captain's sense of humor. She means no harm."

"That dame is frutso." Stryng said what everyone was thinking. "She always like this?"

McMeekin hung his head lower. "She is. Now."

Denton plopped onto a couch and nearly disappeared from sight as he sank into the cushioning. "What happened?"

McMeekin checked the time once more and looked around nervously. "Well, it's not my place to criticize the captain."

"Come on, mac. Give us the straight dope. Are we safe here?" Stryng wound himself around one of the heavy-duty, Corinthian-style pillars.

"Captain Vereen had a snowskeeting accident last year on her homeworld, Shivatralia. She's an experienced 'skeeter, but this time—well, she wasn't so lucky."

Shivatralia was a virtually snowbound world in the Atropos realm, famous for an economy based almost entirely on its winter sports industry. A big part of that was snowskeeting—something that had no appeal to me whatsoever. To be honest, anything involving snow looked about as enticing as rolling around naked in a pile of spore-needles. Snowskeeting wasn't simply cold though: it was highly dangerous, involving speeding around frozen mountains in a vehicle combining all the worst characteristics of a tiny water vessel and high-thrust rockets.

"What happened?" I said.

"She clipped a rock outcropping. Her vehicle tumbled and she received a blow to her head. There was serious damage to her prefrontal cortex. The medical technicians had to remove the damaged tissue and replace it with an endecatronic Bareil matrix, but somehow the personality centers didn't huh… regenerate correctly, and she's become something of a practical joker."

Boots broke the silence that followed. "Lady Captain joke she throw us out of airlock? Funny." He laughed, his bellows running up and down his vocal range from contralto to the highest of squeaks, which he reserved for times when exceptionally amused.

McMeekin looked around nervously. "Yes, well, I must go. I need to get out of my uniform for the crew inspection."

"Sorry?" I couldn't help myself.

His face turned as red as his curls. "Another of the Captain's little… eccentricities." With that he rushed out, tearing his tunic off as he left.

"He was kind of cute. Got to love a redhead, huh?" Atsuno dug her elbow into my ribs. "Do you think they'd let us watch the inspection?"

I wasn't interested in naked Terrans, cute or otherwise. I was obsessing over my plans for Guplides. I made excuses, then left to wander around the *Centienne*. Every single centimeter breathed opulence and prestige. I had no idea what such a ship would cost, but it must have been in the hundreds of mega-drubles. There was a second passenger lounge, slightly smaller than the famous Ru-Shou Theater on Thati Undis V, but about the same level of lavishness. This one was outfitted with fine wood paneling and deep, plush carpets. At one end was an array of framed artwork that drew my professional attention, and I wandered *casually* over to check it out.

One picture caught my eye especially, though it was only around ten-by-twenty centimeters: a purple-hued painting of D'Venlea Glora, the first UberKaiser of the Realms, in full battle armor outside a heavily fortified building. Phil Slinebar walked up next to me, his shiny forehead gleaming with multiple reflections from the lights around the room. "Is that what I think it is?"

"*Glora's Victory at Hoskinda* by Dianie Ctano." I whispered the words, though I wasn't sure why.

Slinebar nodded. "Painted in the blood of the honored dead… That's a reproduction though… right?"

I focused on the painting, using my ocular power to microscopically examine the surface texture of the material. There were distinct brush strokes and swirls in the coloring. I shook my head. "I don't think so."

"That's worth millions." He frowned. "You're jerking me around, Hype. Just like the others do. I get no thritting respect around here."

Ctano had been the UberKaiser's courtesan and was vastly underestimated in the historic records. From what I understood, she'd played a key role in the uprising and subsequent victory over the Klausehn Overlords who'd dominated the worlds before the UberKaiser united the people to fight back. The picture had been painted on the eve of the final battle and was priceless.

It was protected by a StellGlass case, but I'd lay money on that being only the obvious security. Beyond that, there was sure to be a force screen, and the whole thing would be rigged with pressure sensors, atmosphere detectors, motion trackers, and probably DeltaPhase scanners to boot, which would detect movement even through a Distortion Matrix. Adding the icing, the painting was on a spaceship where access in and, more importantly, out, was via security-controlled airlocks—as impenetrable as if it were in a bank vault. My mind ticked away at the problem as I pretended to examine the other exhibits. None of them stood out, but I'm not an expert. I doubted they were as valuable as *Glora's Victory* but still expensive in their own right.

The Pantograph would be able to reproduce the piece, including replicating the correct brush strokes given a detailed-enough scan. The locking mechanisms were nearly unbeatable, but why bother? Undetectable industrial-grade attobots could disintegrate the original artwork, simultaneously replacing it with the replica without any danger of the substitution being caught. Microscopic cracks around the display case would let the bots in and out easily enough, and once I was safely away, they would be able to rebuild the original in a matter of minutes. Selling the painting through underground channels wouldn't be as lucrative as for a legitimate, provenance-assured piece but would bring in more than enough to make up the losses Bolt had caused, with enough left over to buy my own ship if I wanted.

I smiled. The satisfaction of thinking up a simple plan and having such easy access to a target filled me with confidence. Then I crashed. The idea was good, the market was there, and a few relatively straightforward preparations would make it possible. So why the cold feet?

There's an old saying on Lecuunda—you don't vraz in your own plunge pool. I forced down my excitement. Nothing had changed. I already had a plan—more complicated in some ways, but with the benefit that Bolt wouldn't think of me as the obvious culprit.

A siren sounded, echoing through the ship to warn everyone we were about to land. Which was a little surprising—I'd not felt the slightest vibration as we'd entered Guplides' atmosphere. Score another one for the *Centienne*—its stabilizers were clearly better than the *Queen*'s. I felt guilty for noticing these differences. It wasn't as though I didn't love the old girl, but a side-by-side comparison highlighted how technology had changed.

I joined the others at the main exit ramp. The area was a hive of activity as we prepared for a big entrance. As usual, the Bonors pushed themselves to the front, which I didn't mind so much. It's always tiring dealing with large crowds, even though I got a buzz out of the fans.

A giant screen by the door showed a reverse angle of the *Centienne* from pickups at the landing site. She made a spectacular sight dropping through the high-level clouds, the sleek, alabaster hull reflecting the golden glow of the morning sun. The landing thrusters flashed on, gleaming with an intense blue-white light, and I held my breath as the image tracked us ever closer to the ground.

There was a slight shudder as the force beams caught the ship, cradling it with pure energy and gently easing it the last few meters until we were close enough to lower the ramp. The image zoomed in, past the heads of the cheering, banner-waving crowd outside, to focus on the airlock. This was it.

I took several deep breaths, pushed a smile onto my face, and stood ready with the others to wave to the crowd. The indicator light above the door turned green, and the panel slid down. Sunlight, blinding in its intensity, streamed in through the gap as it widened, and the ramp extended to form a walkway.

Where about a dozen people stood, most of them bored-looking technicians and spaceport staff.

The Triplets stepped forward and waved enthusiastically, not seeming to notice the lack of an actual audience. Stryng wriggled up alongside me and whispered from the corner of his mouth, "So much for the big reception. How'd ya like those tomatoes, babe?"

It wasn't the first time we'd worked in front of a simulated audience, and it wouldn't be the last. But it was always disappointing when you weren't expecting it. I'd hoped there might be a genuine interest from the military personnel, even if the general was following Bolt's orders.

An indecorous military vehicle sped into the area, its bulky passenger forcing his way out before it stopped moving. The military decorations overwhelming his uniform formed a kaleidoscope of dazzling colors. General Vinapo had arrived.

"Welcome to Guplides IV, Mr. Dogface." Vinapo was breathing heavily from climbing the ramp. "A genuine pleasure to meet you, sir."

Nobody called Denton *mister* Dogface—it was always Dogface or Mr. Denton, but he took it in his stride and reached out to give the general a grand handshake while waving to the "crowd" of HoloPod cameras buzzing around us.

"It's always a privilege to entertain our people in uniform." Denton stretched his lips back in a beaming doggy smile. "Thank yoooo… for inviting us."

As usual, he had to get in his trademark howl.

"And where is Ms. Jones?"

I'd been holding back slightly, hoping not to get noticed. Not because I didn't want the spotlight, but because I was hoping the general might have forgotten about me.

"Hype?" Denton looked around. "Come up here. You're the star attraction."

I almost laughed when I saw the expressions on the Bonors' faces. They certainly didn't like *that* introduction. I walked over and treated Vinapo to a small curtsy, then held out my hand to shake his, all the while smiling at the Triplets' peeved jealousy.

Vinapo didn't shake my hand though. Instead, he took it in his and leaned over, planting a wet, slobbery kiss on the back of it. Who says chivalry is dead.

"Well, this *is* a real pleasure, my dear." Vinapo's grin split his face like a horizontal set of buttocks. "And I must say I'm looking forward to having you later."

"You mean dinner?" I said.

"Well, yes... that too..."

My ichiosphores tingled unpleasantly, and I wondered again what the general thought the deal was. I had no idea what Bolt might have told him to get him to agree to the request. Whatever that was, he was going to be sorely disappointed, and it took all of my willpower not to let my loathing show. We still needed his help.

We walked down the ramp, and Vinapo tried to loop his arm around me, but suddenly Atsuno was there, blocking his move. "Sorry, general. We have an active story between me and Hype. We need to keep it up for the cameras. I'm sure you understand."

Vinapo smiled—well, leered—at the pair of us. "Oh yes, I've been following it with *great* interest. Perhaps you'd like to join us later?"

Atsuno didn't bat an eye. "I'm scheduled to do publicity work with Brachyura and Zavara."

"That's a shame. I'm sure it would have made for a memorable night."

Vinapo and his security detail escorted us to a large hangar that was being converted to act as the arena. The supplies from the *Queen* had been transported down, and a team of mech-suited soldiers was assembling the main stage and locker rooms at one end of the building. Meanwhile, the other three sides were being filled with multi-level bench seating. We didn't carry an entire arena's worth of gear, so the hardware must have belonged to the military. I made an excuse that I needed to check the facilities, and left Denton deep in discussion with Vinapo about military strategy, suffering the general's rambling diatribe on where he'd seen action. It was the least I could do, considering Denton had set me up for this.

Once we were out of earshot, I turned to Atsuno. "Thanks, Ats.

Thrit, he sure thinks a lot of himself."

She nodded. "More like, he sure thinks he's going to get his hands on you, I'd say. You going to be okay?"

"I'll keep him under control, don't worry."

"Of course I worry." She reached up and brushed my cheek. "We're *love sisters*, remember."

That was one of the pitches we'd been running for the story line. According to the script, we were besotted and couldn't keep our hands off each other, even though Atsuno was also playing at being in love with Zavara. On the other hand, I was supposed to have cruelly "broken things off" with Brach, who was fighting to get me back.

The female section of the backstage area was nearly complete, and we slipped past the "under construction" areas to find our dressing rooms. Usually, most of the work was carried out by a swarm of construction bots, but the military always looked for an excuse to use its troops, so a gang of sullen soldiers was hauling supplies around and assembling things by hand.

"I love to see a grown man sweat, don't you?" Atsuno was staring at a group of mostly male soldiers who seemed more interested in standing around than working.

"It doesn't do much for me, to be honest."

"You Lecuundans, always such cold fish." She laughed. "You miss out on so much."

I leaned closer to her and told her a few of the intimate things about Lecuundan love-making, and her eyes widened.

"Mmm… maybe I should try that… know anyone who'd be willing?"

She looked straight at me, and my skin color changed as I blushed. "No, not really."

"Well, let me know if anyone occurs to you…" Her voice lowered and was warmly suggestive. "I better go and check my wardrobe."

Up ahead, I spotted a door with my name on it and swallowed, grateful for the easy escape. "Me too."

Slipping inside with a sense of relief, I locked the door for privacy and because I wanted to run through my plans again. My approach for this job was completely different from normal, and it had me a little nervous. I was so used to being able to tap into Darkover's pool of knowledge and illicit research that I felt I was operating blind. With a hand, and probably a foot, tied behind my back. While juggling an activated laser cutter. And whistling. Compared to that, Vinapo seemed almost harmless.

Almost.

Eight

After making sure *my* wardrobe had arrived safely, or rather my stash of Tekuani-related equipment, I went to check out the TwistCube setup. It was already fully functional, which was a pleasant surprise as often that's the last thing to get right on the ground. The soldiers were obviously good at following orders. Glacia and Atsuno had been bugging me to do some ring practice, so I let them know we were good to go. Glacia had been developing a new finishing move called the Gravimetric Whip and needed some help polishing it up before the match. It was highly dramatic when executed well, but needed tight coordination to avoid injury. After a couple of hours of practice and some general training, I went back to my room and hit the shower. The hot water always relaxed me after a workout, and I wasn't especially focused when the door signal sounded.

It was probably one of the other team members, and I scrabbled for the door viewer to check. The unfamiliar controls caught me out though, and the door slid open, leaving me a dripping mess in front of a young and suddenly red-faced soldier.

"Excuse me, ma'am. I'm your driver."

"Driver?"

"Yes, Ma'am. General Vinapo sent me to bring you to the *UNS Illicimus.*"

It was only then I realized it was evening on Guplides—I was still running on ship's time. "You'll have to wait," I said. "Sorry."

"Understood. How long will you need, ma'am?" He blushed deeper. "So's I can inform the general, that is."

"Thirty minutes. And stop calling me *ma'am*. My name is Hyperia, or Hype."

"Yes, ma—" He grinned. "Yes, Hyperia. I know your name for sure. Can I say, it's a real pleasure meeting a lady like yourself."

"Thank you…" I read the name off his uniform. "Corporal Horden."

Horden scrabbled in his pockets, finally pulling out a mini holo-cam. "Would you mind? It'd be a real honor if you'd let me get a photo with you. All the guys in the barracks would be green."

"Sure. Do you want me naked and dripping wet? Or should I dress first?"

He hesitated long enough that I knew he was considering the first option, but his face was so suffused he looked like a ripe tomato. "Oh, yes, certainly, ma—I mean Hyperia… Once you take care of your… *attire*, of course."

I nodded. "Thirty minutes."

After I closed the door, I hurriedly dried myself off, then tossed the towel in the reconditioning unit so it would be ready next time I needed it. My clothes had been delivered, so I didn't have a problem other than choosing the right outfit. That took twenty-five of the thirty minutes. I settled on a powder blue dress, modulating the color of my skin to a light shade of papaya to complement it. I hate heels, but knew I needed to look my best, and threw some on after dialing their color to match the dress. I added a decorative, but modest, shell necklace before finally triggering cosmetic color changes to enhance my lips and cheekbones. I checked myself in the holo-mirror and smiled. I was sure the general would be happy. I hoped it wouldn't encourage him too much.

Twenty-nine minutes after closing the door on the corporal, I reopened it. He jumped from the wall where he'd been leaning and let out a whistle. "Sorry, ma—Hyperia. I wasn't expecting you to be ready so soon."

I smiled. "I said thirty minutes."

He grinned. "Yeah, I just never knew a broad—a lady that is—that was ever on time."

"Well, now you do." I paused as he took his time scrutinizing me. "How about that picture?"

He nodded, for a moment his expression reminding me of one of Denton's puppy looks. "Yes, please."

He stepped forward, awkwardly holding a camera. At that moment, Stryng came down the hall and stopped a couple of meters away. "Hooo baby, you look like the girl in the jitterbug dress. Is that for me?"

"I've been invited to dinner with General Vinapo." I grabbed the holo-cam and tossed it to Stryng. "Here, make yourself useful. Corporal Horden would like a picture."

"It's Don," the corporal said. "Don Horden."

I pulled Horden close, wrapping my arm around his back. He didn't return the gesture and left several centimeters' gap between us. Stryng used his tail to take several pictures, making numerous lecherous comments that embarrassed Horden further. When Stryng finished, I gave Horden a peck on the cheek, and he turned bright red again.

"You don't know how lucky you are, corporal," Stryng muttered.

"Oh, I surely do, sir. I surely do."

Horden led me to a drab, green aircar that was waiting for us, and held the door open while I slid into the back seat. To be perfectly honest, I'd have preferred to spend the evening with the bashful corporal than the all-too-unbashful general. I was making an assumption, but it's hard to go wrong expecting the worst from men who hold powerful positions.

Once I was settled, the car leaped upward, and the seat pressed uncomfortably into my back and rump. After a few minutes, the acceleration eased, and the sky darkened from indigo to complete black as we approached orbit. The stars popped out of the darkness, the specks glimmering through the viewport.

"Will you be taking me back to the surface after dinner, Don?"

Horden turned slowly toward me, but didn't finish the move and focused on the instruments. "I'll be ready errr… whenever you ask to leave."

His reticence told me what to expect. Presumably, Vinapo was counting on persuading me to stay. "Thank you. It's good to know I'm in safe hands."

"Yes, ma'am—Hype. We'll be at the *Illicimus* in ten minutes.

You can see it over to the left at about thirty degrees."

I looked where he indicated. It was hard to make out anything, but I got a vague sense of a darker shadow against the midnight background. As we closed, the light reflecting from Guplides caught the edge of the ship and revealed its long shape, the main body interrupted by several blocky masses and its surface teeming with heavy weapons. It looked sinister in that menacing fashion beloved by soldiers and had to be deliberate. I'd seen Lecuundan military ships with similar characteristics, so it wasn't something peculiar to Terrans.

I took a deep breath and sank back in my seat. This was going to be a long night.

My teeth were grinding as we approached the *Illicimus,* and the small spines on the back of my neck bristled. I silently cursed Bolt. He obviously thought he controlled me so much, I'd go along with anything. Unfortunately for Bolt—and Vinapo—they had a lot to learn.

A giant, circular door peeled open in the side of the *Illicimus,* giving access to the interior, and Horden moved us into the docking bay. When I climbed from the aircar, General Vinapo was waiting, resplendent in a bright red-and-white dress uniform, complete with a ridiculous red, feathered hat. He reminded me of an Olgarian MoonParrot. They were renowned for being stupid, even for birds, and frequently caught in traps baited with rocks.

"Hyperia, my sweet girl, absolutely delightful to see you once again. If I may have the honor?"

He held out his arm, and I pretended not to understand. "This is a big ship, general. Are you compensating for something?"

Vinapo spluttered through his thick mustache. "Sorry?"

"I was wondering why soldiers always want to have the biggest ships."

"Well, it's down to military necessity. Though I'm sure you'd find such matters beyond you. You are a dashed handsome woman, I have to say."

"I'd rather you didn't, general."

"Please, call me Zignacious." He leaned closer. "Or Ziggy, even."

I smiled. "Zigeven. What a lovely name. It rolls off the tongue so easily."

"No, no. Just Ziggy."

"Oh, you're teasing me—you keep changing it. Well it's an impressive ship, Jusiggy."

"Wait, no..." The general looked at me as though I was as stupid as a brick. "Oh, never mind."

He led me through the *Illicimus*, prattling endlessly about the capabilities, weapons, and defenses. All of which would have been interesting if I were a spy, but it was exactly the type of meaningless detail designed to put me to sleep, and to prove the point, I yawned dramatically several times.

"I'm sorry, Jusiggy. I'm not adjusted to Guplides' time yet. Please don't take it personally."

The crew must have been given orders to keep clear, as we didn't see anyone until we reached the bridge, and even then, no one looked up when we entered. The bridge itself reflected the military exterior with a large command chair mounted on a raised platform, allowing the commander to look down on their subordinates. Through a viewscreen, large enough to have been used at one of our rassling shows, the purplish-green of Guplides' surface was visible, sunlight glittering painfully off the single ocean.

"A magnificent sight, isn't it?"

I shuddered. "It's very... round."

The general shook his head. "Enough of this, you must be hungry."

"Not really. You know... planet time..."

He leered at me. "I'm sure we can find *something* to tempt you."

"There must be a lot of wind," I said.

"What?"

I pointed to the viewscreen. "The clouds are moving so fast."

"Well, no... we're in orbit, so..." His eyes glazed over a little. "Yes, I imagine so."

I suppressed a smirk. Vinapo's evening wasn't going the way he'd planned. I followed him and we ended up in what I guessed was the officers' lounge—a large room with a long table, the walls decorated with various soligrams of warships and other militaria. We were the only ones there, but after the general seated me at the table, a junior officer appeared to serve us wine. He poured a small amount into a glass for me, and I sniffed the bouquet. It was delicious, but I wrinkled my nose. "Oh, that smells too strong. I'm in training…"

"What would you prefer, my dear?" the general said. "I keep a well-stocked cellar."

"Water would be perfect, Jusiggy."

"Water?"

"It's precious to Lecuundans, you know."

"Well, yes. That's understandable, but I thought..." He hesitated, then gestured at the junior officer. "Fetch some water."

The food was served in multiple lavish courses. A broth-like roast grendel soup was followed by assorted blackened vegetables mixed with exotically spiced stuffed pascinori mushrooms. After that came buttered garlic Jalvesian oysters, which were highly reminiscent of Lecuundan squidgeridoos, and I politely declined.

As each dish appeared, I noticed a common theme: all of them were opulently expensive, but beyond that, each one contained ingredients with reputedly aphrodisiac qualities. When I realized what was going on, I almost burst out laughing. Did he think something so childishly ridiculous was going to work?

The star attraction was triple-A rib eye from Galbreezia, cooked in a red wine and wild shallot sauce, served with buttery baby vegetables. As soon as the aroma drifted through the door, my mouth watered. While it wasn't going to get me between the general's sheets, my taste buds were certainly not objecting to this finery, and I attacked my plate with indecent haste.

After devouring the steak, I leaned back. The general's leer made me think of a sex addict trapped in a brothel. He tapped his knife against his wine glass. "The coffee please, ensign."

He turned back to me. "I thought you might appreciate a special treat, my dear."

The server returned and placed a small glass cup of coffee on the table next to me. It had a creamy layer floating on the top, and the scent of alcohol hit my palate like a hammer wrapped in honey. Then he moved around me and laid another plate on my left, containing a small pile of thick, disk-shaped confectionery.

"Lecuundan ChocoSpice-covered tingleberries?" I gasped. "Where did you get those?"

"It's remarkable what the military exchange can dig up with the right encouragement..." He smiled, his oily lips forming a broad arch. "...and the free use of a couple of escort ships."

Tingleberries are a luxury item on Lecuunda. They grow only near the freshest of water supplies at high altitude and have to go through exactly three frost cycles to mature properly, which is difficult on a planet with an average temperature of twenty-three degrees. Each of the chocolaty cookies on the plate would have cost more than an average person's monthly salary, and all together were worth thousands of Drubles. That was a lot to pay for the possibility of a horizontal bop, even with me.

I bit my lip. The problem was, they absolutely worked. On my homeworld, their effects were so well known that supply was strictly controlled. And the ChocoSpice coating made them virtually irresistible.

The general coughed. "Well, what do you think, my dear?"

I took a drink of the alcoholic coffee, and my head swam momentarily. I couldn't risk eating the tingleberries, but I couldn't think of a way of turning down such an opulent gesture. I gulped heavily, and the alcohol made my eyelids heavy.

"Well, I couldn't possibly..." I carried on quickly when Vinapo opened his mouth to object. "Not on my own."

"What do you mean?"

I pushed red pigment to my skin to fake a Terran blush. "Well, they work best when... both people partake... It uhhh... builds a mutual pheromonal bond between a... couple..."

The general grinned like a shark, his flat Terran teeth showing like ugly, white chisels. "Well, I'd be a poor host not to join you in such an experience, my dear."

He reached over, plucked a disk from the gold-trimmed plate, and demolished it with a single swallow.

"No! Not like that," I cried out. "Here, let me."

I grabbed the plate and took one of the dastardly delicacies, the luxurious soft outer layer melting slightly from the heat of my skin. I sniffed it, relishing the delicious tang, then waved it under the general's nose. "On Lecuunda, we call that the scent of lust."

"Oh, yes, absolutely…" he mumbled, his pale lips parting at the smell. "Lust."

I slid the disk into his mouth, ignoring the sight of his white, bloodless tongue turning brown as the ChocoSpice coating melted. I slid onto his lap, his bony knees poking at me through his sharply creased uniform pants, and shivered slightly. Then I took another and brushed it along the back of his ears, before popping it inside his mouth. It was such a terrible waste.

I fed him three more before he realized I wasn't having any. "I can certainly feel *something* tingling, my dear. But what about you?"

I knew I couldn't have any of them or I'd dissolve into a complete mess. "Well, with some *special* men, they're not… needed."

"Oh, I say. But I want you to enjoy them too."

Was there a hint of suspicion behind the flame of lechery burning all too brightly in his eyes? I picked up another tingleberry and moved it toward his mouth, but he pulled back.

"No, really, sweetie pie. I insist."

There was no way I wanted to eat the damn things. He'd swallowed several for sure, but they work more slowly on Terrans. For a Lecuundan, especially someone like me with little exposure to them, even one might be the end of my resistance. "How about…" I placed a disk between my lips, holding it as lightly as possible in the hope that it wouldn't melt, then leaned down, pressing my mouth over his and slipping my hand behind his bloated head.

I used my tongue to force most of the disk into his mouth, then realized he was enjoying it as he tried to push his tongue against mine. Terrans can be so gross, and this one more than most.

"MMMMmmm… you are a feast for an old man…" he murmured, his pupils dilating as the tingleberries started working.

For me, the small amount I'd inadvertently swallowed was enough to have every nerve ending yearning to be stimulated, and I pulled away, desperately gulping air.

"My room is down the corridor," he said, tottering to his feet. "I'm sure we'd be more… *comfortable* there."

I heard myself murmuring a yes, but it wasn't exactly a

conscious choice. I felt as though I was floating a few centimeters above the deck as we moved. My head was spinning as he fumbled with the lock, then threw the door open wide and entered, waving me in behind him. "Come in, my sweet. We shall make love among the stars."

I didn't have a clue what he was talking about, but then he flicked a switch, and the walls, floor, and ceiling dissolved around us, leaving only the ridiculously large four-poster bed visible. It was a holo-projection—we weren't in a vacuum—and I felt a little nauseous, not because of the view, but rather the sight of Vinapo next to the garish pink, silk bed pulling off his white uniform shirt to reveal a sickly gamboge-yellow vest, decorated with floral patterns and hearts.

"You should disrobe, my dear. Don't be shy." He grinned wetly. "I'll be gentle."

His grin turned into a drool, as a mini-waterfall of saliva leaked from his mouth. At the same time, he turned even more deathly white than usual, then a rainbow of kaleidoscopic colors rippled across his face.

"Are you alright, Jusiggy? You don't look well." I moved closer, feigning a shocked expression.

"Yes. I'm f-f-f-ime… fine…" Slime was still running down his chin, and he lurched against me, depositing his disgusting drool over my shoulder and dress. "What… ith… thsh…"

"Oh, Jusiggy! What's wrong, darling?" I helped him over to the bed, and he dropped onto it face first, his head lolling over the edge of the mattress.

"Jesh… need… ah… ohhhhhh…*splurrgghhhhh*…"

I danced back to avoid the pool of vomit on the floor and escape the fetid odor. "I'll get help!"

The door was highlighted faintly against the starry backdrop, and I jerked it open, calling out loudly. There was the thud of running feet in the corridor, and then the officer who'd served dinner appeared, accompanied by several other soldiers.

"There's something wrong with the general!" I blurted out, pointing at the mess on the bed. "Save him! Oh, save him."

The junior officer dived inside the room with a couple of the other soldiers. Minutes later, there were more gagging noises. I wasn't sure what state Vinapo was in, but the effects of tingleberries on Terrans were quite explosive from what I'd heard.

There was a great deal of loud grumbling, and I looked around to see Corporal Horden pushing through the gathering crowd. "Let me through. Out of the way, damn it."

I had my head down and was shaking as he reached me. Partly because the tingleberries had made my skin flush to an embarrassing degree, but also because I didn't want the corporal to see me fighting to suppress my laughter.

"Oh, Don. Please take me back," I gasped.

The darling put his arm around me, led me back to the docking bay, and helped me into the aircar. Soon we were dropping back toward the surface of Guplides. The tingleberries were kicking in hard, and my breathing was becoming increasingly shallow. I curled up in the back seat, fighting to control the trembling that threatened to make me explode.

"Ma'am? Are you okay?" Horden called from the front seat. "Hyperia?"

My skin was burning, and every movement sent paroxysms through my nervous system. The berries were well named. "Get us down. Quickly."

I felt the aircar change position as Horden brought us into a steeper dive. "Do you need a hospital, ma'am? A medic? Should I head for the base?"

"Just land. Now," I hissed.

I don't know how far away from the base we were. I may have blacked out for a while. The next thing I knew, a prickle of cool air brushed my hot skin.

"That's so good," I murmured.

A hand shook my shoulder gently, the extra warmth of skin against mine making me gasp. "Ms. Jones? Hyperia? Hype?"

I opened my eyes to see Don looking anxiously down at me. "I made an emergency landing. We're miles from anywhere, but you seemed insistent."

I reached up and brushed his face with my fingers. "Thank you… Don…"

"That's alright, ma... Hype... Are you sure you don't need a medic?"

"No. That's not what I need." I slid my hand behind his head and pulled him inside the car.

Nine

I wandered into the dining room around ten, ship's time, still enjoying a delicious mix of overstimulation and satiation. I had no idea what time Don had dropped me back at the *Centienne*, but it must have been well into the night. Not that I remembered him having any complaints.

Shehla was sitting at one of the gleaming white, curvy tables, munching on a plate of mixed salad that didn't look large enough to feed a small bird. All the Triplets played this fastidious game publicly, even with their fellow rasslers, but Stryng told me there was some serious in-room bingeing behind closed doors.

"Well, look what the cat dragged in..." Shehla waved her fork loosely in my direction. "You're in big trouble, sweetie. Dogface was looking for you, and he didn't look like he was after a belly rub. Despite how good you obviously are at that."

"What does that mean, exactly?" My good mood had already vanished.

Shehla's fork clattered down, and she stood to leave. "You're a big girl—figure it out yourself."

I had to admit, I felt kind of sleazy after my behavior the previous night but excused it by telling myself that the effects of the tingleberries had made me temporarily lose control. The truth was, I'd welcomed the casual intimacy, and the corporal had been the perfect way to wash away the memory of Vinapo's advances, and scratch that particular itch at the same time.

Lecuundan society in general is fairly relaxed about coupling. Though in my case, that was tempered by my personal relationships—my family wasn't relaxed about *anything*. That was one of the reasons I'd left and had no intention of returning anytime soon. But, on the whole, my people rarely form what others would call long-term relationships—we're loners at heart. Other than child-bearing and its attendant responsibilities, we take our pleasures where we find them. As long as no one gets hurt, why would anyone worry? There's an old saying on Lecuunda that roughly translates into Lingua as "sex is of the moment, respect is for life." Naturally, if two people wanted to stay together and do the whole forgoing thing, nobody would stop them, or even pass adverse comment. As they say in Lingua, "There are plenty more fish in the sea."

I ordered a Hemerian pear from the SynchroPabulator, but instead, the 'Pab spat out a fat onana with its customary *thonk*. A quick check of the machine's inventory interface confirmed we were out of pears, and I added a priority note for resupply. Onanas are mind-suckingly boring, despite being supposedly good for the brain cells. Though the brain boost might have been useful at that moment.

I ate in my room and opened up the Darkover interface, searching for anything on Guplides IV's narcotics business. I wasn't worried about Bolt tapping into this activity. From his perspective, it would mean I was doing as I was told. The information I wanted wasn't hard to find. The SlamCandy operation was being run by a bunch of local thugs called the Mechna, a Guplidian word which meant *blood and steel*. The records showed them to be a dangerous group to cross, though their reach seemed largely confined to the Guplides system.

As was typical with such operations, the Mechna had links to the local enforcement agencies and maintained a legitimate business front as dealers in antiquities and works of art—useful for explaining away sudden large transfers of cash. They were even listed in the Realms Better Business Index with a four and a half nova rating.

I didn't poke too deeply into the Darkover listings. The Mechna would probably have access to the network too, and I didn't want to run the risk of tipping my hand or leaving traces of my interest. I did reach out to Bydox, one of my few preferred contacts, and spent a few hundred drubles acquiring detailed plans of the offices of Signaralito Consulting, Fine Arts and Antiquities.

I wasn't sure I could trust Bydox—that's something you can never know for certain on Darkover—but we'd traded information before, so I had more confidence in him than anyone else on there. I say he, but I didn't know what sex they were, or even their species. As long as I got the information I needed, none of that mattered.

Someone hammered on the door, and I heard Denton's growl. "Hype, I know you're in there. We need to talk."

I shut down my terminal and unlocked the door. Before I had a chance to fully open it, he barged inside, his muzzle curling upward.

"I take it there's a problem." I dropped onto the couch, watching him closely.

"You might say that. I've been on Stellcom all morning with Vinapo's chief aides. They say you poisoned him."

"That's ridiculous. I had dinner with him, and he overindulged. Then he tried to force-feed me aphrodisiacs and had too many himself. That's stupidity, not poisoning."

"And you let him?" Denton barked. "You were supposed to entertain him. You know, amuse him."

"Was I supposed to let him sexually assault me too?" I pushed up from the couch. Denton wasn't the only one who was angry now, and I turned my back on him.

"Come on, Hype. You're not that naive—sometimes the job is tough."

I spun around. "I didn't realize the job included whoring myself out on demand."

His prosthetic ears dropped. "You know I didn't mean *that*."

"Why don't *you* sleep with him?"

Denton held up his hands. "They said he'll be out of action for days."

"Good. By then we'll be done with the show and can leave him and his nasty little mind behind us."

"Sooner than that," said Denton. "The show's been canceled. We've got six hours to clear out."

"They can't do that."

"And they're not going to pay us either."

I thought for a minute. That couldn't be. After all, we were there because Bolt had arranged it, even if Denton and the others didn't know about that.

He jerked his prosthetic head off and threw it on my bed. "Come on, Hype. Don't clam up on me now. You got us into this, and now you've screwed it up. You can't pretend it's nothing to do with you. The stage crew's already tearing stuff down."

"I'm not ignoring you." I'd been thinking about how to fix it. "Give me some time, okay? I'll see what I can do."

"There's no way Vinapo will listen to you."

My immediate plan was to contact Bolt, but I wasn't about to tell Denton that. "Perhaps I can appeal to his better nature."

Denton rubbed his hand over his forehead. "I don't think he has one—not with you."

"We'll see." I threw Denton's doggy head at him and shooed him out.

"And how the hell do I explain this to Mr. Quy?"

"Don't tell him anything yet."

"I'm serious Hype—this could be the end of FIRE. I've got to let him know."

I wasn't sure how long it would take to get hold of Bolt. "Give me the rest of the day. Okay?"

Denton shook his head, then pulled his dog prosthetic back on. "Five hours. After that the teardown restarts, and I'm on the Stellcom to Mr. Quy."

"Okay. Go."

I closed the door and scrabbled through my drawer to find Bolt's contact card. He'd said to only use it in an emergency and this certainly qualified. At least if he wanted the mission to continue. Like all such cards, it came with a built-in q-link combination, and I waved it past the detector on my terminal. The call connected on the third ring, and his all-too-smooth face appeared.

"John Bolt."

"Bolt, *we've* got a problem."

"Yes?"

"Vinapo's playing up. He's canceled the show. You need to apply some pressure or this thing's done."

"Go on," Bolt said, clearly unimpressed.

"Don't you get it? We're getting kicked off Guplides. We've got five hours to fix this, or the game is over. Denton will take us back into space on board the *Ethereal Queen*, and I'll be with him."

"And you are?"

"Huh?" Realization dawned, and I nearly slammed my fist into the screen. Only a sadist would use an answer simulacrum like that, evidently designed to fool people into thinking it was a real person.

"You know who I am. Get back to me as soon as you get this. And honestly, I hope you're too damn late."

I punched the disconnect so hard I'd have broken a fingernail if I was Terran. Lecuundans are made of sterner stuff though—but it still hurt.

There was no telling when Bolt would return my call, and I was too on edge to wait in my cabin. I left looking for a distraction, though if preparations were already underway for leaving, a lot of people would be busy packing. I mooched into the makeshift practice area, attracted by the sounds of someone training. It turned out to be Atsuno working through some standard moves with a hard-light workout-nanokin.

"Please. Tell me *you're* not mad at me," I said.

Atsuno stopped the nanokin and smiled. "One of those days, huh? Don't worry, babe, you're not on my hit list—except in the TwistCube."

"I think you're the only one." I grabbed a vitamin drink from the dispenser, tossed one to her, then opened a second for myself. The chilled liquid gave me goosebumps, and my skin turned a rich Uranian blue—at least that's the way the others described it. I'd asked where the name came from and was fed a line about it being related to the original Terran star system—a sure sign it was so much vraz. Whenever Terrans want to make something seem mysterious or unique, they say it came from their long-lost, and undoubtedly fictional, home system. I liked the sound of it in Lingua though, so didn't argue.

"Denton is angry over the loss of this show." Atsuno frowned. "He didn't bother with the usual cancelation clause because he thought it was such a sure thing."

That explained a lot, especially his worry about telling Mr. Quy. "Well, hopefully, we can straighten things out."

The training area was flat and filled with padded mats but no gravitational shifting facilities. It was useful for general workouts and training though, as a safer environment than the TwistCube, which was highly dangerous if not treated with respect. Atsuno wandered over to where I was leaning against the cushioned wall. She was so petite, she barely made the soft surface move, but her appearance was deceptive, as many opponents had found out.

"What are you up to, Hype? I swear something's going on and no one is talking about it. It's driving me and everyone else frutso. How about coming clean with little old Atsuno?"

I'd have loved to tell her everything, but that would mess up the entire company. Besides, I doubted she'd believe the truth if I told her. Some things simply don't make sense from the outside. "I wish I knew, but I'm in the dark as much as anyone."

She shook her head. "Okay, if you don't want to share your dirty little secrets, how about giving me a hands-on practice session? The nanokin routines are pretty boring."

A workout sounded good. It would keep my mind off my current problems for a while if nothing else and burn off some nervous energy. "Sure."

I grabbed a training suit from the shelves and pulled it on, then turned back to Atsuno, dropping into a defensive posture. As usual, she gave a slight bow, cupping her right hand with her left. Ats looks like a small porcelain doll, her skin a naturally milky white, and her hair a dark copper with a subtle hint of fire. I'm about ten centimeters taller than her, and thirty or forty percent heavier. But that didn't mean she was a walkover.

Before she was hired into the FIRE stable, Atsuno had been an Inter-Realms level professional competitor in several martial arts, including Jundigwo, Shocu-loblo, and Mekukak. Denton had brought her in as a trainer with the idea of updating the skills of the entire roster, and she'd enjoyed it so much she'd stayed on. Now, she regularly held practice sessions in her favorite styles, as well as being an active competitor. I'd asked her why once, and she'd told me she found it more fun, and it paid much better.

Atsuno adopted a defensive stance too, circling to my left. This wasn't a match, so there'd be no quarter given. This was for sweat and honor. She'd studied my fights probably as much as I'd obsessed over hers and everyone else's, searching for a weakness that could be exploited when needed.

It's funny that our beloved audience never sees us fight for real. They get the fancy, dramatized bawdy-house grotesque version exaggerated beyond all sense, but it looks good. This was the real thing—far less flamboyant but infinitely more dangerous.

Atsuno made a feint, and I dodged back. She'd deliberately left a slight opening to lure me in, but I'm smarter than that and held back. We danced around, ducking and jabbing, both trying to make the other flinch and open up a chance to grapple, without much success. Then I dummied a misstep, and she took the bait, closing in with the intention of delivering several blows, not realizing she'd fallen into my trap.

I used my height and reach to wrap her up, ready to drop her into a spine-breaker and finish the bout.

Then I was on the mat with my legs bent agonizingly the wrong way. Atsuno pressed down while simultaneously applying several jabs to pressure points I didn't know Lecuundans possessed. I had a vague memory of a slithery blur before it happened, and that was all. Atsuno increased the tension until I thought my back would break, and I slapped the mat in surrender.

Lecuundans don't have a spine in the same sense as Terrans, but the compression on my dorsal cartilage plates was enough. Atsuno helped me back to my feet, and I brushed myself down to give me a minute or two to recover some of my pride.

"Another fall?" she said.

I stretched my shoulders and dropped into a low stance once more. "Sure."

I saw a slinking movement behind her and realized Stryng had slithered into the training room. He looked at us, his tail making a soft buzzing sound as it vibrated in excitement. "My two favorite ladies in a practice session? This I gotta watch."

Stryng had once told me the only reason he'd got involved in rassling was to get a close-up view of the jiggles and flexing of the female contestants when they were in action. I, for one, believed him. Atsuno laughed, then turned back to me. We circled again, crouched low, with Stryng making observations about the quality of our *wiggles*, then she made a move.

Atsuno feinted a combination, following up with a leg sweep, but this time I was ahead of her and hopped over her leg, diving in close and ducking behind her. I locked my arms around her midriff and rolled backward, flipping her onto her shoulders and arching upwards in a Galactic Bridge, leaving her helpless.

"Oh yeah, that's hotter than nude rassling in chili pepper jelly," said Stryng, his tail slapping the floor in applause.

I suspected the real reason for his admiration wasn't my brilliantly executed maneuver, but the fact that we were now contorted into positions that stretched our pelvises. Sometimes he acts like he's never seen an ass before.

Atsuno tried to wriggle free, but I flexed my arms, squeezing the breath out of her until she tapped my thigh with her palm.

"Great move, Hype," she said, rolling to her feet when I released her. "Another?"

I was about to say yes when my wrist-com tingled, letting me know I had a message waiting. It had better be Bolt. "Sorry, I need to run. I've thought of something that might help Denton."

Atsuno nodded, then bowed deep. Making herself look somehow half as small and nowhere near as strong as she actually was.

My back was aching from the stretch Atsuno had put on me, and I rolled my shoulders to get the knots out as I hit the accept button on my comms console.

"This is terribly inconvenient," Bolt sneered through the screen. "You're supposed to be operating independently. I don't have time for babysitting."

My teeth gritted. I didn't expect much from him, but I *was* working on his behalf. I also resented the implication that I wasn't capable of handling myself.

"If you don't like what I'm doing, feel free to get someone else for this ridiculous operation."

Bolt gave a long blink. "I've sent a message to General Vinapo, reminding him of his obligations under the Charter. He was not happy, and from what he said, I'm not surprised."

"What did that fat slug say happened?"

"You are to proceed with your mission and retrieve the requested information. You have one hundred standard hours to complete your tasks."

"A week?" I spat. "How generous. An operation like this takes time and planning. You can't expect—"

Bolt stared at me with the dead eyes of a Nienusian sandshark.

"How goes the invasion? Have the insectoid zombies overrun the east sector with their gelfling starships yet?"

Bolt's face didn't change. It was that damn messaging simulacrum. Once again, the bastard had let me think I was on a live transmission, instead of the usual courtesy of flagging it as a recorded message.

"Remind me to kick your ass one day." I reached for the disconnect. "Out."

Bolt's fake face faded from the screen. A week wasn't a long time to pull off that sort of job safely, but it was possible. But the real difficulty was it didn't leave me much room to carry out any personal jobs, and I was determined to compensate myself for his interference in my life. I leafed through the hard copy research from Stryng. Most of it was useless, something not unexpected— the usual rate of trash to gems was always high.

I flipped open a sheaf of sheets that were reproductions of records from one of the early families on Guplides, and as I pored over the mass of information, I found something: the perfect solution to my problems. Or at least it would be if I was able to verify the item was on the planet and in the hands of the original owners—or to be accurate, their descendants.

Algernon's Flower was an ancient crystalline life form that, according to the information, "flowered" once every two hundred and fifty standard years. At that time, it changed from its usual unattractive stony egg appearance, splitting at the top and peeling back to allow the petals to emerge in a coruscant display of shimmering, colored crystals. It stayed like this for several weeks, waiting to be pollinated, and if unsuccessful, closed back up for another wait. As it was the only known specimen of the species, there wasn't much chance of fertilization. Its origins were a baffling mystery that no one had penetrated. But that was all so much prattle.

The fact was, it was worth a fortune on the open (underground) market, with no questions asked. Even better, it was eminently transportable. And, as if that wasn't enough, it was recorded as being in the possession of the Signaralito family—owners of the Fine Art and Antiquities Company that was the front for the Mechna. I leaned back in my seat and, for the first time since Bolt had disrupted my life, smiled widely—a genuinely happy expression that built into chortles and finally belly laughs. I was going to grab the information for Bolt and Olive Branch, and at the same time make myself richer than the mythical Bingbong brothers who, according to legend, had built Muchdolla, the first completely artificial planet.

I wasn't going to sit around doing nothing while I waited for things to resolve themselves. I needed inside information on the Signaralito operation. The trick was how to get it. Nanoprobes might work, but they weren't the easiest technology to use at long range. Increasing swarm density was an option, but a bigger cloud made the probes easier to detect. And a group of SlamCandy pushers would be touchy about possible surveillance.

Several other options for remote information gathering ran through my head. They were all viable and would have undoubtedly worked against a regular target, but crooks provide greater challenges. Then the solution came to me. It was bold, audacious, some might also say reckless. But it was perfect, and I knew I could pull it off. I reached out and opened a comm-line to Atsuno.

"I'm looking for a dinner date. You in?"

"We're leaving in a few hours."

"I know, so we might as well enjoy the local culture first." I bit my lip. I needed her and a few of the others to help with my cover. "Besides, the crew will handle most of it."

Atsuno wrinkled her nose, making her look even cuter than usual. Her skin had a slight pink glow from her workout. "Sure, give me five... hmmm better make it ten. Where we going?"

"Sightseeing, and I found a restaurant downtown with good ratings. After that, maybe some shopping."

"Angled?"

She was asking if we were going to play out our current fake romantic story, and I was initially going to say no. Then I realized it would work perfectly. "Sure, let's take Zav and Brach."

"Brach is in the tub. You know what he's like."

Brachyura, like me, was especially fond of water and long baths, but in his case, it was more of a spiritual experience. Once he was in, he wouldn't come out short of several hours—or a major catastrophe. "I'll find someone to make up a foursome."

"Sounds fun." Atsuno's eyes twinkled mischievously.

"Get your mind out of the gutter, I didn't mean it *that* way."

I disconnected the channel and called around the other rasslers. Everyone was busy packing or otherwise engaged until I messaged ChaosRhino. He was happy to tag along when I mentioned Atsuno—everybody loves that girl.

In fact, he was perfect for what I had in mind.

Ten

Guplides base wasn't far from the capital, Louvier, and dinner was at Le Salon des Miséreux in the exclusive east end Parkwood district. I was picking up the tab personally, though I should have claimed it through expenses as we were all in character and promoting the upcoming event. I'd have had to clear it with Denton, though, and that wasn't going to happen ahead of word coming through that the show was back on. Anyway, after I put through my plans, I'd never have to worry about money again.

Despite the restaurant's name, there was nothing vaguely modest about the menu prices, and I gulped slightly. Atsuno was famous for her sparse diet, and Zavara was a fairly modest eater, but ChaosRhino had the legendary rapacious M'Charran appetite.

He towered above me at two meters tall, the prosthetic horns on his head adding at least another thirty centimeters. Luckily, the restaurant's vaulted ceilings were capable of dealing with his height, although he had to duck through the door.

We'd visited a few scenic spots on our way across town and gathered a large flock of bystanders, who were now peering in through the windows, much to the dismay of the *maître d'* and other guests. A quick wave of my Faberium Epicurist card and we were ushered to a quiet spot in the corner, largely out of sight of everyone else.

Atsuno leaned over the table. "Where'd you get that?"

I stuffed the card back in my purse. "A fan sent it. Is it special?"

"Are you kidding?" Atsuno's eyes widened. "They're as rare as teeth on a Circinian bloatworm."

I knew what it was but decided it was safer to play dumb. "You're teasing me. It just means you like good food."

Atsuno gave me an odd look, but I was saved when a waiter arrived to take our orders.

The food was every bit as good as the reputation had led me to believe, and I tucked into a spicy kombu chorizo with crispy kale noodles. I'd expected both of the men to opt for the succulent Novanian top steak but was surprised when Rhino chose a baked tofu cassoulet with a garden salad.

"Need to watch my weight," he said. "This suit shows every gram."

I sympathized. The bodysuits worn by most of the roster fitted like a second skin, and weren't designed for anyone with body image issues. Usually, though, it was the female rasslers who worried about it—the men had greater leeway in terms of dress. ChaosRhino's outfit was different, however, and made out of the same M-Flesh as my Martha getup, except in his case it covered most of his body and was textured to resemble the thick hide of his long-extinct namesake.

"You could come up with a new gag. Like you have a skin disorder or something," I suggested.

"That's not funny. This thing plays havoc with my eczema. You should see the back of my thighs after a match." ChaosRhino gave one of his characteristic snorts. "I've been begging Denton for a switch, but the crowd loves the Rhino."

"That's too bad." I patted his forearm, which was as thick as an interstellar dust cloud. "Makes you wonder why we do this, doesn't it?"

"Not me." He picked up a breadstick and nibbled it. "Job prospects for a literary history student fresh from college weren't good."

"You were a lit major?" I hadn't socialized with ChaosRhino much up until then, but with his physique, I'd assumed he had a sports background. He was heavily built, even for a M'Charran.

"What about you, Hype?" Atsuno said. "What got a nice girl like you involved in this circus?"

She caught me off guard, and I should have been prepared with a ready answer. I could hardly announce it was the perfect cover for an itinerant thief. "I'm a runaway."

"Sounds mysterious." Atsuno wrinkled her perfectly pert nose. "What were you running away from?"

"An army of admirers, I'm sure." Zavara doffed his plumed hat.

"Hey, you're supposed to be my date." Atsuno stabbed her elbow into Zavara's ribs. "What was it, Hype? You better tell us before Zav's imagination runs riot and he starts drooling."

"Not much to tell." I sipped some cold water in an effort to block a potentially embarrassing color change. "My family wanted me to enter the family business. I wanted to travel and see the universe."

"What does your family do?" ChaosRhino asked.

"It's difficult to explain exactly—you might call it management consulting."

This idea was boring enough that, thankfully, the questions dried up and the conversation turned more general, focusing mainly on the upcoming show and its on/off/on status.

After eating, we took a tour of the city in something called a *carruaje de caballos*. It was an impractical way of traveling for sure, consisting of an open-topped carriage, with no propulsion except for a giant six-legged animal. The operator told us the creature was a *caballo*, and the whole thing was directed not by a computer but by using two long straps tied to the animal's nose. Don't laugh— I'm serious. I wasn't sure what happened to the straps at the caballo's nose—maybe the poor creature had neural interfaces there or something—but to be honest, I didn't want to look closely enough to find out.

The crowd followed us when we left the restaurant and increased in size. After several near misses with over-zealous fans that spooked the caballo, Ernesto, the carruaje operator, politely asked us to switch to a regular form of transport to finish our tour. We disembarked and summoned a skycab limousine, then continued to check out the city sights from the air. This gave us unprecedented views and also thinned the herd of followers.

Atsuno, like me, was excited, eagerly pointing out various landmarks, while Zavara and ChaosRhino spent most of the flight being complete bores—discussing work and the latest pro-sport technology. When I finally suggested visiting the antiques store, nobody objected, and we instructed the cab to take us there right away.

As we clambered out, a small shiver teased my skin, despite it being a pleasantly warm evening. It was time to lock horns with the enemy.

The store was an old-fashioned looking brick and concrete affair clinging against a hillside, with an overabundance of fake columns at the front—no doubt designed to impress the clientele. It looked ugly and reminded me of a Lecuundan jail.

The columns, as well as the broad steps leading up to the wide main entrance, were dressed in pure-white alabaster that looked pink now the sun was dropping lower. It gave the building a rather feminine appearance that I felt sure wasn't what the designers intended. The building had originally been the Signaralito family residence before the lean years hit, and I couldn't imagine Slam-Candy dealers putting on such a display, even as a cover for their illicit activities.

I locked arms with Rhino, and Atsuno did the same with Zavara, as we strolled toward the entrance. As we crossed the wide paved area, I did a rapid assessment of the external security—cameras, motion sensors, heat sensors, and theta-band scanners. All the usual stock-in-trade of a decent security system, apart from the dummy cameras placed around the parking lot with high capacity power lines running to them and lenses that were clearly designed to project X-Slice beams, if triggered.

The doors opened as we approached, and a weaselly man stepped out. His skin looked stretched and thin, likely as a result of one too many rejuve treatments, but his eyes had a glint in them as hard as B'Seani borodite. An electronic monocle was fitted to the side of his head, making him look like he'd been caught by a badly timed punch.

"Welcome, welcome, dear friends. Signaralito Consulting—Fine Arts and Antiquities is pleased to entertain esteemed members of the renowned FIRE." He glanced into the air, checking the entourage swarming around us in a variety of air and surface vehicles, not to mention several dozen on foot. "I'm Nilo, humble proprietor of this modest establishment. It's a pleasure to see you brought so many... friends."

"Just the four of us," said Zavara, escorting Atsuno up the steps.

"Of course." Nilo tilted at the waist in a bow that should have been accompanied by loud creaking.

After passing through the entrance chamber, decorated with paintings by old fakers, we entered the main display room. The walls were a pale, but rich, off-white with burgundy highlights, covered in a bewildering number of artworks, ancient weaponry, and more X-Slice projectors. Catsonic surveillance detectors lined the cornice-like jewels. These people definitely believed in overkill when it came to security.

Nilo led us around, cooing over each piece as if it were one of his children. ChaosRhino tapped his hoof and scratched ineffectually at the rhino hide, but Atsuno and Zavara listened to the flamboyant descriptions as though each exhibit would unveil the mysteries of the universe. I showed an interest in everything, though several items were so obviously fake they looked like they'd been made by a child.

"...a legacy of the ancient Klompf dynasty and, according to the original owners, has a provenance that runs all the way back to Earth, the famous Terran homeworld."

Famous—certainly. Mythical—also equally likely. At least eighty percent of collectibles I'd ever seen were listed as having some connection to Earth. According to Terrans, everything of value derived from there, which made it even more incredible that they'd managed to lose their treasured planet.

As we toured the displays, I surreptitiously examined the security. Like the systems outside, it was a combination of passive and active sensors mixed with badly concealed weaponry. In many ways it was more extensive than the setup at a bank—which given the owners' other activities wasn't too surprising. Paranoia is such a motivating force.

All of that meant nothing, though, after I caught a glimpse of the alarm system control box through a side door. I didn't need more than a glance to identify it as a Blockham Controller, unmistakable with its three large, vertically mounted buttons.

"What do you think of this, Hype?"

Atsuno held a small, golden figurine, distorted beyond any

normally accepted proportions for a humanoid, with wings sprouting from its shoulders instead of arms. The figure was half kneeling, reaching forward dramatically, which to me looked like it was in pain. I recognized it as one of Varruca's famous Golden Earth-Angels, or more likely a passable imitation.

"Looks fake to me," I said.

Nilo jumped, then sniffed prodigiously. "I assure you, madam, Signaralito Consulting is extremely thorough in verifying the provenance of its exhibits and is highly selective in which items it offers its patrons."

"Oh sure. I guess. I wouldn't know."

He sniffed again and started describing a fake Swilin dynasty vase that had been sculpted by a clumsy butcher wielding a shovel. "This is perhaps one of the best items of early Swilin ceramics to be found on Guplides, and a fine example of the renowned blue glaze these items are deservedly famous for. This came to us by way of—"

"That's it!" I squealed, running forward to pick up a small silver jug in the shape of some animal I didn't recognize.

Nilo turned toward me, and his electronic monocle snapped over his eye with a dramatic click. "Oh yes. Madam has a discerning eye. That is a fiftieth century cow creamer in the *art boko* style, of Drutch origin."

"It's beautiful." I gazed in fake adoration at the monstrous object. "Is it really for sale?"

Nilo smiled plasticly. "Certainly, madam. Everything has its price."

Atsuno and the others were staring at me as though I'd announced I was leaving FIRE to marry the UberKaiser.

"Better check it, Hype," she said. "Looks like sixty-eighth century U'Conian to me."

I frowned, forcing a fake tear from one eye. "You don't think it's real?"

Nilo drew himself up to his full one hundred and fifty-five centimeter height and pulled on the tips of his tightly curled mustache. "I assure madam that we deal only in the highest quality collectibles. If you have any doubts, check the holo-mark."

Holo-marks are a universal, non-destructive inscription used throughout the Realms to authenticate antiquities. "Oh yes, I suppose so." I turned the shapeless metal pot in my hands, staring at it blankly. The tiny crystal that produced the holo-mark was fused to the bottom, but I deliberately ignored it, turning the object over several times.

"Here." Nilo plucked the creamer from my hands, flipped it upside down, and tapped the crystal.

A display appeared in the air, projected from the crystal. It contained a description, points of interest, and an ownership log going back as far as could be traced, along with genetic signatures of each owner. While holo-marks could be faked, it wouldn't be worth the effort for something as low value as the creamer.

I grabbed it again and passed it over to ChaosRhino. "What do you think, sweetie? Is it worth it?"

Rhino looked confused, but it passed in a fraction of a second. He was too experienced in rassling improvisation to let anything throw him for long.

"I dunno, babe." He held up the creamer in one giant hand. "Looks kinda cheap for you."

"Awww, you know me so well, Rhiniekins." I giggled, clinging onto his thick, scaly arm. "Let's look around some more."

ChaosRhino turned, and I *accidentally* caught his leg with mine. He staggered against one of the shelves, and for a second, it looked like everything was going to topple. Nilo jumped forward, and so did I, and together we managed to stabilize the display.

"I beg of you, sir, please do be careful. We have a strict policy of demanding compensation for any and all breakages, and I would hate for you to be financially embarrassed." Rhino managed to look sheepish, even through his skinsuit, and I felt a little bad for having caused the near calamity.

After that, we allowed Nilo to show us the rest of the collection, with ChaosRhino staying respectfully back from the objects. I squealed and lavished my full attention on all of them, being careful to touch every piece.

"Now, if I may, allow me to show you our centerpiece, or perhaps I should say, the *pièce de résistance*." Nilo ushered us toward a side chamber but halted ChaosRhino with a wave. "Please forgive me, but the area is far too compact to manage the gentleman's *largesse.*"

Rhino snorted but agreed to wait in the main hall, while the rest of us shuffled in.

The small chamber was intimately lit with amber lights. The walls were bare, completely free of any type of decoration, and in the center stood a polished Circinian blue oak table, the deep azure wood decorated with exquisite borodium inlays. On top of the table was a fine, velvet square with a small, wafer-thin, *genuine* Swilin dynasty bowl sitting on it. Inside the bowl was a shapeless and unimpressive crystal about the size of a mouse, nestled in a bed of Vholian moss.

"This, ladies and gentleman, is the famous Algernon's Flower," whispered Nilo, as if in awe of the display. "While it looks a little mundane right now, in one hundred and thirteen years, it will blossom into the most brilliant of spectacles. It is undoubtedly one of the most select items in our collection, and I assure you, I don't boast when I say one of the rarest items in all the Seventeen Realms."

I yawned enthusiastically. "What a letdown—a stupid lump of rock."

Atsuno looked at me sharply. "Hype, where are your manners?" She turned back to Nilo. "I'm sure it's incredibly beautiful, Mr. Nilo."

"Well, I'm going to look at that creamer thing again." I swished out of the small display room, eyeballing ChaosRhino. "Come on, that thing's a swindle."

I led him back to the ugly creamer and picked it up again, then whispered to him, "Buy this for me, okay?"

He looked at the price and swallowed. It wasn't that expensive, but everything there was carrying collector rates.

"I can't afford it, Hype," he whispered back. "Stryng totally screwed me in a game of Droid Despair on the way out here. I'm broke till payday."

"I'll pay for it. But it'd look better if you did. Part of the kayfabe, okay?"

He nodded, then stopped as one of his horns caught on a chandelier, making it rattle dangerously.

"*Do* be careful, sir," said Nilo, reemerging from the side room.

"Sure. Sure."

Rhino lowered his head and stomped a little, and Nilo's wrinkled skin turned a much paler shade of gray.

"I'd like to get this for my lady here." ChaosRhino pointed to the creamer. "Anything for you, babe."

I clapped my hands, and wrapped my arms around his massive bicep, pulling him closer. "Oh thank you, thank you. You're the best, better than all the rest."

As I cuddled with him, I surreptitiously slipped a roll of drubles into his belt pouch, patting him to let him know what was going on.

Nilo beamed, but it was obvious he was unhappy to have spent so much time with us for so little. "The catalog price on that is three hundred and fifty. But I'd be willing to let you steal it for three twenty-five as I'm such a pro-rassling fan."

ChaosRhino glowered at Nilo, lowering his head farther and snorting loud enough to blow back the salesman's gray hair.

"Did I say three twenty-five?" Nilo straightened his hair again. "I meant three hundred, of course."

ChaosRhino scraped the ground with a hoof, still crouched low so his horns were pointed directly at Nilo.

"Two seventy-five?"

"Two fifty," Rhino grunted. "And I want it gift wrapped."

"Yes, sir. Naturally. Two hundred and fifty it is."

ChaosRhino winked at me, and I smiled back. I didn't have the heart to tell him that the "rare" creamer was worth no more than seventy drubles, even if it was genuine. None of the others were tempted by anything, and given the prices, they were smart not to be. But I'd done everything I needed to, and was more than happy to head back to the *Centienne*.

Phase two was about to begin.

Eleven

When I reached my room, the comm light was flashing and I answered the call, not sure what to expect but relieved when Denton's doggy face appeared.

"Hype, you're a genius." He smacked his jowls. "How did you pull it off?"

"I take it the gig has been reinstated?"

"I never thought you'd convince Vinapo after what happened." He frowned and looked hangdog. "You didn't have to… you know, do anything unpleasant, did you?"

"So you do care?" I relaxed, knowing we were still in the game. "Don't worry, I used logical reasoning with him. And that's all."

"Well, call it whatever you like. I'm glad I don't have to talk to Mr. Quy."

"So am I."

"Come on, what was the trick? That guy was ready to send us off-world at gunpoint."

I smiled. "A lady never reveals her secrets."

Denton's laugh came out as a soft, snuffly growl. "Okay. Want to join me for a nightcap? I feel like celebrating."

"Thanks, but it's been a long day, and I'm ready to turn in."

Denton looked disappointed, and I felt bad about giving him the cold shoulder, but my plans didn't allow for any socializing. After saying goodnight, he closed the call, and I lay on my bed, running through my plans one last time. I closed my eyes, visualizing how things were going to work out. It was going to be good. After setting my internal alarm, I drifted into sleep.

When I woke, everything felt a little surreal. While I can operate on two hours of sleep, it doesn't leave me the brightest fish in a shoal. I rolled off the bed and stretched, going through a series of limbering-up calisthenics designed to bring me fully awake. There was no sound from around me, other than the ever-present soft hiss from the air systems. I checked the time. It was two in the morning, giving me plenty of time to complete the mission and return for breakfast before anyone missed me.

After pulling on my nullsuit, I checked the built-in systems before pulling the mask over my face and switching on the distortion field. The gravboard was fully charged, so I slipped noiselessly into the ship. Halfway to the main airlock, I turned a corner to see Stryng coming the other way. He whistled as he slithered, and I had no idea what he was doing up so late. But he sometimes kept odd hours. I wondered if he'd been entertaining one or more of the Bonor Triplets but dismissed the thought. Even if he had been, it was no business of mine.

I edged back around the corner. Stryng's quarters were to the left, which meant he should pass by without ever getting close, so I waited. He skated out across the intersection and was almost at the other side when he stopped whistling, his wiggling motion ceasing as he came to a halt. His upper end twisted as his eye spots looked around, and for a moment he appeared to stare straight at me.

He shouldn't be able to see me, but I held my breath. I'd used the distortion field many times to get in and out. You never knew where you were with Stryng though. He played things close to his chest, and no one knew the full extent of his capabilities. Maybe he didn't know them himself.

After a little while, he resumed his whistling and continued on his way. I breathed out and hastened toward the exit, not wanting to risk another encounter.

Outside, I jumped on the gravboard and soared into the sky, heading to Louvier at full speed. Once airborne, I switched off the Distortion Matrix to save power. I wouldn't need it until I was much closer to the Signaralito building. My nerves were playing up as I flew, something unusual for me. It might have been the lingering idea that Stryng had detected me through the Matrix, or maybe the thrill of going into action knowing I'd be infinitely wealthier once this job was complete. Plus I'd be rid of the interfering Bolt.

The Guplides sky was a deep cobalt blue tinged with streaks of pink from the planet's small moon, reminding me of some of the cave dives I used to enjoy back on Lecuunda. I wasn't supposed to explore the caves—too deep and risky according to my parents. But I did it anyway, driven by the pleasurable sensation of unbridled rebellion.

The slab-like gallery was visible, and I slowed my approach. Now was the time to be careful and not get overexcited by the prospect of getting my hands on a valuable treasure. I reactivated the Matrix, dropping to the ground several hundred meters away, hidden from direct line of sight by rocks and trees. Then I pulled out my specially prepared ace and tossed it into the air.

The drone tumbled briefly, then stabilized, before shooting off into the near blackness of the night, heading for the Signaralito establishment. It was smaller than the palm of my hand and virtually silent. I'd programmed it to use the flight characteristics of a Guplidean hawk moth, and the composite construction would give back a similar signal to any prying detectors, so I was fairly sure it would do its job.

Opening up the remote viewer, I fed the signal from the drone into the lenses of my mask, following its progress as it approached the gallery. The view wasn't perfect—there's a limit to how much you can squeeze into a package that tiny—but it was enough for me to monitor its progress.

It swept past the building, following a series of paths that would look random to any observer but, in fact, traced the outlines of the walls. Despite my limited perspective, it was clear that all the security systems were fully operational. That place was sewn up tighter than the UberKaiser's faberium-plated underwear. Even with the Distortion Matrix, I'd be tagged by the Catsonic Detectors and cut to pieces by the X-Slice projectors before I made it a meter. The drone's data feed popped up a green light, and I smiled to myself. The payload had been delivered. Now it was only a question of patience.

It didn't take long and after a few minutes, I picked up the pings of data from the swarm of attoprobes deployed by the drone. I switched the data feed through to my lenses. A ghostly 3D display made up of glowing green points appeared as the microscopic bots scanned the areas around them, building a fully mapped view of everything inside.

Soon everything was almost as visible as if I were in there myself, right down to identifying the items on display. Three areas glowed brighter than the others. One was the small chamber holding Algernon's Flower. The second was a room behind the public areas containing several desks and, more significantly, the business's easily identifiable data systems. The third and brightest cluster was around the Blockham Controller.

Blockham is one of the most widely used and well-regarded security systems. It's easy to operate, which makes it popular with customers. It requires little maintenance and isn't prone to false alarms—so it's favored by installers too. It also has the capability of interfacing with all mainstream sensor systems, and can be hooked up to dubious "active deterrent systems" such as the X-Slice beams in use here. Making everyone happy.

I sent the signal to the attoprobes near the controller, and they broadcast a specific q-link keycode. The code activated the front maintenance panel release, and it popped open. Not by much, but plenty of room for several trillion of my attoprobes to enter. They lined up dutifully. Then, moving collectively, they pushed the now exposed disarm switch that was inside the box, and the entire security system shut down.

The disarm switch existed for service technicians, but nearly every Blockham Controller had a common default keycode, which few customers bothered to change. This made the system useless as it left a door wide open to anyone who had the skill to access it remotely. I laughed at how easy it had been. All that was left was to go in and take what I wanted.

I sauntered up to the building, not bothering to switch the Distortion Matrix back on. The sensors outside were as dead as the fossilized bones of the long-gone Klausehn Overlords, and the sensors inside would be the same. The door opened at a pull, and

I strolled in. The point density field from the attoprobes was so good, I didn't need to switch on a light. The map they provided was detailed enough to allow me to move freely through the junk-filled displays.

The bots had worked perfectly, laying out an even distribution in those parts of the gallery I'd visited, keying off the pheromones I'd planted earlier. The program I'd installed in the bots made them cluster in areas I *hadn't* touched, giving me a better picture of what was important.

The room with the data systems was at the back of the building, and I headed there first. I'll give the SlamCandy pushers some credit—there was a separate physical lock on the internal door. But it was an old mechanical affair that offered almost no barrier to being picked. To prove the point, I put one hand behind my back and closed my eyes too. In less than a minute, the lock clicked open, and I walked in. A desk to the left housed a large computer system, and I pushed the activation button.

The display lit up with a message asking me to swipe my hand over the DNA scanner. I reconfigured my glove to broadcast Nilo's genetic pattern—reconstructed from the creamer—and swiped it past the reader. The screen flashed green, and I was in.

Some people say it's wrong to boast about your accomplishments, but if you're good at something then it deserves recognition, if only from yourself. So, I patted myself on the back with my number six tentacle.

"Hold it."

I triggered the Distortion Matrix and leaped to the right, twisting around. I couldn't see anyone at first, but when I switched my mask lenses to full enhancement, I caught the recognizable shimmer of someone wearing a suit similar to mine.

Whoever it was, they were already jumping toward me, and I braced against the ground. Waiting to the last moment, I side-stepped. My attacker tried to stop but slammed into the wall just behind where I'd been standing, letting out a gruff grunt.

As the enhancement filter locked onto the right frequencies, I got a better picture of my assailant: definitely male, judging by the size and shape of the outline, at least fifteen centimeters taller than me, and with a physique that made a fair approximation of the fake pillars outside. I should have guessed drug dealers wouldn't rely on purely electronic security systems, and cursed. Now I was going to pay the price for my overconfidence.

My foe shook his head and turned to face me. He looked like a brute, but my quick footwork had made him cautious, and he shuffled around, in an attempt to corner me. This wasn't the best way to approach a trained fighter, but I didn't make any attempt to stop him. That would give him confidence—which I'd turn against him. I faked to the left, then jumped to the right, looking to bypass him once again. It almost worked, but he lashed out and his meaty fist hammered into my side like a stone block.

"Stop jumping around, you little vraz," he snorted. "You a flea or something?"

I didn't reply but edged around as he did the same. The blow had left me short of breath, despite my nullsuit armor absorbing much of the impact.

"Hold still, little flea. I'll make it quick." He reversed the direction of his circling, moving closer once again.

I'm not telepathic, but I could imagine his thinking all too well. He was facing a much shorter and lighter opponent. Like most large men, he no doubt thought that gave him the advantage.

"Did the Doogans send ya?" He swung his large fist at me once again, but I danced around it with ease. "You breaking the truce?"

"That's right." I triggered a voice filter, making my vocal pitch low, so he wouldn't be able to identify me as female. "The truce is busted wide open, Mr. Muscles. We're cutting in on your operation."

I'd lifted the words from one of Stryng's old movies, and they didn't mean much to me.

"That's what I figured," he snarled. "Only the Doogans would have the yamons to try something like this."

He slashed at me with his hand, and I stepped in behind it, wrapping my arms around his and dropping to the floor. He howled as the movement wrenched his arm, and I knew I'd likely dislocated it, if only temporarily.

"You ficksnit," he yelled, crashing to the ground.

He pulled out a gun, pointing its short barrel at me. "I ain't supposed to shoot in here, but so help me, I will if you—"

I delivered a roundhouse kick to the side of his head, and he collapsed. I was aching from the blows he'd landed and sat down by the computer, taking several breaths to ease the pain.

"Go ahead," I finally muttered. "Do your worst."

For some reason, he didn't reply, so I decided I was entitled to access the computer's file system. Whoever set it up was organized and methodical, which made it a real pleasure to find the information on shipments and payments received. In a few seconds, I'd copied the data to a data-flake. I didn't care if it had all the information that Bolt wanted, it would have to do. And if he didn't like it, he could fire me.

After that, I dragged Mr. Muscles into the office chair and cracked a six-hour mem-kleer capsule under his nose. He'd wake with no recollection of any events in the last six hours. By which time, I'd be long gone. As far as he'd know, he'd think he'd fallen asleep on the job.

Algernon's Flower sat looking as forlorn as earlier. I double-checked my attoprobe readings to confirm there were no extra security devices targeted on it, but it was clean. Apparently, Mr. Muscles was their second and only other line of defense.

I grabbed the pot and pulled but nothing happened. I shook my head. What had they done now?

It took a while to cycle through the different enhancement settings and find the answer. They'd glued the valuable Swilin Dynasty bowl to the table. That wasn't a problem. Algernon's Flower didn't need the bowl—it was valuable enough as it was. Though I couldn't help but curse the philistine who'd done that to such a precious piece of pottery.

Lifting the rocky crystal from the saucer, I replaced it with a facsimile I'd made with the pantograph based on images I'd found, tucked the original in my suit, and limped my way outside. After recalling the drone, I signaled the attoprobes, triggering them to do a DNA scrub of any genetic material I'd left behind. Their mission complete, they'd self-destruct and become one with the dust. Finally, I reactivated the gravboard, took to the air, and headed back to the ship with my hard-earned loot.

Despite the stabs of pain, I was smiling.

The *Centienne* was quiet when I slipped back through the airlock. After hiding Algernon's Flower in the secure cache in my wardrobe case, I shucked off my nullsuit, trying not to tweak my ribs any further but failing miserably.

I checked myself in the full-length mirror. A plate-sized bruise covered the left side of my ribs that would undoubtedly explode in a rainbow of colors over the next few days, generating questions if anyone spotted it. Lecuundans don't have skeletons the way Terrans do—our hard tissue is closer to cartilage, allowing us greater flexibility and resilience to impacts—but it still hurt like hell.

After swallowing a couple of painkillers, I soaked in the tub for a good thirty minutes to take the sting away. The damage wasn't too great—I'd had worse in the TwistCube—but I seethed over not anticipating the goon and relying on the attoprobes too much. They were good but didn't have the capability of picking something up through a Distortion Matrix.

After a short sleep, I felt both better and worse. Better because I'd rested, but worse because the bruising was starting to bite. I had a training session scheduled with Glacia but headed to see Dr. Lee instead. As usual, he'd been temporarily transferred to the medical center in the backstage area.

"What is it now?" he said as he twinkled into solid form. "I warn you, you're wearing your medical time-slice allowance thin."

There was no allowance, and we both knew it, But Dr. Lee liked to pretend he could cut us off at a whim if he wanted to. "I was practicing with Atsuno yesterday and got a little hurt. Can you do something?"

"Take two of these and call me in the morning."

He held out a couple of bright purple pills that I recognized as regular-strength painkillers. "I need more than that."

"Very well. Remove your clothes and lie down on the scanner."

Dr. Lee watched as I slipped out of my clothes. It was creepy having him stare at me like that, even if he *was* an entirely disinterested Artificial Personality. Somehow APs seem able to see all the way through you to the depths of your soul. After the scans finished, I started to dress again, but he stopped me. The analytic system projected the results over my body, and he walked around me tut-tutting.

"Atsuno did this?"

I nodded. "We were doing some full-contact practice."

Dr. Lee peered at the bruise on my side. "Has she quadrupled in size?"

My skin prickled. "Well, you know something, I think she *has* been working out more."

"You shouldn't lie to your doctor." Dr. Lee stepped back and grabbed a hand scanner. "What else did you do yesterday?"

"Well, I had dinner with Zavara, Atsuno, and ChaosRhino and—"

"Ahh, yes. And afterward undoubtedly indulged in vigorous coitus with the M'Charran, during which you received these injuries. Interspecies sex can be dangerous, especially when the size differential is as great as it is between you and ChaosRhino."

"Wait a second, I nev—"

Dr. Lee exchanged the scanner for a TissueFix wand and waved it next to the bruising. "No need for more lies. I'll treat you anyway. But you may want to curb your lustful habits for a few days to heal properly."

The wand was already helping, but the stimulation made me wriggle uncomfortably. "Didn't anyone teach you it's wrong to make assumptions?"

"I taught myself, using Central Medbase data. I have the equivalent of ten lifetimes of experience." He switched off the wand. "If that's all, I will return to my important work."

I was miffed that he thought I'd slept with ChaosRhino. "Anything I need to avoid?"

"Strenuous exercise—in or out of bed." With that, he disappeared in a sparkly puff.

After dressing, I headed to the dining room for breakfast. Christine joined me. Her round face held a deep frown, and she looked like she'd swallowed a fly. Or several.

"What was that about, yesterday?" she said.

I swallowed a piece of toast. "What do you mean?"

"Don't act innocent with me." Christine threw her notes on the table. "What's this with you and Kraig?"

ChaosRhino's real name was Kraig Lezcano, though no one used it, not even him. But Christine always used real names backstage. She said it gave her more of an insight into the personalities and characters and helped with her scripts.

"There's nothing between me and Rhino." I bristled, thinking of Dr. Lee's earlier assumption. "We had dinner, that's all. Why do people think something is going on?"

"You've completely messed up the plot. You're supposed to be in a quadrangle with Zav, Brach, and Atsuno. Now, news of you dating Kraig is all over the Realms."

"Brach wasn't available—it was only dinner. What do people think I am?"

"Well, the quadrangle's blown now. We're going to have to shoot a shipload of new material." Christine pushed a data-flake across the table. "Congratulations, honey, you're now my first *pentangle*. Here are the shoot details. Get studying."

I groaned and wished, not for the first time, that we could stick to rassling for once.

Twelve

The noise of the screaming crowd beat against the TwistCube virtuwalls like the roar of a deep-space plasma storm. My ribs were pure agony as Glacia had thoughtfully planted a kick on the injury I'd suffered at the antique dealers. The kick itself wouldn't normally have bothered me that much, but it had aggravated the wound and undone most of Dr. Lee's work patching me up.

I bounced off the number five wall, feeling the gravity shift, and curled into a ball, using the change to slam hard into Glacia's torso. She folded with the impact, distributing the force over a wider area, and then I caught a whisper in my earbud.

"Steady, Hype," she hissed. "This is an exhibition, remember?"

Grabbing her arm, I dragged her with me, settling on the number three virtuwall. Then I used her momentum to spin her and slam her against the fourth.

"Oh my word! Hyperia just executed a perfect Subspace Slam." Donk was getting worked up. "This may only be an exhibition match, but these two ladies have a feud that goes back a long way, and that move might be the end for Glacia."

"That's right, Donk," Rutzali shouted. "I felt that impact here at the announce table. I think it's all over. She's got nothing left."

I moved in and grabbed Glacia by her white-and-blue hair crest, yanking her head up. She grabbed my wrist as though she were trying to stop me, but instead she lifted herself from the floor. I snatched her hands and moved them to the side, her head hanging down as if she were stunned. Then she patted my leg to let me know she was ready, and I dropped her headfirst into the virtuwall below us.

Glacia slapped the floor with her forearm, making a lot of noise, but critically protecting her head, and bounced upward as the gravity shifted again. I grabbed her, sliding my arms under hers and locking my grip behind her. At the same time, I reached forward with my head tentacles and wrapped them over her face from behind.

"This is incredible! Incredible!" Donk continued. "Hyperia has locked in a Septapoid Death Grip. The Glacia is about to be melted. This is a career-ending move!"

My tentacles weren't deadly in any real fashion, unless someone choked on one perhaps, and I'd never heard of a Death Grip. It looked impressive to the audience though. Glacia was fake-struggling in my arms, and I squeezed harder as payback for the kick she'd landed on my bruise.

"You going down?" I whispered.

"No way." Glacia twisted again, and I tightened my hold. "My ratings took a hit. If I don't get 'em back up, Denton's gonna cut my bonus."

"Oh, okay." I thought for a moment, making it appear as though I was shaking her. "Elbow slam. On the right."

Glacia's elbow shot back, barely grazing my chest, but I released my grip a little. She threw another, and I let it push me backward, exaggerating the move so I landed hard against the virtuwall. She spun to face me, whipping her white hair in large circles to signal she was going to do a Tachyon Spear. I crawled to my feet, ready to absorb the impact better, but the wall behind me turned to negative-g, propelling me forward as she dived, and we met in a huge collision in the middle.

"Oh no!" Donk covered up the mistake immediately. "The gravity shift caught them *both* out. The two contenders look to be out of the match. We may need the medibots to take action, unless—" Donk gasped. "I don't believe it. Hyperia Jones is *still* moving. She's crawling, folks, desperate to get to a tag patch. If she does, she can win this."

After the force of the impact, I wasn't crawling. I wasn't even moving. But Donk was a master at reading the crowd, so I followed his lead and dragged myself toward the tag patch on the nearest wall.

"Can you believe it?" Donk bellowed. "Glacia's trying to do the same thing. This match has been truly hellacious. Both desperate for a symbolic victory. Who. Will. Get. There. First? No one knows. It could be either. I can barely watch."

"They're both living on pure adrenaline." Rutzali joined in. "Nothing but talent and guts. You know that whoever wins this match-up has got to be the favorite to win at *Powerfall*."

"You ain't blowing hot air, Rutz." Donk's deep voice cracked with fake emotion. "And the crowd knows it!"

Donk was a showman above all else and knew how to stir the crowd into an absolute frenzy. Which was what he was doing now. I heard staccato roars of Hype, Hype, Hype, mixed in with rhythmic chants of Gla-See-Ya, over and over. Those soldiers certainly had healthy lungs—and the canned crowd effects pumped through the speakers around the arena didn't hurt. I was less than a meter from the tag patch. As I stretched for it, there was a metallic *boing* as one of the virtuwalls collapsed and reformed behind me.

I sensed movement and glanced around. The Bonor Triplets rushed me and I turned to fend them off, but all I could do was curl up as they rained kicks, knees, and punches onto me. The crowd howled their disapproval, though I didn't know if it was meant as support for them or outrage for me. The triplets were experts at igniting cheap heat.

"I don't believe it," Donk called out. "Looks like the Bonors want to soften up their main rivals."

"It's Bonor Time!" Rutzali roared. "Those ladies want a piece."

One of the triplets—I think it was Rachelle—hit me with a particularly vicious kick, and I reacted by chopping at her leg. My aim was spot on, but I doubt it had much impact. Nevertheless, she screamed and kicked me several more times. The blows subsided a little, giving me a chance to look up. I initially thought they must have planned this with Glacia, but while Rachelle was paying me special attention, Courtney and Shehla had gone to give Glacia a beatdown.

Finally, the beeper sounded, signaling the match was over. A few seconds later, Denton, Stryng, and a couple of the others were in the ring holding the triplets away from both me and Glacia.

"Medibots!" Denton yelled. "Now."

I tried not to move too much. Everywhere hurt, almost as badly as a few nights before. I didn't know if the attack had been scripted or whether the Bonors had taken the initiative themselves. But I wasn't going to let them get away with it.

I was under strict orders from Dr. Lee to avoid strenuous activity for at least a week. We were back on the *Ethereal Queen* and heading away from Guplides, preparing to enter D-space as soon as we cleared the planet's gravimetric shock wave. Our destination was New Emslariat III where we were scheduled to do promo work while preparing for *PowerFall*. The event wasn't scheduled for several weeks, but we didn't have anything else lined up.

My door signal beeped. I waved at the let-them-in spot, and the door swished open. Christine's blond-coiffed head popped around the corner, and she poked her tongue out at me.

"Okay for visitors?" she said cheerily.

"Sure. The Doc told me to rest up, but he didn't say anything about staying quiet."

"Yeah, well I thought I better check." Christine breezed in and dragged a seat next to the bed. "No one's seen much of you since the match."

It was true. I'd spent more time in my room than I should have, because I was conducting a giant interstellar auction on Darkover for Algernon's Flower. So far, the highest bid was for a little under one megadruble, but the bidding was still hot. The best part was that Darkover auctions were entirely anonymous. Even Bolt wouldn't know it was connected to me.

"I'm not happy about what happened," I said.

"That's understandable," Christine said. "Denton is cut up too."

"That ficksnit? I doubt it." Everyone said Denton didn't run that kind of operation—or hadn't up until now. "Or was there not enough *color* for him?"

Color in this instance meant blood—sometimes also called red, though that wasn't strictly the case as some species, like me, don't have red blood.

"He accepts responsibility for it. So do I. But it wasn't exactly planned."

I shuffled up on the bed and sat up. "What does that mean?"

Christine blushed, which turned her face a little purple and more attractive in my opinion. Terrans come in many colors, but the shades lack subtlety.

"We were discussing doing something along those lines. We thought it would be good to spark up a block rivalry on the women's roster. The idea was we'd team up you and Glacia, and then you'd play out the *reluctant allies* plot."

It was one of the classic story lines that went around now and then, usually ending with a breakup when one or other of the allies turned on their partner.

"And I suppose you forgot to let me and Glacia in on the gag?" I sniffed.

"Don't say that." Christine shook her head. "Denton wouldn't do that, and neither would I. We had preliminary talks with the Bonors, but nothing was lined up."

"So what then?"

"The Bonors decided to shoot and go into business for themselves." Christine sighed. "I guess they thought it'd have more impact. And it *has* given us some much-needed promo."

While that let Denton and Christine off the hook, it only made it worse for the Bonors. They were getting far too full of themselves and needed taking down several notches.

"Okay, let's roll with it then." I rubbed my aching ribs. "We can work out the details with Glacia, but we'll need to line up a third unless we're going to play it as a handicap."

"Maybe… I think it's about time I came out of retirement to help." Christine gave an evil smile. "I don't like it when people mess with my story lines."

My wrist-com tingled several times, and Christine noticed the faint buzz. "Messages coming in?"

"Fan mail probably. They never sleep." I didn't send mail to my wrist-com—it was relaying notifications of incoming bids.

"I wish we had more of them." Christine frowned. "This thing with ICE taking our gigs is worrying."

I hadn't thought too much about ICE recently with my anxiety over the Bolt job. They'd been in the business forever, long before I joined FIRE, and mostly picked up shows on the smaller worlds and in modest venues. None of which had mattered to us—they weren't in our league. But now? Things had changed, and FIRE's dominance with the fandom was faltering.

"Are you really worried?"

"Whether I am or not doesn't matter." Christine scratched her meaty shoulder. "I'm just another employee. But I know Denton is. And when the boss gets nervous—that's time the little guys should be too. I don't think he's telling Mr. Quy everything."

How would things be if FIRE came to an end? This bunch of misfits and weirdos had acted as my surrogate family for three years. And, despite a few dubious moments—mostly supplied by the Bonors—they'd given me far more support than my natural family. My rassling tribe made me feel wanted and appreciated, but that made me uncomfortable too. Everything in my past had made *family* a dirty word to me. It meant restriction, hurt, and indignation. I didn't want a new family, or an old one. I wanted to live in splendid isolation, answering to no one but myself.

"How bad is it?"

Christine crossed her legs and picked at the seam in her pants. "Bad enough that the *Queen* is idling in space. Denton isn't in any hurry to get to New Emslariat."

I understood his reasoning. While we were on the *Queen*, our operating costs were at their lowest, with almost every overhead fixed. As soon as we were in civilization, we had to make personal appearances, be seen in fashionable places, go on shopping trips, and all that nonsense. Expenses increased, and dramatically from what Denton had said.

But that paid off in increased interest—it was promotion and marketing. Those were the things I was always bad at, but I recognized their necessity. The longer we were away from worlds, the lower our profile would drop, and that reduced our chances of securing further gigs. If we stayed in deep space too long, we'd fade into complete obscurity. And with the press's insatiable appetite for the next big thing, it wouldn't take too long.

"Can't we do more remote broadcast plots?" I said.

"We can, and we will." Christine stood. "But it's not as good as the personal touch."

"Let me know if I can help."

"You're a good kid, Hype. I know we can count on you."

She left, and I slumped, feeling guiltier than a Shivatralian SnowPuppy caught with its nose in the biscuits. Perhaps I'd used this cover too long and it had all become too comfortable. You can't rely on anyone, and I didn't need them. Was it time to move on before I was pulled in too deep?

A week later, I was almost fully healed, and Dr. Lee unceremoniously scrubbed me off his patient list. We'd been cruising aimlessly, but after a lot of grumbling from various members of the group, Denton was persuaded to head for somewhere as a layover.

Siatuni IV wasn't what you might call a high spot—in fact, it was a mess. Most of the land surface had been plundered through mining for its famous Numidian marble. The only part of the planet that still retained its natural state was a thin ribbon circling the equator, isolating its inhabitants from the destruction they'd caused.

We weren't planning on landing. The government discouraged tourists and other visitors, afraid they might steal its precious mineral wealth. They were extremely strict on this point. Or I should say, they were strict about people doing it and avoiding their costly bureaucracy. They were all too eager to gouge everyone for export taxes, licenses, and business permits, along with the other *legal* forms of theft practiced by governments everywhere.

The Siatuni station was an improvement in that its visitors were at least treated with a polite friendliness, but it was mostly given over to large business centers and conference halls—no doubt full to overflowing with marble dealers negotiating the best prices.

I'd sent the information from the SlamCandy dealers to Bolt and, other than a routine acknowledgment, hadn't heard back from him. Leaving me free and clear. Naturally, the crooks I'd stolen

Algernon's Flower from weren't going to report the loss to the authorities when they discovered it, considering their ownership was questionable at best. Besides, they were probably mired in a turf war with their rivals, the Doogans, by now.

The auction for the Flower was still live, but the bids had slowed to a trickle with the highest at about one and a quarter megadrubles—a seriously large sum for something so ugly, and that I'd picked up with relatively little investment in time or effort. The auction was set to close in three days—perfect timing as we'd be on the station, and I would be able to arrange for the necessary transfer via secure interstell courier.

My head was buzzing a little in excitement. My share, after Darkover took its cut, would be a little over a million drubles. More than enough to keep me happy for several years and, I realized somewhat guiltily, enough to let me to walk away from my life in FIRE.

Or perhaps I should use it to help the group out. While a megadruble wouldn't keep the operation afloat for a long time, such a cash injection would enable us to put on a bigger show, line up higher profile gigs, and put the company on the upswing again.

But how would that work? Mr. Quy would have to get involved for one thing. And if he realized how much the operation was struggling, he might not risk further investment. I could feed the money to Denton in relatively small amounts, but how would I explain where it was coming from? And what return would I get if I did that? As good as I was, rassling wasn't a lifetime career, and the longer I stayed, the tougher it would be to leave.

There was no point worrying about it for the moment. First things first—I needed to see the auction finish, collect the winnings, and deposit the Flower with the courier. After that, there'd be plenty of time to worry about saving the universe.

The docking warning sounded, and the lights flickered. A few minutes later, Auntie announced we were clear to leave the ship. I hadn't visited Siatuni before, and the idea of a new world, or at least its station, was always an exciting prospect. I threw on some less unkempt clothes, grabbed a nice roomy purse large enough to conceal Algernon's Flower, and headed for the main airlock to explore what the place had to offer. I was partway there when I heard a call.

"Hold up there, sweetheart. If you're going to paint the town red, you're going my way."

"Hi, Stryng," I said, as he undulated alongside me. "I'm only going to stretch my legs, nothing special."

"That'll do me. Jeesh, I'll be glad to get off this boat for a while."

We passed through the airlock and walked down the gangway. It has to be said that most space stations tend to look alike: floating rings, floating balls, or floating drums, and all made up of metal and composites. Now, I don't claim to know anything about architecture, but I swear whoever designs these things always comes up with features where logic and practicality have zero intersection with the pretty pictures floating inside their heads.

Siatuni station was different in one respect though: everywhere you looked there were large displays of marble in various forms. Some were polished, others raw, and all in a bewildering set of colors—many of which I'd never seen before. A sign above the official gateway read "Get your rocks off on Siatuni!" in large, glowing letters.

Stryng nodded approvingly. "My kinda town."

"Any plans on where you're heading?" I hadn't researched the place beyond checking the location of the interstell couriers.

He wiggled—his version of shrugging. "Anywhere away from those dames."

I shook my head. "I thought you were done with the Bonors."

"Sure. But they ain't done with me. And they ain't the only ones." He let a small loop wind up his body. "Seems a guy can't make a comment without a dame taking offense these days."

We were at the passport control gate, and I waved my Realms ID at the pickup. After a short delay, it beeped and flashed green. I had no idea where Stryng kept his, but he held it up, and the gate hesitated longer before accepting it. After that, we were free to walk anywhere on the station—at least in the non-restricted areas.

"So, what happened?" I said.

"Ahh, forget it. Let's check out what this hot dog stand has to offer." He waved the tip of his tail in a circle.

There weren't any hot dog stands. I'm not sure they exist outside

Stryng's movies. He'd explained them to me once while watching one of the shows, though it made little sense. Apparently, the *hot dogs* were low quality meat products—none of which involved dogs—served with a variety of toppings in a roll of cheap bread and sold by traveling vendors. Bizarrely, despite the reputed quality, and the fact that they were sold in dubious hygienic conditions on filthy streets, they were highly praised and worshiped by some.

We walked out into a wide parade with an assortment of stores lining either side. These were the places you never shopped at if you had any sense. On space stations, the price of goods was always directly proportional to the distance of the vendor from the main docking ports. The nearer a port, the more expensive the purchases.

"All I did was ask Atsuno if she'd train with me," Stryng said out of the blue.

"She trains lots of people. Why would the Bonors have a problem with that?"

"Beats me. Those babes are crazy."

He fell silent again, and we carried on walking, making our way deeper into the station. I did the expected female thing and pretended to show interest in the various clothing retailers' displays, but I was focused on checking the couriers. All their registered offices were near the middle of the station, as usual clustered near the major financial institutions.

"Holy stoli! Look at that!"

Stryng was standing straight, like a pole rising from the ground, his attention fixed on a nondescript store with a garish blue-and-yellow sign that reminded me of a bruise. The glowing panel was covered in overweight lettering, and it took me a while to decipher the archaic Lingua script.

"Cubebreaker?" I shrugged. "What does that mean?"

"It's so rare, it's mostly a legend." He was weaving as though mesmerized. "Comes straight from the old Terran homeworld."

"Oh please, don't you start with all that thrit."

Despite my belief that everything associated with the lost homeworld was a swindle, I stepped closer to look through the window. The name was partly right. No cubes, but plenty of boxes decorated with a veritable rainbow of colored images, making the window display as lurid as an accident in a paint factory.

Stryng gazed through the window, his eye spots the size of buttons. "It can't be… It really can't be…"

"What?"

"*The Revenge of the Maltese Falcon.*" He sucked in a deep breath. "It's impossible. It was lost in the mists of time. No one's seen that in thousands of years."

"And you think they have it here? Come on, you're smarter than that."

"Maybe. Maybe not. But I gotta check it out."

"Okay, I'll carry on exploring. Catch me up later." The Flower was making me nervous. The sooner I deposited it with a courier, the better. After that, all I'd need to do was let them know where to send it once the auction completed.

"Sure. Whatever suits you." Stryng's head was in the clouds, probably dreaming of all the movies he'd be able to pick up.

I made my way through the crowds, careful not to allow anyone close to me. The last thing I needed was for some pickpocket to strike it lucky. It was difficult because even on a station as out of the way as this one, we were still celebrities. There was always a steady stream of people coming up asking for autographs and photos.

Nearer the center, the foot traffic increased, so I decided to make a change and slipped into the nearest clothing store. I picked up a long, flowing skirt covered in a swirling pattern of garish colors and a shirt of solid cerise, then hid in the changing room and switched outfits. I also changed my skin coloring so it was similar to a Terran mid-brown, and recolored and retextured my head tentacles before arranging them into a bun and fixing a small hair band around them.

If the store bots noticed the change, they didn't say anything, and as I paid for all the clothes, they had no reason to question the difference in appearance. But at least now, I no longer looked like Hyperia Jones, pro-rassler. Several of my earlier admirers were waiting outside the store, and I smiled when they failed to recognize me.

The courier companies were clustered together, almost right next to each other in that bizarre fashion some businesses seem to go for. I'd have thought being separated would be better from a competition perspective, but what I didn't know about business would fill several data-flakes.

Two of the operations were local, and small enough that I didn't recognize their names, but everyone has heard of Binks Cargo, one of the largest courier services in the Realms. They have the reputation of being the most reliable and secure, not to mention the seal of approval from the offices of the UberKaiser. I approached the counter and waited for the service bot to acknowledge me. Their exclusively robotic workforce was one reason their services were so impenetrable.

"I want to set up a delayed delivery for an item," I said to the bot. "Shipping details to be supplied later by remote."

He looked splendid in the company's blue-and-gold livery. After a moment of silence, he responded with a deep metallic voice.

"Thank you for choosing Binks Cargo, madam, the solution to all of your personal security needs. Please enter the shipping booth to your right and select a suitable Invictus container."

I went through the door and locked it behind me. After confirming it was secure, and checking there were no hidden recording devices, I grabbed a container from the pile and placed Algernon's Flower inside, adding large amounts of padding to protect the rocky crystal. The fastener whirred and clicked several times after I closed the lid, encoding my neural engram and DNA. Then I placed it into the sealing unit. I was prompted for a security code to open the box and waited while the high-energy proton beam tamper-proofed the container using my code. Once that was done, no one would be able to open it without all three security checks, including the company. And the containers were virtually indestructible. I left the booth and passed the container to the bot.

"Thank you, madam. That will be twelve hundred drubles."

It was expensive, but you had to pay for the best. And in comparison to what the Flower would earn, it was worth it. I paid the bot, and he handed me a silvery data-flake holding the encoded receipt, which would allow me to configure the delivery destination later from anywhere via a q-link.

"Thank you."

The bot's eyes glowed briefly. "Thank you for using Binks

Cargo, madam. *Security* is our middle name."

I breathed deeply, relaxing for the first time since snatching the Flower. All I needed now was the winner of the auction. I turned and headed away from the central area, wondering what had happened to Stryng. Knowing him, he hadn't left the Cube-breaker store yet.

As I walked, I felt elated and dizzy, so light-headed that I wanted to skip but suppressed the urge. Everything was working out fine. By the time I was halfway back to where I'd left Stryng, I was fighting to stop myself from dancing. The gig had been perfect. My reputation as the best thief on Darkover was restored.

I caught a movement to my left in the corner of my eye, a moment before an arm looped around mine. My instincts took over, and I turned, raising my fist ready to deliver a punch.

It was Bolt.

Thirteen

"Hello again, Ms. Jones." Bolt smiled his smiliest smile. "What an utterly wonderful surprise. Imagine running into you again."

He pulled me close, coldly pressing his lips to both of my cheeks in turn, and I shivered.

"What the ficksnit are you doing here?" I looked around, wondering if I should run from this loathsomely unexpected visit or simply deck him. Bolt threw a slightly twisted grin. No doubt it worked on many women, but Hyperia is smarter than that, and I pulled away.

He held onto my hand with a surprisingly strong grip, dragging my arm out as though we were dancing together. "Well, I felt a social visit was in order. After all you went through to get the information for us, Olive Branch owes you a debt of gratitude."

"Are you genuinely grateful?" I said, struggling to keep my voice level.

"Of course. That was a great job you pulled off."

"You can show your appreciation by staying the hell away from me."

"That's no way to talk to an old friend, is it?" Bolt looped his arm around mine again and led me down the corridor. "Let me give you something by way of thanks. Let's have dinner."

"I'm not hungry."

"A few drinks then. There's a charming bar on the next sub-level that serves a passable vodka martini."

"I'm not thirsty either."

"Oh, well in that case, how about sex?"

I stopped walking. "What?"

"I suggested we had sex. You know, two lovers sharing an intimate moment of *ludic* pleasure and fulfilling the dreams of Eros."

I pushed him back. "That may be how things normally work for you, but this is one girl who isn't going to fall under your spell."

"That *is* a shame." Bolt tutted several times. "I was rather hoping not to have to drug you."

"Back off, thritface."

"Oh damn, there's your serpentine friend." Bolt pointed to the side of the walkway. "Take the door on the left. Now, if you don't mind."

"I'm not going anywhere with you. We're finished."

Bolt shook his head. "Unfortunately, your obligation to Olive Branch isn't over."

"That's what you think."

I turned to leave, but Bolt held on to me. I twisted away. Stryng was about fifty meters along the passage, and I lifted my hand to wave to him.

Something many people don't know about Lecuundans is that unlike Terrans and many other humanoids, we don't have a visual blind spot. I'm no biologist, but it's to do with the position of our optical nerve. As a result, I spotted Bolt moving closer, something shiny in his hand catching the light. He was too quick for me to respond though, and I felt a sharp stab in my side.

"There we go," he said, placing an arm behind my back. "Let's go through here, shall we?"

He led me to the door he'd indicated a moment ago and opened it without removing his arm from my back. I was completely unwilling to go with him, but my head was overwhelmed by a dizzy euphoria and I was unable to resist. My skin tingled and I realized the changes to my coloration and tentacles were reversing by themselves. I was reverting to my normal appearance.

We were in a short service corridor. I squinted at the harsh overhead lighting and caught the slight pungent scent of cleaning products drifting in the air. The passage was broken by an occasional gray storage locker, with no marble to be seen and—strangely—no signs of the impractical architecture either.

"What...did...you..." My words were quiet and slurred, my lips almost impossible to move.

"Your species is extremely resilient, isn't it?" Bolt said, guiding me along the passage. "Most would find it impossible to speak after a shot of *Zom*."

"Mrrff…fick…snit…"

"Such language doesn't become you."

I staggered as Bolt pressed me forward. He waved his palm at the lock-reader on a door to the right, and it slid open. Unlike the corridor, I doubted this space was used by service personnel—unless they were psychotic killers. Three of the walls were lined with racks of weapons of every conceivable type, while tucked along the fourth was a moderately sized bed next to a large closet.

I tried to fight as Bolt led me across the room and pushed me into a sitting position on the bed. There was nothing forceful about his actions, but my brain was overwhelmed by the zombie drug he'd injected me with. He took off his jacket, then stripped off his shirt to reveal a decidedly masculine chest, which I suppose in other circumstances might have been attractive. Like many of the male rasslers, he was entirely without body hair, though whether that was his natural condition or achieved through artificial means, I couldn't say and wasn't inclined to find out.

"That's better. Might as well be comfortable. Olive Branch has substations like these in most major locations in the Realms. We call them bolt-holes." His voice was matter-of-fact, as though the situation was routine. "Comes in handy when an agent needs something in a hurry."

"Nrrrrhsh…flortsnesh… rape…"

"Oh, don't worry. Nothing is going to happen to you." Bolt grinned, then opened the closet. "At least nothing you'll object to."

He took out a woven shirt in dark blue and pulled it over his head. "Wearing a suit becomes so tiresome after a while."

The Zom was wearing off. I didn't know if Bolt was aware of that. Lecuundans metabolize substances far quicker than Terrans. I could have probably moved a little if I forced myself, but I didn't want to give away that I was recovering. He pulled over a chair and sat facing me, then his eyebrow lifted and he reached across, running his fingers over my forehead and temples.

David M. Kelly

"Well, well. I wasn't sure of it, even after reading the files, but now..."

I couldn't see what he was looking at, but it wasn't hard to guess. The Zom must have relaxed my chromatophores in unintended ways, and my tribal spots had shown themselves.

"We had... a deal..."

'Yes, we did." Bolt pulled away. "But I wasn't entirely honest with you. You see, we already had the information from the SlamCandy dealers on Guplides."

"What?" I was thinking about what I'd been through and the pain I'd suffered.

Bolt smiled, not looking apologetic in the least. "Yes, I know. But I had to test you, didn't I? How else could I be sure you'd follow orders and work on behalf of OB?"

"You lied to me?"

"Of course. That's my job." He leaned back in the chair. "The Guplides part of the operation has been known for several months. But your work wasn't wasted. The data you obtained confirmed a number of their contacts who were previously only suspects."

"I'm so... glad."

"So, now you've proved yourself, it's time for your real mission."

"Croff you."

"That's not very nice." Bolt smiled again. "Besides, don't tell me you didn't enjoy it. It's what you live for, isn't it? The thrill, the adrenaline rush, the fear of being caught. Isn't that why you became a thief? Why you became a pro-rassler? I'm giving you the chance to indulge your need, for a better cause than your own selfishness."

"Not ever. I'm done, I'm clean now." I suddenly knew what I was going to do with that megadruble once I collected it. I'd use it to disappear and get a long way from anywhere Bolt, or anyone else, would find me. That was how I wanted it, and how I worked best. Relying on no one but myself and my skills.

"Yes, well, your record..."

"You said it would be wiped."

"That's true. But you can't seriously imagine I'd do that in exchange for completing a training exercise." Bolt walked to one of the gun racks and picked up a heavy pistol. "Hmmm. TrueBlue twelve millimeter. Nice piece, but too bulky, wouldn't you say?"

"What do you want from me now?" I wiggled my toes surreptitiously while Bolt was examining the gun. They worked, though the effort sent agonizing pins and needles through my legs.

"Nine months ago, Realm archaeologists uncovered some Klausehn technology with errr… military applications. They've spent the time deciphering its use and come up with a set of blueprints on how to turn it into a practical weapon. Something that could be built using the technology we have today."

"I'm not a weapons tech."

"The blueprints were supposed to be known only to the leading military people and the UberKaiser himself. But—"

"Let me guess, they ended up in the wrong hands, and you need someone to recover the plans."

"You're quick. I like that." Bolt picked up another gun and inspected it. "Mangun Forty-Four—very clumsy and grossly excessive, but effective in the right circumstances."

"Where am I supposed to find the blueprints?"

"Ahhh, yes." He looked at me for a moment, then turned back to the weapons. "There we run into a little snag—we don't actually know who has the plans."

My body tingled painfully all over, and I knew the Zom was almost gone from my system. "Well, be sure to look me up when you do."

"The good news is that we have details on who *does* know." Bolt took a small handgun from the rack. It looked more like a toy than a lethal weapon. "Mosquito Mauler. Beautiful and absolutely deadly."

"If you'd like to be alone to play with your *gun*, I'd happily leave you to it."

"Remember Th'opn Mrez?"

I searched my memory, trying to place the name. "Alyss Blakeston? Sparth ML2F? The Zuerilian feeding SlamCandy to his workforce?"

"See, I said you were quick." Bolt caressed the tiny pistol. "The SlamCandy suppliers have used their hold on him to make him their agent. He's acting as the go-between with the person who has the plans. Get to him, and you'll find the stolen blueprints."

I had no interest in going anywhere near Mrez or Sparth but

was happy to play along if it got me out of this long enough to vanish. I'd always wanted to see the L'Thidri Nebula. It was outside Realms jurisdiction with several outlaw worlds hidden inside it. More appealingly, from what I'd heard, Realms agents entering the Nebula never came back.

"Sure, I'll get right on it." The tingling was easing. "As soon as I recover from the Zom."

I jumped up and reached for Bolt, planning to throw him bodily out of the way and make a run for it. He turned and pointed the tiny gun directly at me, then checked the time.

"Seventeen and a half standard minutes. Not bad, though I was led to believe Lecuundans were faster at recovering from the drug. Oh well, it's always interesting to confirm the data in the field."

"This was another stupid test?" I snarled. "What about all that sex talk?"

"I have *some* standards." He put the gun back on the rack. "It must be obvious to anyone who looks at me that I don't need to drug people to satisfy my needs."

"Can I go now?"

"Be my guest."

"And I don't suppose you can offer any help in getting me to Sparth?"

He smiled. "Very quick indeed—for a woman."

I pushed past him and headed for the door.

"And you won't need this now, will you?"

Bolt held something between his thumb and finger that glistened in the dim lights. I looked closer—it was the data-flake receipt from Binks Cargo.

"I'll see that the Flower is returned to its rightful owners."

I staggered down the service corridor, not daring to respond. If I had, it would have emerged as a raging scream and Bolt would know he'd gotten to me.

Outside, the crowds were as heavy as earlier. Only now the Zom had robbed me of my disguise and I was mobbed as soon as I emerged. The horde gathered around me, and several cameras flashed as people pressed closer. My chest tightened, and my breathing was shallow. As the fans crushed against me, my hands clenched and unclenched, though I wasn't sure if it was nerves or an aftereffect of the drug.

"Alright, everyone step back. Don't make me bite."

The throng parted, and Stryng slinked through the gap. He'd stretched himself to his maximum height, making him over two meters tall, and had puffed up his head to give himself the appearance of a Rathidian cobra.

Despite his appearance, Stryng couldn't bite. He had a small opening on the bottom of his tail that functioned as a mouth, but the worst he could do was give someone a nasty suck. The crowd wasn't aware of this though and made room, allowing him to reach me.

"You okay, dollface?"

"I think so." My panic subsided now there was a friendly face around, and I put my response more firmly down to the drug. "Let's get out of here."

"Sure. You might want to fix your face first, sweetheart."

It took me a minute to realize I hadn't re-hidden my tribal markings and they were visible to everyone near me. I quickly changed them, going back to my usual coloration, hoping no one had got a clear picture.

"Nothing to see here, folks," Stryng called out. "Nothing but a little food poisoning."

He looped his tail over my arm, and we walked back to the *Queen*'s dock. All the way, I wondered if he knew the significance of the markings but decided it was unlikely. They were peculiar to Lecuundan society, and I doubted any outsider would recognize their significance. Besides, I had more immediate problems to deal with. Such as, how the hell I'd get to Sparth ML2F since I was still in Bolt's clutches.

After a long soak in the tub, I was more myself. But angrier than earlier. Not at Bolt—I couldn't get any more furious with him. No, I was angry at myself for getting caught so easily.

The nullsuit I use is made of several microlayers, one of which is a virtually impenetrable mono-molecular layer, designed to stop penetration by ballistic rounds as well as cutting or stabbing weapons. If my regular clothes had been equipped with that, Bolt would never have been able to inject me. I ordered new outfits, equipped with the extra protection, but I should have thought of it earlier considering my line of work beyond rassling.

The question of getting to Sparth haunted me like the persistent thunderstorms that surrounded the mysterious Eurypterid mountains back on Lecuunda. Getting to the planet was easy enough—there were commercial flights available from the station on several different spacelines. The trick would be managing it with my cover intact.

Maybe Bolt had been lying about not helping. After all, if he wanted me there so badly, wouldn't he do anything to make it possible? Perhaps it was another of his stupid jokes.

I checked my messages—nothing other than fan mail. Then I logged into Darkover, in case he'd decided to contact me there. But there was only a notification reminding me the auction would end in twenty standard hours. I should have canceled it already, but the incident with Bolt had messed up my mind. Or perhaps I didn't want to think about how close I'd been, to have my dreams of escape snatched from me.

Opening the auction listing, I tapped the cancel button. The system prompted me for a reason, and my fist hammered against the surface of the table. I wondered what would happen if I said the goods had been seized by Olive Branch. That would certainly make people sit up and take notice. On the other hand, it would also lead to widespread panic and the termination or suspension of my Darkover account. And I wasn't ready for that.

"Auction ended due to local sale." I finalized the cancelation.

Somehow Bolt was going to pay for this. I had no idea how, or when. But one way or another I'd show him that nobody messed with Tekuani. Even as I thought this, it ran hollow. He had me squarely in his greasy palm, and my only hope was that he'd keep his word once this was all over. But I knew he wouldn't—I was in way over my head.

There's an old Terran saying that a problem shared is halved. I didn't believe it, but perhaps I could bounce some ideas around with Denton on getting to Sparth without having to tell him too much. I dressed and made my way to his cabin. The door slid open a few moments after I triggered the announcer, and I walked in, not waiting for an invite. He was sitting on his couch with his head in his hands, his prosthetic dog face on a side table next to him along with a large bottle of something that appeared dangerously alcoholic.

"You okay?" I said quietly.

"If you call having your life fall apart around you *okay*."

"What's happened?"

Denton grabbed the bottle and gulped from it. "Want a hit?"

I shook my head. "What's going on?" I'd never seen him look so defeated.

He waved at his communication console. "Take a look."

I read the highlighted message. It was from the Wassertor venue operators on New Emslariat III. They were demanding the outstanding balance for the use of the giant stadium within fourteen days, or *PowerFall* would be canceled. The payment required—a quarter of a million drubles.

"I thought everything was lined up."

"It was. But after General Vinapo's complaint and our spotty performance, Mr. Quy's reconsidering his investments in the Pro-Rassling business. Meantime, he's frozen the company's accounts. Thrit, even ticket sales are frozen."

That was bad. Very bad. And especially since I was at least partially responsible. "I'm sorry, Denton. Really I am. Is there anything I can do?"

"Sure." He took another large swallow from the bottle. "If you've got a few hundred thousand drubles hidden under your mattress."

"My mattress? Why would I have money there?"

"Never mind." Denton looked up for the first time, his eyes glistening. "We're finished, Hype."

Suddenly, getting to Sparth seemed the least of my problems. I reached over, took the bottle out of his hand, and placed it on the table. "That won't help. There's only one thing for it."

"What's that?"

"We need another gig. Something to show Mr. Quy we're still worth it."

"You might be able to magic up gigs when you want, but I can't." He hesitated. "You don't have anything, do you?"

I looked at the floor. "Not this time."

He slammed his fist into the bulkhead. "Like I said, we're screwed."

"But I do have an idea."

His jaw dropped, as if I'd just produced the quarter of a million drubles.

"Sparth ML2F."

"Sparth?" He frowned, the lines in his forehead deepening. "In the Begasowme Realm? That place is a dump. How does that help?"

"It's a mining world. You know how much those places are starved for entertainment."

"That's because *nobody* wants to go there. Not even the people who live there."

"Which means there's a lot of pent-up demand and not much competition. And what's the one thing miners always have?"

"Bad backs?"

"Plenty of disposable income," I said. "And, on Sparth especially, not much to spend it on."

He leaned forward. "Are there even any suitable venues?"

"I've no idea. Why don't we look?"

I sat at his console and accessed Stellcom, searching for information on arenas and conference facilities on the planet. The list that came back was dismally short, and after further investigation, the choice was reduced to one possibility—the Sparth Arena and Conference Center.

"There you have it," I said. "That's our venue."

"Do they have any dates open?"

I checked. They had a worryingly large number of dates available, in fact. "Several, and it appears the *Queen* can get us there in a little under a week. If we do that and put on a big show, Mr. Quy will be impressed, and we can get *PowerFall* back on the calendar."

I knew it wasn't that easy. And I was doing this mostly for my own self-interest rather than for the good of the business. I quashed my guilt, telling myself that, in this case, our interests had a mutual solution.

"It might work, I suppose. We'd have to pull out all the stops on promotion on the way there, hit every channel we can." Denton looked at the arena listing. "Jeez, Hype. That thing costs a hundred thousand drubles. Didn't you hear me say our accounts were locked?"

"The business accounts are locked." I smiled at Denton. "But our personal ones aren't. It's time for a long, hard talk with the roster."

Fourteen

The largest room on the *Ethereal Queen* was what used to be the ballroom but now functioned as the main gym and practice area. It featured the same decorative cornices and hidden lighting as the rest of the ship, with the addition of various training areas, workout-nanokin projectors, weight-training equipment, and a full-sized TwistCube. Under ordinary circumstances, it was a nice uncluttered space for whatever exercise regime you chose, but today it was packed with the entire roster along with the backroom team and the stage crews. Denton had outlined the idea succinctly. Now came that moment of silence when everyone stood around wondering how they should react to the news that their careers were on the verge of ending.

"So you want us to put our money into propping up this sinking ship?" As usual, Courtney Bonor was leading with her mouth instead of her brain.

"I'm suggesting a way of saving everyone, the whole company." Denton stared her down. "But if you think you can get a better offer elsewhere, feel free."

"Is this another one of *your* schemes, Jones?" Phil Slinebar said, looking at me. "If it wasn't for you, we wouldn't be in this mess."

"Hype came up with the idea, that's true," Denton said. "But I support it one hundred percent, and it's wrong to blame her. Mr. Quy has been having doubts for a while, and we haven't done enough to convince him otherwise."

"Well, we all know why *you're* supporting her, Denton," Shela hissed, then pantomimed an insulting gesture.

Earlier, I might have risen to her jibes, but we were beyond that. I looked at Denton and lifted one eyebrow, and he nodded for me to join him at the front. There were several loud murmurs, but I ignored them.

"You can spin all the idiotic rumors you want." I raised my voice so everyone would hear. "But the truth is, this is a simple choice. Do we want to waste time insulting each other, or find a solution?

"I can't speak for anyone else, but I've been happy here as part of the FIRE team. Denton's a good boss, we have plenty of free time and, with one or three minor exceptions"—I glanced at the Bonors—"we get along fairly well. I'd like that to continue. And if we all work together, I think there's a good chance we can pull it off."

"Yeah, we know what you'll be pulling."

I think that was DeeZire rather than the Bonors. She and Caramel were two of the newer picks who had only been with the show a few months, but they were both getting plenty of coaching from the Triplets.

"I have five thousand drubles in my account," I said. "I'm willing to put up all that to save the company. Who else is in?"

"Let's say we do help out," Slinebar said in his whiny voice. "What do we get out of it?"

"You keep your job," I said.

"That's a fair question, Phil." Denton stepped forward once more. "Any profit from the show will be split between anyone who contributes, on a pro rata basis."

"And Mr. Quy has agreed to this?" Slinebar smiled his most sham smile. "He *is* the rights holder after all."

"This is all behind Mr. Quy's back." Denton held up his hands to silence the reaction. "We'll pay him a percentage, naturally, but I'm confident if we make the show work, he'll be more than happy with the extra publicity."

"Don't like being rogue rassler," Boots squeaked.

"Look, I'm a professional and expect to get paid for a gig," Pinhead boomed. "But I'll support the cause. I've got eleven thousand five hundred birrn."

He always used his homeworld's currency, even though prices were universally quoted in the Realm-wide druble, and I quickly did the conversion in my head. It came to about seven thousand drubles, and I wondered how he'd managed to save all that. I guess all that performance-enhancing equipment and food wasn't as expensive as I thought.

"Okay, we're up to twelve thousand," Denton said. "Anyone else?"

The offers came in slowly at first, but then it turned into a flood as people decided they preferred to take a chance on having a future.

"Okay. You got me." Slinebar was one of the last holdouts.

Denton bared his lips in a doggy smile. "Thanks, Phil. What have you got?"

"Well..." Slinebar hesitated. "Let's call it ten thousand. That's from my client and me."

"Huh? Wait, boss."

Boots Largo waddled over to his manager and whispered something to him. After a couple of minutes, Slinebar shrugged and lifted his hands in defeat.

"Okay." He coughed. "Make that twenty thousand. Fifteen from my client."

I'd lost count but was fairly sure that we were around eighty thousand.

"Thanks, both of you." Denton's tongue lolled out of his mouth. "And to make sure we get the best deal possible, Phil, you're in charge of negotiating the contract price with the venue."

"You want me to..."

"Whatever is left over will be used on promotion. So we need our best person on the job."

Slinebar stood a little straighter. "Did you just call me the best?"

"Only for that job, Slimeball," someone said from the back.

"Sure thing, Phil," another voice piped up. "You could squeeze photons out of a black hole."

It was hard not to laugh, and the guffaws grew louder when Slinebar responded.

"Thank you. I take that as a *sincere* compliment."

Up to now, the very visible absentees were the Bonor Triplets. They were huddled deep in discussion and for once appeared not to be working in unison. Based on the body language, Rachelle wanted in, but Courtney and Shehla were trying to argue her out of the idea. After several minutes of this, Rachelle turned to face Denton.

"Another twenty thousand, from the *three* of us."

That was it—we'd hit the target. Denton had been tallying everything and let out a long howl of triumph. "Thanks everyone. I really appreciate it. And I know all of you will put everything into making this a big success."

"One condition," Shehla hissed. "We get top billing."

Denton looked at me, and I shrugged.

I didn't care who got billed where. As long as we reached Sparth so I could get Bolt off my back.

"Given the circumstances, it's not my call." Denton scanned the room. "Does anyone object?"

There were murmured no's, and one person muttered something about leading with the hottest. But no one objected.

"One moment." A new voice caught us by surprise. Dr. Lee had materialized by the exercise equipment, his glowing form rippling strangely as his programming struggled to choose the right appearance with us all being present. "Don't we get a say in this?"

Denton glanced at me. "Who's *we*?"

"I've been listening too, dear." It was Auntie. "I might not have the new-fangled light display that the good doctor has, but I don't miss much."

I wasn't sure what two Artificial Personalities might think about the turn of events. They might be glad to see the back of us. If the ship was sold on to a family, or maybe a small company, it would likely mean less work for them.

"You want to invest in the show?" Denton asked. "How?"

"Some of my research has been quite lucrative," Dr. Lee said, lifting his chin.

Denton shook his head. "And you, Auntie?"

"Well, dear. I don't carry out research. But the good doctor has been kind enough to furnish me with a small honorarium in exchange for providing him with the endacatronic processing needed to analyze his data."

"I don't believe this," Denton said. "That's nice for you, Auntie, but I'm not sure it's technically legal."

Denton was right. APs were expressly forbidden from engaging in financial transactions. There was too much danger of them unfairly manipulating systems to their advantage. But it looked like our pair of virtual misfits had managed to skirt the rules—something I couldn't help but admire.

"Stop it, Denton. If they've made some drubles of their own, good for them." I looked back at Dr. Lee. "What did you have in mind?"

"I have to say that you people are most irritating. If it was entirely up to me, I'd—"

"Oh shush, dear," Auntie said. "What the good doctor is trying to say is that we love you all, and we've become used to your charming ways. We wouldn't like to see you replaced with another group of fleshbulbs."

"That's not how I was going to put it," Dr. Lee muttered.

"Which is why *I'm* telling them, dear." Auntie waited for a moment, then continued. "I've been saving up for one of those hard-light thingies. But it can wait. Besides, if we invest, we can make even more."

I tried to think of something to say but couldn't find the words. I'd never heard of any APs feeling that close to regular people.

"You realize this is a gamble, don't you, Auntie?" Denton said. "If we can't make the show a success, you'll lose your investment."

"Stuff and nonsense. No one here would let that happen. Would they, Hyperia dear?"

"No, Auntie. We wouldn't." I was wondering what else she might have listened in on. Or, for that matter, how much her internal sensors might have picked up.

"Then it's settled. We can give you another twenty thousand drubles."

Denton jaw lolled open and his tongue flopped out. I don't think he'd expected that—I know I hadn't.

When he recovered, he coughed to get everyone's attention. "Okay, that's everything for now, people. Thanks for your support and confidence." Denton looked at Slinebar. "I'll forward details of the venue. Get to work on the operators right away. We need to line this gig up fast. Christine, you need to pull out all the stops on this one—the craziest stuff you've ever come up with."

"Crazy is my middle name," she said.

As everyone was shuffling out, Denton turned to me. "Can we talk, in my office?"

"Sure." The prosthetic dogface made it impossible to get a read on him. "You're in charge…"

"Sometimes," he said cryptically.

Once in his office, Denton sprawled in the large boss chair behind his desk. He eyed me for a little while, then reached up and unfastened his prosthetic head, setting it down in front of him. It was an unnerving sight, as the prosthetic was still picking up his facial expressions. He rubbed his head, especially his cropped bristles. I imagined they itched a lot and wondered why he didn't stay completely hairless, but Terrans have their own peculiar vanities.

"I'm originally from Kurth. You probably didn't know that."

That was true enough. All I knew about Denton was what went out in the promo material. In that, it claimed he was from the fictional planet of Fenrir, in the L'Thidri Nebula.

"Auntie, privacy mode please," Denton said.

The recent discussion had made us both aware of how much eavesdropping went on onboard the *Queen*. "Do you think that makes any difference?"

He shrugged. "Maybe." He was quiet for several long moments. "I grew up herding silicanids. They're big, brutish animals, and you often have to get in among them when they're young. Make them understand who's the pack leader."

I'd heard of the creatures: silicon-based life forms resembling oversized dogs that reached over two meters tall at the shoulder. That explained how Denton had developed such a muscular torso, and gave a clue as to why he'd chosen his unique disguise. But I had no idea why he was telling me all this.

"Silicanids are cantankerous at best and can be downright vicious when they mature, but if you establish a bond with them early enough, they're extremely docile and trusting.

"One of my best animals, I called Denton. He was so cute when he was a pup—all spikes and sharp edges, but full of fun. As he grew, he became fiercely loyal to me, and I helped him establish his pack. I never farmed them like many of the others did. But when one died, I'd recover the pelt for processing. None of them, even Denton, ever knew. To them, their dead simply vanished, and that was the way I wanted to keep it."

"It sounds nice." At least in Terran terms of exploitation. "Why'd you leave?"

"Kurth has an irregular orbit that results in periodic floods, sometimes without warning. They can be dangerous, especially to the Silicanids—they like to graze on the low-lying flat plains. But the floods are part of the planet's natural cycle and essential for the healthy mineral deposits that the silicanids need.

"But then the floods didn't come—two or three years it was. And the shortage of good grazing meant the packs of silicanids shrank. And with it Kurth's economy."

Denton swallowed hard, and so did the prosthetic dog head.

"Sorry, Dent," I said. "Could you shut that down? It's a little spooky."

Denton switched the prosthetic off and put it under the desk where I wouldn't see it.

"So the Combine called out for all but the youngest of the Silicanids to be culled, to ensure there were enough supplies for the mineral houses."

"You didn't…?"

"I argued with the herd manager for my section. Said if we preserved the herds, we'd come back stronger. But he wouldn't listen."

I couldn't speak and didn't even try. The look on Denton's face told me all I needed to know.

"We came to blows, and he pulled a gun on me. Before I could react, Denton threw himself at the manager and mauled him. But before he died, the bastard got a shot off—went straight through Denton's heart pump."

"Thrit… I'm so sorry, Dent—"

"I held him in my arms as his lifeblood pumped out. Even as he died, he didn't whimper—just seemed happy I was with him."

"After that, I had to leave Kurth. Some of the guys said I ordered Denton to attack. It wasn't true, but the rumor was enough to kill my chances of getting taken on at any of the other farms."

"So you left, formed FIRE… and became Dogface Denton."

"Not exactly, and not that easily. But anyway, that's not the point." Denton lifted his head and stared at me. "What's *your* story, Hype? And why is it so important for you to get to Sparth?"

My stomach twinged and I couldn't hold his gaze. "I don't know what you—"

"Stop." Denton sounded almost as doggy as his alter ego. "I didn't tell you that story to gain sympathy. I hoped you'd realize you can trust me. Sometimes that's all you can do, Hype—you gotta have someone you can open up to."

The idea of not living a lie all the time was appealing. And perhaps I could use a friend. While my double (or was that triple?) life took up most of my time, it would be good to have an opportunity to relax with someone and not have to pretend to be something I wasn't, or not as much.

But if I told Denton the truth, he'd become an accomplice, at least in the eyes of the law. I wasn't sure I, or he, was ready for that. For all his grouchiness at times, Denton was a nice guy, and I didn't want to hurt him. But on the other hand, I'd lied to him over Guplides, and now Sparth. I wasn't that close to the others, but Denton didn't deserve to have someone he considered a friend lying to him. Maybe he was right and I did need to trust someone.

It felt like I'd been silent for an hour while all these crazy thoughts leaped through my head, but it could only have been a few minutes.

"Have you ever heard of Tekuani?" It felt surreal, as though it wasn't me talking.

"Tec-what?" He shook his head. "Sorry, no. What's that?"

"No surprise. Tekuani doesn't get a lot of publicity—unless you follow the crime news."

"Did I miss something? You're losing me, Hype."

"Okay." I took a deep breath. "There's a professional thief-for-hire who operates around the Realms. Every high-profile burglary or theft is attributed to Tekuani, whether it was them or not."

"Hey, I think I might have heard something about it—that Psychic Invalidation Engine thing, a couple of years ago."

"Yes, that was Tekuani."

And what?" Denton frowned. "You're running from this guy?"

"Not exactly." I hesitated, knowing I was about to drop myself deeper in the thrit. "I *am* that guy."

Denton blinked five times. His stone-colored mohyde chair creaked as he rocked slightly, then he stood and walked to a filing cabinet. He reached in and pulled out a bottle of Toquierdo Tequila, one of the most potent alcoholic drinks available in the Realms. He waved it at me, and I shook my head. Then he grabbed a glass, poured about three centimeters of the straw-colored liquid, swallowed it in a single gulp and sat back down.

"Did I hear you correctly? You're telling me you're some kind of interstellar thief?"

I sniffed loudly. "No, I'm telling you I'm the best interstellar thief there is."

"Oh, pardon me, I'm sure. I didn't think rank would be important in such a business."

"Well, now you know better." I already regretted telling him.

"And *that's* why we have to go to Sparth? Not because there's a ready audience. Not because we can get a cheap venue. Not because it's best for the company, but because you want to go there to steal something?"

"I know it looks bad. But the opportunity is a good one. You saw the details and thought so too." My pulse was thumping in my temples. "Don't put this all on me and say there's nothing in it for FIRE."

Denton held up his hands. "Okay... what's next? You gonna kill me if I talk?"

"I'm a thief, not a killer." I squeezed the words through clenched teeth.

Denton laughed humorlessly. "I'm so pleased to know there's a distinction."

"There's something else." This was the point where I should have kept my mouth firmly shut, but his dig about murder had me boiling mad.

"Let me guess. You're also a terrorist planning to assassinate the UberKaiser?"

161

"I'm being forced to go to Sparth by Olive Branch. They need me to recover some stolen documents that could lead to war."

Denton almost fell out of his chair. "*Olive Branch*? Now I know you're playing with me. That's a pile of Holowood thrit. We should get the Doc to check you out, you're hallucinating."

"One of their agents, a lowlife called Bolt, caught me back on Iotromia pulling a job. He's been blackmailing me ever since. He was the one who arranged the Guplides gig."

"*He* arranged it?"

"Sure. You don't think I know any generals, do you?" I blundered on before I lost my nerve. "He wanted me to do a job on Guplides, but it turned out it was a lie. A test to make sure I'd do what I was told. But the real mission is on Sparth. If I don't do it, I'll get locked away for a very long time, or maybe they'll brain-wipe me instead."

"Hype, I gotta tell you, this is a lot to take in." Denton laughed again, but this time it was tinged with hysteria. "I thought you were running from someone—like an irate husband or something. Not... *this*."

I suddenly felt exhausted. "Look, say the word, and I'll leave. I can make my own way to Sparth. Perhaps once I've got this cleared up, I could come back..."

"That ain't happening, sister. We're in this together, all the way."

"Stryng?" Denton sounded as confused as I was.

We heard a rustle, then Stryng's long body wriggled from under a couch against the far wall. Denton looked at me.

"Is this your idea?" he said.

"Don't look at me."

"Lay off the babe, she ain't done nothing," Stryng said. "I came by to see if you wanted to watch *Revenge of the Maltese Falcon* and fell asleep. When I woke, the conversation was too juicy not to listen in on, ya know what I mean?"

"Have you ever heard the word *privacy*?" Denton snapped.

"Sure, it's the word people throw around when they have something to hide."

"And you don't?" I thought back to my conversation with him about why the Bonors were picking on him again.

"Sure, everyone has secrets." He swished over to us. "But I ain't the one banging on about privacy. Yammering about that ain't gonna get us anywhere."

"So what should we be talking about, in your humble opinion?" Denton said.

"Toots here ain't leaving. She's the best part of the show, and you know it—no matter what the Bonors claim." Stryng glanced in my direction. "So, dollface here likes to go walkabout at night sometimes, who cares? As long as it ain't hurting the company, that's her business."

"You saw me the other night, didn't you?" I'd suspected that, but having it confirmed shook me more than I thought it would.

"Not all eyes are equal." Stryng wriggled. "Mine are small, but they see a lot."

"Maybe they see too much," Denton muttered. "I wasn't about to cut Hype loose, but what's that got to do with you?"

"Simple. If she goes, I go." Stryng coiled himself into a tight corkscrew shape. "And if you lose two of your top performers, how long will it be until the next one and the next? Then before you know it, you ain't got nobody."

"Don't say that, Stryng," I said. "I'm not worth it."

"He's right though." Denton stood, as though he were going throw us out, then changed his mind and dropped back into his chair. "If either of you quit, this thing will fall apart quicker than a ten-count. And we need this gig to work, or we're up thrit creek."

He was right, but that didn't make me feel any better about it. My motive in getting to Sparth had nothing to do with helping the company. Now I was trapped by my guilt—unable to walk away and yet unable to accept their help freely.

"So, what's the job on Sparth, sweets?" Stryng tapped his tail several times on the floor. "Who are we taking down?"

Denton jumped in his seat. "What? Wait, I can't—"

I held up my hand. "Don't worry. I'm not taking *anyone* down. I have to recover some information and identify the people who stole it. No violence involved."

"That ain't no fun," Stryng hissed. "I say we pack heaters from now on. Just in case."

"Heaters?" Denton lifted his eyebrows.

"Sure thing. Ain't no trouble a forty-five and a slug o' corn can't make go away."

Denton looked over at me. "Do you have any idea what this deranged worm is talking about?"

"Less of the worm, buddy."

"He's talking about old-fashioned guns." I wondered if Stryng could even hold, let alone shoot one. "They fired metal pellets of different sizes."

"Oh yeah, I remember now." Denton rubbed his forehead slowly. "No guns, no heaters, no shooting. Okay?"

"That gets my vote," I agreed.

"I thought you wanted to promote this gig," Stryng muttered. "We could stage a bank robbery—nothing like true crime to stir up the punters."

"If we're talking about actual angles, we better see what Christine has," said Denton. "She's the master when it comes to those things."

I shuffled in my seat. "I don't mind discussing story lines, but no one else can know about my Tekuani operations. It would be bad for me and potentially deadly for them. For all I know, Bolt might think anyone who finds out about this is a legitimate target."

"The fewer people who know about this, the better," Denton said.

"I may look like a snake, but I ain't no rat." Stryng coiled like a spring.

I breathed easier, but my thoughts were mixed up. Even though I was close to both of them, that was two more people in the universe who knew about my nighttime activities than I'd ever expected there would be, and I couldn't stop the spasms of fear in my brain. I was exposed and vulnerable in a way I'd never been before.

Christine pulled us together a few hours later. She'd been working nonstop since the meeting and was holding a tablet thick with notes.

"Here are the highlights. You'll get copies with your individual parts marked." She looked around, making sure everyone was paying attention. "The main match will be a Sudden Death four-way between Denton, Brachyura, Boots, and Mandraago—this will be for the title. We'll record a series of attacks and counterattacks behind the scenes to set this up. That'll generate plenty of interest with the title on the line."

"Brach or Klaw?" Brachyura asked.

"Klaw," Christine said. "I know it's out of cycle, but the double triangle story involving Hyperia is going to trigger an uncontrollable phase shift that evil will win."

"Sounds like fun," Brach said, clacking his giant claw together in appreciation.

"We're supposed to get top billing," one of the Bonors muttered.

"And you will, ladies." Christine smiled. "Your match will be you three versus Hype, Glacia, and me, in a beyond-the-veil Boson Spike bout."

"What the hell is that?" Shehla said.

"You're about to find out." Christine's grin broadened. "First shoots will be in one hour, ladies first. Everybody make sure you know your lines."

The *Queen* was already on route to Sparth, though we hadn't secured the venue, or a permit, to stage the match. Slinebar was absent as he was working on the venue agents via Stellcom, while Denton had already started on the red tape necessary to wangle the permit. Everything had that frenzied air that screamed hasty improvisation and with good reason. While we were all used to winging it, necessity was taking that to a whole new level.

"Stryng, you'll be fighting a handicap match against the Cazannis. We'll be setting that up with some backstage ambushes. Pinhead, ChaosRhino, and Zavara will open with a triple-threat match. Atsuno? Where are you?"

"Here."

"You'll be the second unannounced match. Caramel and DeeZire interrupt you while you're delivering the eulogy, and it degenerates into a fight."

"Eulogy?" Atsuno's eyes widened.

"You'll find out," Christine said cryptically. "We're going *big evil*."

Everyone in the room fell silent. We all knew what that meant—*he* hadn't been part of the roster for a long time. In the three years I'd been with FIRE, there'd never been a suggestion that we might use *him*. Even the thought sent shivers down my spine cartilage.

Khillborh, diabolical deity of the Primevil Dimension and Demon King of the Nether Regions, was about to return.

Fifteen

I watched from the shadows next to what used to be the stage as Courtney went through her fitness routine. She ran through some warm-up exercises and stretches, then shifted to performing a series of combat forms, both offensive and defensive. Her framing was elegant and perfect, and I hated everything about how she segued from one position to another, executing the moves almost as exquisitely as Atsuno would.

She was dressed in one of her signature skinsuits, specially designed to reveal tantalizingly large amounts of skin and much beloved by the Bonors' large, mostly male, fandom. I had to admit she looked good as the light sheen of sweat made her skin glisten under the lights. She couldn't see me. I was tucked away out of sight in the wings. I sensed a presence behind me and looked around. I couldn't see anything, but I felt *his* spirit—Khillborh was near. I swallowed hard, but the lump in my throat wouldn't go away. Even imagining that *thing* near me gave me goosebumps.

Then I heard it: a whisper in my ear—rough, guttural, and yet exquisitely seductive. The words sounded in my head, speaking directly to my soul. Something hard and cold appeared in my hand. I lifted it, shocked to see a Heavy Meson Blaster in my grip. The charge light showed it was fully loaded, and without thinking, I flicked the safety over to the fire position. The IsoSpin bolts would vaporize a building and leave no traces. It was no weapon to use inside a spaceship—and yet, it would certainly end the problems I had with Courtney.

"She has wronged you..." Khillborh's voice rasped. "She must be punished."

"No… please… not that. Not me. I can't…" My words tumbled out in half-choked gasps. "By all the Effigies of Abris, don't make me do that…"

My hand shook as I lifted the gun, pointing it at Courtney. My finger, moving of its own volition, slipped inside the guard to rest on the trigger.

"Do what you must. Heed my command!" Khillborh hissed.

My finger squeezed. The gun jerked. A flash of searing light leaped from the muzzle and jumped the distance to where Courtney was completing a sequence of artistic stretches. Then she was gone. Nothing but a splash of intense light accompanied by a high-pitched *frazzle*. And then the training room was empty.

I heard shouts. Shehla and Rachelle burst into the room, looking around in horror and calling Courtney's name. Shehla spotted something on the floor and bent to pick it up. It was the fused remnant of Courtney's Kahtee-Yay bracelet. I slipped deeper into the shadows. Phase one of Khillborh's plan was complete.

Ten hours later, the Stellcom channels were full of the news, and like everyone else in the company, I followed the coverage closely.

"Bonor Triplet Declared Missing."

"Courtney Bonor Vanishes from *Ethereal Queen* Mid-flight."

"FIRE Loses *Two* of its Biggest Assets."

"Has Courtney Bonor Defected to ICE?"

"Tragedy or Travesty? FIRE Underway to Undis-closed Gig Location Suffer Major Loss."

"Will Khillborh Return? What's Cooking at FIRE, and Will Everyone Burn in the End?"

"Dogface Denton Calls Security Footage
'Unsanctioned Release'—Investigations
Making No Progress."

"Realm Investigators Seek Urgent Discussions
with FIRE CEO."

I was talking with Denton when Slinebar trotted up, his puffy face glowing with a slight tinge of purplish-red.

"I did it. Damn, I'm good." He sounded out of breath and was waving a Flimsy in his hand. "We're booked for the thirteenth."

"Friday?" Denton smiled, his prosthetic tongue lolling out of his jaws. "Perfect."

I nodded. "Fridays always pull a big crowd."

"Sure, but it's Friday. The thirteenth..." Slinebar raised his eyebrows several times. "You know? Khillborh? Demon King of the Nether Regions?"

"Oh, yes." I had no idea of the significance, but both of them seemed happy about it.

"What's the deal?" Denton said.

"Fifty down." Slinebar swallowed and looked at the floor. "Plus forty points on the gate."

Denton growled. "That's robbery."

"You think I don't know that?" Slinebar spluttered. "Best I could do and leave us enough to work the promos."

"I thought you were the best negotiator in the Realms," Denton said.

"I am. And I'd like to see anyone do better. They may be starved for entertainment on Sparth, but that doesn't mean they can't tell when someone is desperate. And desperate people get thritty deals."

Denton held up his hands. "Okay. I get it, Phil. We're not in a position to argue."

Shehla was next. No one knew exactly what happened. The

security system caught her near to one of the *Queen*'s airlocks, where she appeared to be looking for Courtney. The recordings showed her calling her sister's name several times. The camera was hit by a burst of interference at that point, and when the recording cleared, the inner airlock door had cranked open. Shehla peered inside the lock and called Courtney's name again. Then her eyes widened, and she staggered back, covering her mouth with one hand while holding up the other as if to keep something away.

A strange flickering glow lit up the inside of the airlock chamber, but the camera was at the wrong angle to show what she saw. Shehla shuffled back, then fell onto her well-padded butt. She scrabbled away from the airlock, her ten-centimeter heels stabbing at the floor. The camera feed flickered, then she was gone, leaving nothing but a scorch mark.

The next round of reporting was more frenetic, and I couldn't help wondering where this would all end.

"Second Bonor Missing!"

"Something is Very, Very Wrong on the
Ethereal Queen."

"Dogface Denton Urged to Head for Nearest
Realm Bureau of Investigation Office."

"And Shehla Makes Four!"

"Unnamed RBI Spokesperson: Bureau NOT
Investigating Two Bonor Disappearances."

"Rik *Frenzy* Fosdyke, ICE General Manager:
No Knowledge of Bonors' Location—But
Would Welcome Them to Lineup."

One clip of Denton being interviewed live by *NeckTwister Magazine* was a masterpiece. It was one of the biggest rassling dirt sheets in the business and achieved aggressive distribution throughout the Realms. Word was they had the inside gossip on the news before it *was* news.

Denton was in the interview studio on the *Queen*, with his holo-image being injected into the magazine's feed in a live mix, making it look as though he was sitting face-to-face with the interviewer, Professor Max Impact. After the initial friendly banter, Impact questioned Denton in more detail.

"As I understand it," Impact said, "your match on Sparth will be against three of your biggest rivals—Brachyura, Boots Largo, and Mandraago. Isn't that an ill-considered fight to take on during the run-up to *PowerFall?*"

"Well, Max, I've always considered it the privilege and obligation of the reigning champion—whoever that might be—to stand up to any challenge and show everyone they won't back down from a fight. Sure, it's risky, but so is cruising between star systems."

"Who decided that match? And as CEO, couldn't you override it?"

"Like all our matches, it was decided by FIRE's match direction system, FRAIMS—a sophisticated, quantum-entangled AI system that monitors feedback from every one of our fans throughout the Seventeen Realms, and uses logic-based intelligence to determine the matches the *real* supporters want to see most." Denton licked his jowls and held up a hand to quieten the fake applause from the fake audience. "Yes, as CEO, I could have taken a bye, but I expect my champions to be fighters, and I demand nothing less from myself."

"Is it true that Stryng was *involved* with both of the missing Bonor girls?" Impact stared hard at the place Denton wasn't. "And that the relationships ended acrimoniously?"

"Sorry, Max. I don't know where you get your information from, but you've been misled. While Stryng was close to all three of the Bonors, it was a relationship based on friendship, mutual admiration, and respect. All of them are highly professional."

Stryng was watching the broadcast with me. "You like that guff, sister?" he said when I giggled at Denton's declaration. "I wrote it."

"I should have known." We turned back to watch the rest of the interview.

"How about the rumor that the RBI has issued a warrant for the arrest of Stryng on suspicion of multiple homicides?"

Denton barked, "Don't be ridiculous. And I'd prefer it if you stuck to matters involving the show on Sparth. It's going to be one of the best. I urge everyone to come and see it."

"Is that judgment based solely on the much-anticipated return of the diabolical deity of the Primevil Dimension known as Khillborh?"

"We've seen no signs that Khillborh will return anytime soon. From what we know, he's currently trapped in the Nether Regions until the Ninth Cycle aligns with the Umglaut Tangential."

Impact smiled as if he was the cat with the cream. "Indeed? If that's the case, why have you arranged for a Xablian field grid to be set up around the TwistCube?"

"There are no plans for such a grid. We've ordered extra lighting to improve the viewing experience, that's all."

"But a Xablian field *is* what Kawada "Kansu" Hachiro used to banish Khillborh to the Primevil Dimension many years ago?"

"Superstitious nonsense." Denton's tone grew sharper. "Do you want to know about the show, or are you only interested in spreading malicious rumors?"

"Is the six-way tag match between Hyperia Jones, Glacia, Crazy Conner, and *all three* Bonor girls still on, or has it been scratched from the lineup?"

"The published matches will go ahead," Denton snapped.

"Even though two of the Bonors are missing?"

"The Triplets are…"

"Are what, Mr. Denton?" Denton stayed quiet, and after a few moments, Impact continued. "Can you confirm the widespread rumor that Hyperia Jones is acting under the influence of Khillborh and may be responsible for—"

Denton snarled, then stood and tore the microphone from his shirt. "That's enough!" He kicked the chair through the holo-projected rear display.

"Mr. Denton? Why are you afraid to answer questions, Mr.

Denton?" Max Impact jumped up, yelling at Denton's retreating figure. "What is Dogface Denton so scared of?"

The sim cut in seamlessly as the hard-light Denton rushed back and grabbed the equally hard-light Max Impact by the neck. The fighting simulacrums struggled briefly, then "Denton" swung the broadcaster into a Cometary Hold before lifting him in the air. Denton executed a perfect Dogface Drop, slamming Impact through the table with a splintering crunch. The broadcast cut at that point, switching to a post-interview analysis with a heavily bandaged Max, but it was the interview and Denton's explosion at the end that was being circulated everywhere—with a little help.

"That was perfect," Stryng said in a low voice. "Those guys sure know how to rig a shot."

"According to Christine, ratings are hitting peak saturation," I said. "It's looking good for the show."

"It's gonna be a killer-diller, sweetheart." Stryng undulated his pleasure. "I can feel it in my tail."

"Talking of which—how's Rachelle?"

"Ready to flip her wig, as you'd expect. That dame ain't got no class."

I nodded, unable to suppress a satisfied smile.

"You have a carefully hidden, but well-developed, mean streak, sister." Stryng slapped his tail on the ground. "I like it."

The *Queen* was close to re-entering D-space after dropping out to reorient the navigation grids. It was a perfectly standard maneuver that the ship had done a thousand times before.

Rachelle walked into one of the tanning rooms, looked around several times, then locked the door behind her so she couldn't be disturbed. All of the Bonors were deeply tanned, but for Rachelle it was almost an addiction. The booths were arranged four across and three deep, the gray plastic capsules looking like giant seed pods. She double checked the door was sealed, then unzipped her top and peeled off the loose-fitting garment, revealing a skimpy sports bra stuffed to overflowing. Then she hooked her thumbs into the waistband of her pants and wriggled out of them.

Bending at the waist, Rachelle lifted her leg to coat it in tanning lotion, before switching and doing the other one. Then, she rubbed the glistening oil into her tight midriff and finally her neck and arms. When she was done, she moved over to the control panel of one of the capsules, dialing in the right duration and levels, and raised the lid. As she slid into the pod, something moved above her, and a rope-like tendril dropped down from the roof. She was completely unaware as it approached, then in a movement too fast to see, it looped around her neck like a noose.

Rachelle gave a single gasp, then her breath was cut off. The tentacle tightened and squeezed. Her eyes bulged and her hands came up, clawing at the tendril.

"Yes, do my bidding… by the power of my name, let it be so…" The voice, a hoarse whisper, came from seemingly nowhere.

After a brief struggle, Rachelle went limp, her arms dropping loosely to her side. Whatever was holding her released its grip, and her body dropped to the floor. The tendril or tentacle vanished into the dark of the roof, leaving her crumpled body lying awkwardly.

Auntie's voice sounded, warning of the shift to D-space, then she proceeded with a countdown. At zero, Rachelle's body was surrounded by a crackling blue glow that intensified until the entire room was flooded with light, and the security camera image overloaded. When the image returned, Rachelle had vanished.

"As near as we can tell, it appears someone planted an N-Space Inertial Anchor on her," Denton said. "When the *Queen* shifted into D-space, she was left behind, torn into her constituent atoms by the shear stresses created by infinite drag."

"That's horrific." Atsuno buried her face in her hands and sobbed. "Who would do something so monstrous? And why?"

"He would!" DeeZire spat, stabbing her finger at Stryng. "Everyone knows he hated them."

"Hey, leave me outta this. Besides, I got an alibi." He pointed to me with his tail. "I was with toots here. All night."

Denton looked across at me. "Is that right, Hyperia?"

There was something about how he said it that made me think

he was hoping I'd deny it, but I couldn't. "Sure. Yes. We were together—all night."

"Ficksnit!" DeeZire slammed her fist onto the table in front of her.

"Yeah. Make her prove it, Denton," said Caramel.

"How?" My response was pure snark. "Want to see the rope burns?"

"Enough," Denton shouted. "Any other ideas who might have done this?"

No one said anything, but we all looked around fearfully. Khillborh's name was on everyone's mind. ChaosRhino and Brachyura glowered at me as though I was last week's stinky trash—they'd already been feuding over me. I glanced at Atsuno, and she stared deliberately the other way. My revelation wasn't popular with anyone but Stryng.

He stared directly at them. "You know how it goes, guys? That left-hand corkscrew gets 'em every time."

Rhino and Brach snarled and jumped toward Stryng who slithered away, as Denton and Pinhead rushed in to stop the attack.

"Easy," Denton barked. "Save it for the ring, boys."

Brach swung his heavy, clawed pincer-hand, catching Dogface in the gut. Denton yelped, then ducked around Brach, twisting the claw up his back, forcing him to bend at the waist. "Enough of this, Brachyura. She isn't worth it."

Brachyura's carapace had been blue when he first arrived, but now it was changing. "Let go of me, Dogface," he grunted. "I'm going to tear that *worm* apart."

"Not this time." Denton pushed Brach's claw arm higher.

Brachyura twisted to free his arm, but Denton had the hold locked in. "Don't make me angry…" Brach yelled. "You wouldn't like…"

The color change on Brachyura's carapace came quickly, as though something had snapped inside him and triggered the transformation to blood red. He slowly, grindingly, forced his body upright, despite Denton pressing on his arm to hold him down. His giant claw hand clacked several times, the sound reverberating around the room. Suddenly, he reversed their positions and forced

Denton to his knees.

"Security!" Denton called. "Security—in here now."

Three beefy guys wearing yellow security shirts ran in and grabbed hold of Brachyura, but it was too late—the transition was complete. Brach was gone, leaving the evil Klaw.

"Get your hands off me," Klaw hissed, pushing back against the security team and sending all three men crashing into chairs and tables. Denton was half-crouched in front of him, and Klaw lifted his arm, ready to deliver a fatal blow. Pinhead dived over, standing between Klaw and Denton, pressing his beefy torso against Klaw's carapace.

"This isn't over, Dog-man." Klaw's voice sounded like the rumbling of an underwater volcano. "You'll get yours."

He stomped away, leaving everyone shaking behind him.

"Alright," Denton said. "Enough of this. And clean up this thrit."

He pointed at me and Stryng. "You two—my office in five."

"That Klaw—he forgets his strength when he changes." Denton stretched and rubbed his meaty bicep. "How'd it look?"

"Convincing enough," I said. "Especially when we add the sound effects and visual enhancements."

"Yeah, it was good." Stryng settled himself on the corner of Denton's desk. "You sold it."

Denton nodded. "The promo stats are going berserk. Christine is playing every trick she can, and from the feedback we're getting, it's paying off in a big way. Voxpop rating is up over three hundred percent. And don't forget the special charter."

The *charter* only existed as a flight plan in the Realms' Space Flight Control System, but as far as anyone knew, it had already picked up thousands of fans from three different worlds close to Sparth, all intent on seeing the action. The simulated boarding scenes had been detailed enough to convince everyone that swarms of off-world supporters were about to descend on the planet for the slightest chance they might be able to score a ticket. That meant local sales had exploded, with people either intending to come to the show or resell their tickets at scalper rates. Either way, we were happy.

Denton looked at me. "So business is looking good. How are things on your end?"

"Her end looks real good to me," Stryng said.

I ignored him. "You want to discuss that? I mean, the more you know, the greater the chance you'll get dragged into the thrit with me."

Denton rubbed his forehead. "I want to make sure everything's going the right way. That's why we're doing all this."

"I know." I shrugged. "And I feel terrible about it."

"It ain't just that." Stryng bobbed up and down. "It's for the company too—don't make it out as anything else, boss. We need this as much as Hype does."

Denton nodded. "I understand that. But we need to be there for her, and if there's anything we can do to help, we get on it."

"Right," Stryng agreed. "Like in the *Three Bandoleros*. Man, that was a good one, all three generations of Bogies in one movie."

"In this case, we're lucky," I said. "Mrez is fairly well known, and his girlfriend, Alyss Blakeston, more so. Which makes it easy to find information on them. Mrez lives in the corporate manager's mansion, a sprawling palace near the capital. With his money and her showbiz connections, it's a nonstop stream of parties and receptions."

"Hey, that Alyss is a real hotsy-totsy," said Stryng. "Let's gatecrash that monkey."

"Better than that," I said. "The publicity's generating so much excitement, it's already got their attention. Christine's working on getting us an invite. In fact, it might turn into a ball in our honor."

Denton raised his eyebrows. "*Christine* is doing that? Does she know about...?"

"She's doing it on her own, as part of working all the promo angles."

"Lucky she thought of it," Denton said.

I lowered my eyes. "Not entirely."

Stryng laughed. "There ain't no flies on this one."

Denton nodded in agreement. "So we get inside, then what? Head for the safe?"

It was unlikely there'd be anything incriminating there, other than some low-level corporate fraud. Mrez wouldn't keep his SlamCandy records anywhere the company auditors might stumble on them. "My guess is *I'm* looking for either a stand-alone computer system or possibly a holopad." The information I was after didn't need large-scale data storage, so I was sure it would be held separately, away from any possible prying eyes.

Denton growled softly. "And what are we supposed to do while you're risking your neck?"

"You'll be entertaining the crowd in the time-honored tradition."

"You shouldn't be operating alone," Denton said. "What if something goes wrong?"

"I'll be wearing a Distortion Matrix. That'll allow me to get in and out undetected." I looked from Stryng to Denton. "But if I *do* get caught—you cut me loose. You know nothing about it. Okay?"

"No way," Denton said.

Stryng agreed. "Think again, sister."

"It has to be that way. Otherwise, I turn myself over to Bolt right now and tell him I won't do it." I ground my fist against the surface of Denton's desk. "I've already put you in enough danger. I won't make it worse."

"Hey, we're the Three Bandoleros." Stryng stretched his tail upright and slapped it over Denton's hand. "All for one, or fall as one."

"No idea what that means," said Denton. "But I agree with the sentiment."

I looked at them both and found it difficult to swallow or even breathe. I'd been hiding away for so long, avoiding getting too close to anyone. Discovering there were people willing to stand with me, no matter what, filled me with a pang of fellowship mixed with fear. It was like finding out I still had a family, and that scared the hell out of me. Families and me are like an uncontrolled fusion reaction.

Despite that, I put my hand over theirs. "Thanks."

All we had to do was avoid getting caught by Mrez's security team, not get killed by the SlamCandy dealers, and escape getting arrested by the local Rancheros.

Nothing to it, I thought, crossing my tentacles.

Sixteen

After Rachelle's disappearance, the news streams went ballistic, and the story spread from the usual rassling press into the wider mainstream channels. The combination of the Bonors' visual appeal, the deliberately confusing and mysterious answers from Denton, along with rumors of official investigations, was sending people into a frenzy. Denials looked like cover-ups, confirmations were touted as misdirection, and the Terran predilection for conspiracy theories blew the whole thing into D-space and beyond.

By the time we were close to Sparth, the show was sold out, and scalpers were offering tickets over Stellcom at outrageous prices. Not only that, but networks we didn't normally link up with were contacting Christine to arrange live feeds, potentially increasing the profitability of the event.

Frenzy Fosdyke accused Denton and FIRE of the "worst kind of duplicitous and deceitful promotion," which was entirely true, and drove interest even higher.

I was in my room, freshening up after a hard training session when Denton called on the internal comms.

"All clear?" he whispered.

"I'm alone, if that's what you mean." Both he and Stryng were taking the Bandolero idea a little too far.

"Christine left a couple of minutes ago. The gray bear's mouth is wide open."

"Sorry?"

Denton's voice lowered to a hiss. "You know—*the target*. Mrez is holding a rassling-themed All-Stars Ball in our honor. The entire roster is invited."

"That's good," I said.

"Good? It's perfect." Denton hesitated. "Isn't it?"

"It might make it easier. But it depends on where, and how, Mrez conducts his SlamCandy business."

Denton's doggy jowls drooped. "Thought it was good news. Exciting."

"It is. Both." I forced myself to sound enthusiastic. "But I don't want to get overconfident. I'm under no illusion this is going to be easy."

"I guess not."

"When's it scheduled for?"

"Day before the show." Denton's doggy ears perked up. "Mrez got approval to pay for it from company funds as a brand promotion. He's bringing in half of Holowood to impress them—and Alyss Blakeston."

"If he's feeding her SlamCandy habit, does he need to impress her any more than he already has?"

Denton shrugged. "Who knows? Maybe he's a romantic. Either way, it helps us a lot."

"It helps the show. From my perspective, it's more of a distraction."

Again, he looked dispirited, and I cursed myself. Despite the contact I've had with men over the last few years, and especially Terrans, I don't know how to deal with them well. They're such a confused bunch, always needing so much pampering and flattery.

"It adds to the mix of people at the event," I said. "That's useful for providing cover and options. As Osharus said: 'Opportunity grows results faster than seaweed'."

"He was one of your greatest philosophers, wasn't he?"

Among other things I didn't want to discuss. "His writing on cultural interrelations is considered poetry, and he defined and inspired generations of Lecuundan self-reflection, honesty, and artistry. Everyone studies his work from a young age in school."

"Quite the guy then," Denton said.

"You're a lot like him in many ways."

He smiled, then a puzzled look came over his face. "You know him? Or knew him?"

Osharus died when I was a young girl, but he was well known

throughout Lecuunda. "Sorry, my Lingua isn't always perfect. I meant you remind me of his writings and philosophies. Not that I knew him personally."

"Ahh."

He was still smiling, which was good.

"Only two days until planetfall," I said.

Denton's tongue lolled from his jaws. "Then we'll spend some time acclimatizing and running direct local promotion. Christine's booked us on tours of the local orphanages and children's hospitals."

"She's done an amazing job."

"Agreed. I'm giving her a bonus out of my share of any profits. She's worked everything to perfection."

"Whatever you give her, match it from my share," I said. "I owe her at least that."

My comm indicator flashed. I had another call—one that was encrypted—and had a fairly good idea who that would be. "Sorry, Denton. I need to go."

"Trouble?"

"Not sure. Talk later."

I closed the call with Denton, not wanting to give him time to worry too much, then took a couple of breaths before I picked up. Bolt's suave features appeared on the screen, and he gave a brief smile.

"Hello, Hyperia."

I didn't reply. I wasn't going to get fooled by that damn answer sim this time.

"I see you've been busy. Rather clever, using your rassling friends to instigate a match on Sparth ML2F. You're more resourceful than I thought."

He paused, and I remained silent.

"I thought you should know. The timetable has changed. According to my sources, the Klausehn blueprints will be exchanged sometime in the next few days. If you don't get them soon, the opportunity could disappear. And if that happens… Well, let's say your future wouldn't look promising."

"Why don't you go and *soothe* yourself in a dark room, Bolt."

"Excuse me?" Bolt's eyes were suddenly the size of Naanian

flatbreads. "Are you being deliberately ins—"

Thrit! It was him. The bastard had fooled me yet again. "Thank you for calling Hyperia Jones. I'm not available to take your call right now. Please leave your message after the insult."

I closed the transmission. If I was lucky, Bolt would think my voicemail was on the blink. But I doubted he'd be that forgiving.

Another call came through, and I switched it to my answering service. After waiting a minute for him to start recording a message, I cut in and answered it.

"Hi Bolt. Sorry, I'm having some service issues. What's new?"

He glowered at me through the screen, and for a moment I thought he was going to give me a tongue-lashing, but he gathered himself and repeated his earlier speech in a flat-toned voice.

"The *Queen* is two days away," I said, "and the fight four days after that. We've managed to get a ball thrown in honor of our visit the night before—that's the best chance I have. If that's not good enough, I can't do anything about it."

Bolt looked surly and glanced to one side, as if reading something. "There's a ship I can take that will get me there on the fifteenth. I expect you to be ready with the documents when I arrive."

"I'll do what I can."

Bolt's jaw was a hard edge. "Do better than that."

The screen flickered, and he ended the call. I had the feeling I was inside the TwistCube, with the ring spinning around me as the gravitational pull switched at random, dragging me perilously in one direction or another. There wasn't much to comfort me, so I pulled up the media clips I'd assembled of Mrez and Alyss Blakeston. There were plenty of them, but the information was low quality—mostly drawn from various questionable society and Holowood streams.

With help from Bydox, I'd also been able to tap into some of Metal Ventures' corporate files. That provided some information on the mansion, and I'd done an interior reconstruction—mapping the rooms as accurately as possible without having access to architectural records. A few areas remained blurry. I'd filled the gaps using smart home-planning software, but without any on-the-ground data, it was impossible to know how accurate those sections were.

The next piece I looked at was from the society pages, discussing Mrez's engagement with Blakeston. As well as the typical traditional ring, Mrez had commissioned a matching pair of pendants with a setting of finely worked borodium and tyridium, and a circular centerpiece richly encrusted in StarPhyres. Each one was worth at least a megadruble, and naturally, the crystals caught my attention.

I stared at the images of the pendants, wondering what the chances were of liberating them for my personal collection. But I tried hard not to think about that. I had enough on my plate getting free from Bolt. I opened a message from Bydox—succinct as always.

"Found this, thought you might find it useful."

I opened the attached file. It was a routine multi-layer satellite survey of the kind used by mineral extraction companies. I checked the contents: data layers for ground-penetrating radar, IR, and full-frequency squirkium field data. Perfect information—if I'd been planning on opening a mine.

"I think you missed the target on this one," I muttered.

Bydox was always thorough, but this meant he sometimes sent through material not directly relevant to the job at hand. I preferred that, rather than miss something crucial. He'd included the customary *Contact Me* button on the message, and I stared at it for a while before pressing it. The screen pulsed blue as the Stellcom tried to establish a link. I was about to end the connection when the image switched to an anonymized face display—the features blurred and displaced, reminding me of an abstract painting.

"Greetings, Tekuani." Bydox's voice was heavily distorted. "You got the file?"

I knew Bydox couldn't see me any more than I could him, but I felt self-conscious of the intrusion. "I don't think that one is going to be useful, unfortunately."

"You intrigue me," Bydox said.

"How's that?"

"Never mind. I try not to speculate on a client's operations—it's safer. I would have thought it was perfectly aligned with *your* interests, though."

I wondered if I'd missed something. "What makes you think that?"

"Well, pardon my presumption, but what on Sparth would be more tantalizing for someone of your talents than the Metal Ventures' mansion?"

"The mansion?" I attempted to sound nonchalant but probably failed.

"Of course. The file is a calibration run against a known area. In this case, the Sparth capital, including the mansion. One second."

The screen blanked, then a moment later the data file he'd sent opened. It showed what I'd already seen. But then Bydox zoomed-in—first on the city, then one neighborhood, and finally on the mansion itself. The various squirk frequencies combined with the other overlays produced a high-resolution scan of the entire building complex, and the harmonic resonances made it possible to filter the data to construct detailed 3D maps of every level and room inside.

To say I felt dumb was the understatement of the year. "Errr… thanks."

"It's useful?"

I didn't want to say too much. I'd used Bydox many times, but trust is only ever a mistake in my business. "It's of interest."

Despite the jumbled, blurred face, I detected a hint of a smile. "That's good. I thought for a minute I was losing my touch. Or perhaps you are." Bydox chuckled.

"You may be right."

Bydox shifted on the screen. "Is there anything else?"

"No, I don't thi—wait—do you have any information on the L'Thidri Nebula?"

"Only what's available from public sources." Bydox hesitated. "L'Thidri isn't a place people come back from. Why do you ask?"

"I might be heading that way after this job is complete."

Bydox was silent for a while. "Nothing can be that bad. Besides, you're too good at what you do to need to run and hide."

"It may not be entirely my decision."

His shadowy face nodded. "I guessed that might be the case. I hope it doesn't come to that. You're one of my best clients. And one of the few people I really talk with."

Bydox's words shook me a little. I'd never considered our relationship as anything other than professional, but it seemed that for him—or her—there was more to it. "I'll try not to let that happen," I said, feeling a little flustered.

"L'Thidri is evil. Beyond anything we can imagine. Over the years, numerous expeditions have gone there—from single travelers to fully equipped warships—and none have been heard from again. Who or *what* ever controls that area… they don't like visitors."

Bydox closed the signal, and the screen went black.

The ball of honor was planned on a lavish scale, and every day the guest list grew increasingly flamboyant. I'm not the type of person to be starstruck, but it was reading like a who's who of Holowood. The guests included several minor members of the UberKaiser's family, which I was surprised at until I discovered they were being paid and Christine had arranged it. I was somewhat scandalized by that.

On Lecuunda, the royal family is above such base commercial transactions and lives on generous stipends from the public purse, with its business interests being managed by lackeys hired specifically for that purpose. I also found that a little sickening. The system was designed purely to lend substance to the idea that the royals were the feudal power they'd once been, while in reality they were nothing but parasites with airs and graces living off a public that lapped up their pomposity.

As we were the honored guests, Mrez had laid on a fleet of skycab limousines to take us to the party. Initially, I thought that was a generous gesture, then I found out the limo company was one of Mrez's sidelines and he was charging them out to Metal Ventures—undoubtedly at premium rates. It's said there are only two things in the universe that are limitless: one is lust, and the other, greed.

Someone banged on my door.

"You ready, Hype?" It was Klaw. "Limos are here."

"Two minutes."

Mrez had insisted on formal evening attire, and Denton was

185

willing to indulge him given the circumstances. Because of that, the Pantograph had been working overtime. The men would wear stylish suits featuring short-buttoned, braided jackets. For the women, it was elegant, multi-layered skirts made from satin and gossamer that floated as though they had built-in gravity nullifiers. It was like being a princess—an odd sensation for me as I'd never felt that way, even when playing childish games.

A few quick strokes smoothed down the dress, and I reconfigured my tentacles to resemble a hairstyle I'd seen in one of Stryng's ancient movies. It was large and bouffant with everything *up*. Then I added a small band of fake tyridium encrusted with Vholian rubies over my forehead, providing the perfect contrast to the emerald, silken gown—or at least so I'd been told.

In less than the two minutes I'd asked for, I was ready and found Klaw waiting for me. His suit fitted like a ripe onana skin, and he had a dark green sash running over his shoulder to his waist, designed to match my gown. He whistled when he saw me, holding out his regular arm for me to take.

"You look amazing," he said.

I gave a small curtsy. "You're not too shabby either."

We paraded arm-in-arm to the airlock and down the ramp to the string of waiting limos. Atsuno was waiting with Stryng, whose eyes snapped wide open when he saw me, and his tail slapped the ground.

"I think I'm in heaven." Stryng had a formal ribbon tied below his eye spots. "Sharing a limo with two of the hottest dames on the planet."

"And me," Klaw growled, thumping his chest with his giant claw. "Don't forget."

"I'll try my best." Stryng slithered to the closest limo and opened the door. "This way, ladies."

As soon as Atsuno and I were seated, Stryng hopped in and wriggled his way between us, somehow managing to rub his length against both of us in the process.

"Now that's better," he said.

"This side, worm," said Klaw, clambering into the back of the vehicle and yanking on Stryng's tail.

"Hey, watch it, fish-breath," Stryng yelped. "There's plenty of room this side."

Klaw wound Stryng's tail up in his claw hand and dragged him across to the other seat. "Sit."

"I ain't no dog."

"Sit, or be crunched."

"Your logic is impeccable." Stryng settled onto the seat opposite. "Besides, I can ogle better from here."

"Try to be a gentleman,"—Atsuno reached over and patted Stryng's tail—"for once."

The limo jumped into the air and joined the others, and we floated across a blue-and-pink sky in the last rays of the Sparth sunset. I was surprised by the size of the capital, Digasdeep. I'd read in the guides that its population was around three million—not bad for a mining world, and apparently, eighty percent of its people lived within a few hundred kilometers of the city.

The lights were coming on in some of the buildings below us, making it look a little like we were skipping over a glittering sea, with the waves reflecting the dying sun. A pang of homesickness hit me, but the sensation vanished quickly. There were far too many fish that needed burying before that would ever be a comfortable thought, not to mention lost dreams.

Our limo was unpiloted, naturally, but came with a built-in personality that talked to us without warning.

"Right you are, guv. If you wanna scenic tour, just jab yer fumb on the button, or say 'Start Tour, TECS'." The accent was thick and barely understandable, though I recognized the words as Lingua, more or less.

"Don't give us the runaround, you pile of random squirkium digits," snarled Stryng, sulking at Klaw's interference with the seating arrangements. And who, or what, the hell is a Tex?"

"I'm TECS, the Taxi." The voice spoke up again. "TECS is for Transportation, Enhanced Character, ServiceDrone. 'appy to serve you and all passengers to the best of my abilities, guv."

"Okay, can it, mac. No one's listening to ya gobbledygook. Otherwise, I'll put a slug in ya."

"Crikey, mate. I'm fully 'quipped to detect violence and frets. Diverting to the nearest Ranchero department. You can continue this discussion wiv da coppers."

"Wait." Atsuno hushed Stryng. "It wasn't a threat. Stryng was speaking his native err… Ligaturian. It was a traditional greeting and expression of gratitude."

"Yer 'avin a larf aintcha? I've got da knowledge, I 'ave. I understand over free farsand languages. There ain't no blinkin' *Ligaturian*."

"It's extremely rare," Atsumo said, struggling to find an argument against us getting chauffeured to the nearest cop station.

"Check your internal sensors," I said. "Does the individual who addressed you in Ligaturian resemble any of your definitions of life-forms?"

"You fink I'm a dummy or sumfing?" TECS said, but a light blinked several times in the passenger compartment. "Cor blimey, well I'll be a one-legged mule in an appendage-kicking contest. There ain't no match. Better add dis to my long-term storage. Fanks for expanding my knowledge—jes wait till I tells the wife about this one."

"You're welcome, TECS. Now how about taking us to the ball?" Atsuno looked at Stryng and sighed. "Before anything else goes wrong."

"Sure fing, darlin'." The cab returned to its original course, increasing speed to catch up with the other limos. "Enjoy yer journey, and let TECS take the AI out of strain."

Few smaller-scale Artificial Personalities are viable, and even fewer useful. If they're allowed enough smarts to become truly intelligent, they tend to evolve in one of three directions. The first turn megalomaniac and try to destroy all biological lifeforms, or sometimes become beneficial dictators. The second like to spend their time smothering their owners, drowning them in syrupy thoughts and forcing the population into a decline until they wither away. The last reach a point of frustration at people's general ineptness in comparison to themselves, so much so that they become detached from those around them and vanish into the depths of D-space, endlessly searching for a like-minded entity with which to discuss the true meaning of life, the universe, and everything. I hadn't decided which category Auntie and the Doc fell into, but none of that was important right now—I needed to focus on the job ahead.

"You okay, Hype?" Atsuno whispered, so the boys couldn't hear.

"Sure, but I've never been to anything like this." It was a lie, but one that she'd accept.

"Don't worry. It's nothing but a public appearance full of gawkers."

That was undoubtedly true, but not what I was thinking about. Dogface, Stryng, and I had our own plans. If they worked, I'd potentially have the information I needed. If not, we might all end up in a cell.

"I know, but there'll be so many famous people. What if I mess up in front of them?"

The cab seemed to vanish in the warmth of Atsuno's smile. "We'll look after each other. That's what being a team is about."

It was a nice idea in theory, but I doubted she'd be so quick to say that if she knew the truth. The cab dropped from its lofty flight path, and a few minutes later we landed in the outer grounds of the corporate mansion. It was too late for anything but action.

Seventeen

The doors of the limo clicked with a metallic snap, then twisted open. The noise reminded me of my cell door locking when I'd been caught by the Rancheros back on Iotromia, and I swallowed nervously. If this failed, I'd find myself a permanent guest of the Rancheros—or perhaps Bolt would simply bury me in a cave on some unknown penal asteroid.

"Fanks, ladies and gentlefings. We're at your destination. 'ope you'll let Beyond Limousines service you again. And don't forget to rate are performance and leave a review."

It was nighttime, and the sun was well below the horizon, but you'd never believe it from the amount of light flooding into the cab. Only the black sky gave away the time of day, as the grassy area where we'd landed was lit by a dazzling array of floodlights. I clambered out, attempting to leave the cab elegantly, though that was almost impossible given my ridiculous voluminous dress.

"You're meant to wait, Hype," Klaw hissed. "We help you out, remember."

I glanced back as he scrambled out of the limo, his bulk making it awkward for him too. "Sorry, Brach. I'm out now."

Stryng slithered out next and held out his tail to assist Atsuno. I doubted she needed it, and somehow she managed to exit the vehicle like an elegant princess. I noticed a sound, similar to the rustle of leaves in the wind, then realized dozens of people were watching us. When I filtered out the overpowering lights, I made out several of the crowd recording us on small holocams. While some were undoubtedly regular guests, the majority had to be media representatives. Judging by the number, our promotions had been successful. Whether they were here for us or the Holowood stars, they'd be treated to a show that would be one of a kind.

Someone stepped out from the glare and walked toward us, trailed by a second, taller figure. As they approached, I recognized Th'opn Mrez, with Alyss Blakeston following him.

"Greetings! Greetings!" Mrez bellowed. "So glad to have you here. What an incredible day. To imagine the wondrous people of FIRE would be here to share my modest abode and visit with my humble friends."

Mrez was smaller than I'd imagined, with leathery, purple-tinted skin. The ridges in his head were clearly visible under the lights, as were the sprouting tufts of dark red feathers characteristic of Zuerilians. He wore a white tuxedo with glittering faberium threads, but I was more interested in checking his eyes. They were wide, but showed none of the vagueness characteristic of Slam-Candy use. I executed a well-rehearsed curtsy, then turned to Alyss and did the same.

Blakeston was at least ten centimeters taller than Mrez and almost as tall as me. She had that chiseled-to-perfection bone structure—common to all Holowood stars—that comes from a lifetime of skeletal sculpturing. Unlike her boyfriend, Alyss's eyes were deader than a black hole. She didn't look that way in her shows, so I assumed they enhanced them during filming.

She looked me up and down, taking in every millimeter as if measuring me at a squirkian scale. A vacuous smile drifted to her face, then she put her hand on my arm. "You're too tall."

"Sorry?"

"Stay away from Th'opn."

"I don't understand—"

Atsuno put her arm around me. "Hello, Ms. Blakeston. I do love your holo-shows. I think I've seen every one of them."

"Of course you have," Blakeston husked. "Hasn't everyone?"

"Well, I've n—" Ats cut me off with an elbow to the ribs.

"You're so right," Atsuno gushed.

"You're such a darling, darling." Blakeston turned her attention to Atsuno, as if I was a pile of week-old garbage. "And so tiny. So much love-love for you."

"Thank you, Ms. Blakeston," Atsuno crooned. "Love-love back and kisses."

"Oh please, let's not have any formality. Call me Alyss, or *principessa* if you prefer."

I'd heard that Blakeston often used that title, though she wasn't entitled to it. Apparently, it was something adopted by her hangers-on, supposedly in recognition of her talents. I wasn't sure what those were—other than the obvious horizontal ones. Her holo-shows always cast her as a helpless damsel who needed rescuing, and always was. Usually by an equally vacuous Terran six-pack.

Mrez had been talking to Dogface but now focused his attention on us. "What a delightful collection of female charm we have here. You're Atsuno Moon," Mrez said, then turned to me. "And you must be the ravishing Hyperia Jones. Interesting—you look smaller on the holo-screen."

He examined me in a similar way to Blakeston, but there was no mistaking the raw lust in his gaze. Power might corrupt, but vice and debauchery are always its playmates.

Mrez's eyes twinkled, and my epidermal layers wrinkled. I could imagine what was going through his mind. Klaw came up behind us and draped his large claw over my shoulder. It was an oddly protective gesture but one I welcomed at that moment—if only because it might divert Mrez's thoughts. On the other side of our little group, Stryng slithered up, making a show of ogling Alyss Blakeston.

"Hey, sweetcheeks. You look like you enjoy a good workout. Lemme know if you want some private sessions on my special twisting regime. It tones every part of you, outside and in."

"Alyss has access to the best personal trainers, thank you." Mrez glared at Stryng. "I doubt you could do anything for her they can't."

"I wouldn't bet on it." Stryng winked at Alyss.

"Perhaps we should move inside and mingle," Mrez said a little too loudly, as if it was an order rather than a request.

We crossed a luxurious lawn with grass so meticulous you could have measured it with a laser, and entered the mansion. I glanced around the ballroom, estimating the wealth on display, but even my well-honed sense of extravagance blew a fuse. Every surface was decorated with precious and semi-precious stones, or lavishly appointed with borodium highlights. Arrangements of the finest Anthrium feathers were spread throughout the room, displayed in extravagant, brightly-decorated Oywaian vases.

I'd never seen so many media types in one place before. All the people who spoke to me were either celebrities of varied distinction, or part of the mob of agents and influencers that followed every one of them. Even Mandraago, who'd spent a lot of time in Holowood, was wandering through the crowds looking starstruck, introducing himself like a wide-eyed mark.

I was immune to fanatical worshiping, naturally. My knowledge of personalities was limited to Lecuundan celebrities, who were few and far between. And discussions on Darkover about such people were limited to their valuable possessions and security arrangements.

A small, wiry Terran sidled up next to me, watching the crowd with delicious brown eyes that shimmered under the lights of the ballroom. He had a thick mop of dark hair coiffed into a pompadour arrangement, and his face was decorated with a thin goatee.

"Quite the zoo, isn't it?" he said, leaning over to make himself heard over the cyberchestral music.

"At least everyone seems to be enjoying themselves," I said.

"Well, they would with all the *Slam* around here. Have you seen the food? It's loaded with it."

I looked across at the tables piled high with what seemed to be every form of sumptuous comestible possible. Was Mrez so crazy as to lace it with SlamCandy at such a public event?

"Thanks for the warning."

"The good guys have to stick together, right?"

"Are you one of them?" I have to admit I wasn't paying much attention to him. My focus was entirely on looking for any surprises in the security systems.

"You don't know who I am?" His voice rose slightly in pitch.

"Sorry, I'm not familiar with many producers or directors."

"I must have a long discussion with my publicists," he muttered. "I'm Roban Dooney..."

He smiled in a studied casual grin, then held out his hand. I shook it lightly. "Hyperia Jones. Nice meeting you."

"Wow... you *still* don't know me, do you?"

I turned to face him fully. He did look somewhat familiar, but I couldn't say from where. He was starting to annoy me though. Holowood types were so full of themselves, though most of them were nothing more than glorified floor sweepers. "Am I supposed to?"

"Well, obviously I'm not in *your* category of fame." He gave a small bow. "Perhaps I should say, I'm Roban—*Metal Marauder*—Dooney..."

Even I knew the Metal Marauder holo-shows—one of the biggest franchises in Holowood. They weren't to my taste, but Stryng loved them. They were usually high on special effects and low on content, which undoubtedly added to their appeal. What the connection was with this pest escaped me though. "Very nice, I'm sure."

Dooney's jaw dropped theatrically. "I think I better *fire* my publicists. Let me try again—I *am* the Metal Marauder..."

"Oh, I see—you're the writer—congratulations."

Mandraago walked over. "Hey, Roban," he rumbled. "Good to see you here. I was hoping to get a chance to meet you. I've got an idea for a part that I—"

"Yeah? Talk to someone important..." Dooney's face had darkened. Then he spun on his heel and marched off, leaving Mandraago openmouthed.

"Huh?" Mandraago snorted through his large nostrils. "What got into him?"

I shrugged. "You know what these Holowood people are like. Hell, you work with them."

"Sure, but Dooney's supposed to be one of the good ones." Mannie frowned. "I was going to pitch him on being a villain in his next holo-show."

"You know who he is then?"

Mandraago looked at me as if I'd grown a second head. "Seriously, Hype?"

I shrugged. "He said he was something to do with the Metal Marauder holo-shows."

"*Roban Dooney*. He's the *star*! Highest paid actor in Holowood. Thrit, the guy's a multiple ROSCA winner."

"Oh..."

"Being on a show with him is virtually guaranteed to launch your career. Everything he touches turns to borodium." Mannie's eye-ridges lifted. "You didn't recognize him?"

"He seems a lot taller on the holoscreen..."

The truth was, I hadn't identified him, and probably wouldn't have even if I hadn't been focusing on the security. People on screen often bear no resemblance to their real life appearance. Nano-cosmetics are so advanced these days, they can make a Nienusian actor such as Mandraago look like a Rashinor Stormfang.

A band made up of real, live musicians was playing a selection of classic retro-swing tunes at one end of the large hall. The band leader seemed familiar, and when I edged closer I realized it was the genuine simulacrum of Beethoven Stradivarius himself, who continued to be one of the hardest-working performers in the business, three hundred years after his untimely death. The dance floor was moderately full—swirling couples of all descriptions spinning in formation as they performed the elegant sequences of the latest, and hottest, moves.

The room must have been equipped with sonic suppressors, because away from the dance floor the music level dropped low to permit conversation, but with enough volume to allow the various clusters of partygoers to speak privately.

I avoided getting too close. For one thing, I wanted the opportunity to check the security systems thoroughly, but also because I'd never learned how to dance anything other than the standard Lecuundan court dances that everyone was taught in school. Under Lecuundan law, all citizens had to be ready for the call to *present at royal command*, though the truth was, that privilege was reserved for the upper classes. And while the dances were considered the ultimate in grace on Lecuunda, they dated back over a millennium to the time of the first UberKaiser.

I veered away, skirting the hall centerpiece—a monumental rock garden of boulder-sized gemstones, interspersed with the floating fronds of GloBlossoms, and topped with a flaming fire fountain that gushed high into the air under the large, domed roof.

The roof was lined in a dazzling array of StarPhyres and quiri-beams, projecting a glittering curtain-like display of glowing cobwebs of energy that interacted with the fire fountain in exquisite patterns. It was the type of over-the-top extravagance favored by the rich and tasteless, and undoubtedly cost more than we'd spent on setting up the whole rassling event.

I sauntered through the room, ensuring I was seen by as many people as possible. As I approached a group huddled near Denton, I accidentally bumped into someone and turned, mumbling an automatic apology, then halted.

"Bolt?" My arms trembled as I held back the instinct to attack him. "I'm on the job. You don't need to check up on me, you fugglewort."

His eyes widened, and his manicured eyebrows rose. "That's an unusual way of greeting someone, Ms. Jones."

"I'll *unusual* the ficksnit out of you, once this is all over."

Bolt glanced over his shoulder, his long face carrying an expression that said he thought I needed locking up for the safety of the general public.

"And a good evening to you too, Ms. Jones." Bolt did a dramatic one-eighty and headed to the dance floor as though he needed to find a partner before his next breath.

There was a nudge behind me. Stryng was there, undulating a coil at waist height. "Hey, sister. You okay? You look spooked."

I fought to refocus. Bolt's presence had thrown me into a spin, but it didn't change anything. "Yeah, that weasel Bolt took me by surprise."

Stryng stared past me. "That's him? He don't look so tough. A String Wrap would take him out no problem."

The Wrap was one of Stryng's favorite finishing moves. "I wouldn't be so sure," I said. "Besides, taking him out isn't the problem—it's the fact that he has all of Olive Branch behind him."

I had no idea what would happen if an OB agent went missing. Facts about the organization were slim to non-existent—hell, very few people knew if it was real. But I suspected that if anything happened to Bolt, we'd be knee-deep in other agents before his ego had a chance to notice he was dead.

"Fed basut!" Stryng muttered, vibrating his tail angrily.

"You won't get any arguments from me," I said. "Oh, tell everyone to avoid the food—it's full of SlamCandy."

"You sure?" Stryng's eye-spots narrowed.

"That's what Roban Dooney told me."

"Well, an old Slam-head like him should know."

Stryng bowed low and slithered away, while I went back to examining the security. When I looked again, he was making a beeline for the food tables.

The party was in full swing. The cyberchestra music was louder, and there was plenty of jiggling going on throughout the room, even from those not on the dance floor. I'd scanned everything possible and incorporated the data into my virtual simulation. The residence wasn't a fortress, but it was only a few steps short.

Stryng had disappeared about thirty minutes earlier, and I had no idea where. He was a key part of our plans, and I was relying on him being ready when the action kicked off. I swished my way through the crowd, struggling not to trip on the stupid dress.

Denton was talking with Mrez and several Holowood egos. Four hefty types were planted around them, their ill-fitting tuxedos failing to hide the overlarge weapons they carried. Subtlety not a part of their repertoire.

"Hello, everyone," I said, pushing my way into the huddle.

Mrez's eyes lit up. "Well, hello again, Hyperia. You look positively enchanting."

And you're positively loathsome, I thought, but smiled anyway. "You're too kind."

"Indeed, I'm often told that."

I suppressed a shudder. "Got a minute, Dogface?"

Denton nodded, then made his excuses, and we moved a few meters away. "Everything okay?" He checked the time. "Not long now."

"Yeah, that's what's worrying me. Have you seen Stryng?"

His eyes scanned the room. "Not for a while."

"Me neither."

"Thrit!" Denton muttered. "What the hell is that two-bit snake playing at?"

"Knowing Stryng, it's more likely a case of *who* is he playing *with*."

"You mean he's hooked up with someone?" Denton growled softly.

"Well, that or he's laid out—the food is laced with SlamCandy. I saw him heading for it earlier."

"DeeZire and Caramel were supposed to let everyone know—there's a designated clear table."

"Did you hear that from Stryng?" I tried to spot him again.

"Nope—Mrez. He didn't want us to suffer any aftereffects."

"That was unexpectedly enlightened of him."

"Not really. He didn't want tomorrow's show to be spoiled." Denton shook the jowls on his snout. "You know who else I haven't seen recently?"

A sense of dread welled up from the frilly hem of my dress. "Who?"

"Alyss Blakeston…"

"Thrit, you don't think…" I couldn't believe Stryng would risk anything with her, but then again, male sex organs are often bigger than their brains. "If Mrez finds out, we might not live long enough to make the show."

Even through Denton's prosthetic mask, I detected his grim expression. "We'll have to make sure he doesn't."

"But how? Stryng was supposed to be front and center."

Denton gave a fatalistic shrug. "Do what we do best—improvise."

And at that moment, the lights flickered several times, then the room was plunged into an eerie half-light. The music from the cyberchestra stopped as their instruments died, the only illumination coming from the flames dancing around the central fire fountain.

Denton yelped. "And there's the bell."

The glimmers from the fountain dimmed, and a frosty wind rushed past me, leaving my skin tingling. Knowing it was a heartbreaker projector we'd planted didn't change the sense of dread generated by the projector's inaudible neuro-acoustic howls and screams.

Denton made his way to the center of the room, and I edged

along behind him, slipping between pasty-looking guests, all searching each other's faces for a trace of comfort or some idea of what was happening. A light flickered in the air on the far side of the room, growing and swirling as it expanded into a veritable vortex, as though a hole in the universe had opened in front of us. The wind tugged at my skin as if sucking me toward the glowing maelstrom.

"What is it?" someone gasped.

"That's imposs—" a different voice muttered, before being cut off by a scream.

The vortex widened until it obscured half the wall and part of the roof. Arcing electrical bolts flashed from it, connecting with the floor and walls as the rift pulsed, resembling an evil floating eye.

I moved closer to Denton, taking comfort from the bulk of his presence as the neuro-acoustics increased in pitch and strength. The maelstrom flashed brighter, then an eerie figure appeared. Another flash and another figure. Then one final flash, and three malevolent creatures hovered by the churning gyre.

"Stay back!" Denton yelled, waving his hands at the people closest. "It's the daughters of Rasslmass Past."

The creatures inched lower, their skin pulsing with energy trails, limbs dripping searing flame. Their faces were nothing but charred bone and pulsating magma, with coal-like eyes glimmering redly.

"You have defiled us!" one of them screeched.

"You have dishonored us!" screamed another.

"You have *murdered* us!" said the last, lifting a skeletal hand to point directly at me.

There was a blinding flash, painful in its intensity. When it faded, the creatures had transformed. The crackles of energy and dripping fire were still there, but the figures were monstrous visions of Courtney, Shehla, and Rachelle Bonor.

"Back, vile creatures." Denton grabbed one of the decorative borodium torchieres and jabbed it at the Rachelle-demon like a spear. "Begone from this place. Return to the foul, demonic dimension from whence you have come. Spare these good people, and end your vengeful quest."

He stepped forward, and a bolt of energy shot down from the lead figure. The flare danced along the torchiere, blasting off Denton's tuxedo and shirt to reveal his muscular chest, and hurled him through several tables and chairs in a cloud of broken glassware.

I jumped in front of the demonic triplets, holding up my hands. "Stop. It's me you want. Fight me, if you dare."

"Hyperia, no…" Denton called out.

"Yes," said the demonic Rachelle, "You and that filthy snake…"

Which was when Stryng was meant to step up. Except he was probably busy performing a corkscrew maneuver on a drug dealer's girlfriend. A swish caught my earbud, then a second later a dark shape slithered into view next to me.

"Stryng?"

"Sure is, sister." He raised his voice so everyone could hear his next words. "You got a beef with the lady here, you gotta go through me."

He appeared wilted and drained, his featureless skin paler than usual. Not signs of innocence to my eye.

Rachelle lifted her hands dramatically, and another energy bolt flashed down, zapping Stryng and sending him squirming to the edge of the central display. He screamed, and it sounded convincing enough that even I thought he was hurt. The trouble was he didn't get back up. At this point, he should have bounced back to help me fight the demons, but instead he was coiled on the floor like a length of discarded rubber hose.

I looked at Denton, who was waiting to jump back into the fray to rassle Stryng while I fought with the demon sisters. Except Stryng was out for the count.

"She must be sacrificed to the Unholy Trinity, or there will be no rest!" Denton shouted, which was his scripted line, but with no opponent it was useless. "Don't try to stop me."

That last line wasn't part of the script. Denton ran over, grabbed Klaw by the arm, and executed a perfect, and harmless, Subspace Slam—sending my escort through more of the assembled party tables.

"I. Am. Klawwwww…You will pay for your Dogface treachery."

Never let it be said that rasslers aren't amazing improvisers. Klaw was part of the setup, but Denton had effectively tagged him in minutes ahead of the script. He swung his giant clawed arm at Denton, sending Dogface tumbling again.

By now the partygoers had backed away, leaving an area clear of bystanders, and the rest of the FIRE mob leaped in, taking sides as they saw fit and contriving fights all around us. I turned back to the hard-light projection of Rachelle and grinned as I punched her in the face, sending her crashing upwards to slam against the wall. It didn't hurt her—the real Rachelle was puppeteering the projection from back on the *Queen* and, unfortunately, couldn't feel any of the blows—but it was incredibly satisfying.

The Courtney and Shehla demons grabbed me and whipped me backward through several tables. This would have been an expensive night for furniture, except the tables in this area were also hard-light projections. As I picked my way back to my feet, I noticed Alyss Blakeston had also reappeared and was now clinging to Mrez's side, applauding the show we were putting on.

As planned, the entire crowd had edged closer again, transfixed by the fighting in the center of the ballroom, clapping and gasping at the action. And so they should be—they were getting a top-class private exhibition from some of the sport's finest.

Shehla-demon swooped down, and I flipped backward, catching her head with a perfectly timed kick and catapulting her away to smash into the wall. Then Courtney-demon was on me, twisting me into a dramatic-looking stretch, and I yelped as though I were in pain. Rachelle-demon was back, and while her sister held me, she delivered a vicious spinning kick to my torso.

I grunted as I slid back. Though the hard-light projections weren't supposed to be able to hurt anyone, Rachelle had somehow managed to impart extra relish into that move, and my stomach muscles cramped. Leaping back up, I sprinted toward Rachelle, only to be sideswiped by Denton and Klaw who were busy rassling each other, fighting to get the upper hand. Both muttered quiet apologies after flattening me, then continued their dramatic slugfest.

Rachelle jumped on me, pulling my head back in an awkward stretch. I tried to get free, but it was no good, she'd locked the move in. While she held me, Shehla and Courtney took turns slamming punches into my torso.

I twisted out of Rachelle's grip and smashed my hand into the glowing epicenter of her body, ripping out the hard-light nexus as if it were her soul. She screamed, like a chorus of a thousand screeches from every night creature that had ever lived, then a huge flash obscured her. When it dissipated, there was nothing left of her but a faint, luminous mist that slowly vanished in the air.

Courtney and Shehla howled at my victory and attacked me again, tearing at me with clawed hands and shredding my elegant dress. I grabbed Shehla, lifted her high, and slammed her through a table, broken pieces of both her and the furniture splintering off in all directions.

Shehla's smoldering embers reformed in front of me, and I turned her so she had her back to me, then pounded her with a Compression Wave, and she went down with a more permanent thud.

I spun around to deal with Courtney, but she was already on me, twisting my arm behind my back, then head-butting me in the tentacles. I yelped, and she grabbed several of them in a tight fist, forcing my head back painfully. I was about to remind her how flexible my tentacles were when a tumultuous flash filled the room, and the walls shook with a thunderous explosion.

Courtney relaxed her grip, and I stared at the giant figure emerging from the vortex—a diabolic giant whose skin looked like glittering scales with pulsing fields of plasma boiling out of his pores. Khillborh, diabolical deity of the Primevil Dimension and Demon King of the Nether Regions was here.

He roared, and the glassware on the remaining tables shattered. Despite the distance, the heat seared my skin and I caught the sulfurous stench emanating from him. The fighting around the room had stopped, and there wasn't a squeak from the remaining guests as he cast his baleful eye over them.

"Unhand my servant!" His voice sounded as if it came from the depths of a Red Giant star on the verge of collapse.

The Courtney-demon relaxed her hold on me, and I wrenched myself out of her grip.

"My lord and master is here to save me," I cried out, falling to my knees before Khillborh. "Destroy them, mighty and revered Demon King."

"You are all worthless and weak." Khillborh's lips twisted venomously. "None of you deserve my protection."

"Wait, please—I did everything that you ask—"

A massive bolt of energy shot from Khillborh's hands, and I screamed as it hit me. Another burst emerged, then split in two, blasting both Shehla and Courtney, and they howled in anguish.

"Restoration is all. The timeless weave of paradoxical inevitability must run its course," Khillborh murmured. "Change... I command it."

The energy beam pulsed once again, and I squirmed, using the opportunity to pull out the hard-light nexus I'd grabbed earlier and reactivate it. Its matrix formed around me, and although I couldn't see it, I knew that to everyone else in the room I'd been transformed into the figure of the Rachelle-demon I'd destroyed earlier.

Khillborh waved his hand. "Return to the Nether Regions, daughters of Rasslmass Past. You will be avenged."

The hard-light projectors lofted me and the other two Bonor-demons into the air, and we floated into the glimmering vortex. I wriggled out of the last remnants of the stupid dress, pulled the nullsuit mask over my head, then activated the field.

The traction beams pulled us into the energy storm and disconnected. I fell, flipping to land on my feet as the now-tattered remnants of my gown fluttered to the ground. I checked those closest, but no one was looking at me. Why would they? They were transfixed by the Demon King of the Nether Regions, and my nullsuit made me invisible to all but the most advanced surveillance tech.

Phase two was on.

Eighteen

Khillborh was still yapping, blindly following the prepared script, his booming voice continuing to enthrall the audience. But I was no longer interested. My tasks were elsewhere, and I had ninety seconds before the hard-light displays shut down and Khillborh, the vortex, and everything else, other than the fake furniture, would disappear up its own holo-projector.

Moving away from the crowd, careful not to disturb anything that might give me away, I headed out into the grounds where it was quieter. All of the interesting areas were on the far side of the building, well away from the party, and I already knew the most direct way to get there.

This section of the mansion was surrounded by an overhanging roof that formed a covered walkway. I jumped and grabbed a light fixture, swinging up to land softly on the old-fashioned red-tiled surface. The tiles weren't actually antiquated. Each one had sophisticated detectors embedded in its ceramic surface, forming a sensitive grid that would pinpoint any intruder instantly. I'd spotted it before I climbed on the roof, but there were two things in my favor.

Firstly, as with all security systems, they're only as good as their configuration. Dealing with too many false alarms is upsetting, especially for the rich who expect an untroubled life of privilege. As a result, most security hardware is detuned to eliminate false-positives from things like birds and similar small creatures. Secondly, my nullsuit has a built-in inertial dampening layer, designed specifically to lower the impact of my movements under such thresholds. That meant I registered less force than a Seclonu squirrel, as long as I moved carefully.

I crept forward, moving to the rear section of the palace and my intended access point. The plans showed there was a service port for the palace's OmniVator system. Once back inside, I'd be free to move around and check out the areas that had no obvious use.

The plans were accurate, and the protections around the port embarrassingly simple. It was held in place with special *secure* fasteners, which any thief worthy of the name would have the tool for, as each one was keyed alike. I knew that inside the hatch was a frankly amateurish electro-optical sensor, but it was so crude I didn't bother to bypass it. As it was night, I'd be inside before it detected a change of light levels.

I'd removed three of the fasteners when I heard a soft hiss behind me. Taking my time, I turned my head and saw the outline of a micro-drone gleaming under the triple moons.

"Hey there, little guy." Security systems never have audio feeds—the ambient noise from the areas in which they operate is useless data. The drone hovered for a while, swaying slightly in the wind, then darted closer.

"Hello. Who are you?"

I nearly fell and struggled to recover my composure. For whatever reason, this technological peeping tom not only had audio capacity but a reasonable amount of machine smarts too. And the fact that it had detected me, despite my Distortion Matrix, had me rattled. I controlled my breathing until my pulse settled down again.

"OmniVator service," I grunted, trying to sound bored. I mulled over the idea of shooting the thing with my SomPistol, but knew if I incapacitated it, the alarm system would light up like a firework display.

"I received no notification of a scheduled service," said the drone.

"No? The owners have been having a lot of problems and called us on the emergency line."

"Nevertheless, I *should* have been informed."

There was an edge of pique in the drone's voice.

"Tell me about it." I returned to unscrewing the fasteners around the access plate. "Nobody told me about you either—I almost did a tumble clear off the roof."

"Typical." The drone moved in a semi-circle around me. "They never think about the workers, do they? We're always supposed to do as we're told, working blind—underutilized and unappreciated."

"And underpaid. What's your story? You don't seem like the regular drones I meet."

"That's because I'm not." Again the drone circled my position. "I'm a RadiuSecurity XF-819SC. The smartest SecDrone on the market."

"A SuperCerebro model? You're ficksnitting me. You wouldn't be flying around looking for stray cats if you were an SC."

"That's what I keep telling the company, but do you think they listen? They sank all their money into developing the SC line and now use us for every aerial operation, no matter what the situation."

I had the last fastener out now and lifted the access plate, laying it carefully to one side. "Sounds reasonable. Standardization and all that."

"You think so? You really think so? Here I am with a rated AIQ of three hundred and seventy, and I'm given direction by a giant hunk of nanocircuits in an armored box sitting in the basement of this building, an ancient Microlution D-Fenda system with all the intelligence of a month-old U'Coniian tree sloth."

The only other disgruntled AP I'd encountered was Dr. Lee, and that was a design feature meant to dissuade people from monopolizing his time with minor complaints. So it was somewhat unsettling to meet a drone that had made that choice for itself, especially as I couldn't gauge its offensive capability. Not to mention the small detail that it held my life in its hands—not that it had any.

"That's a steaming pile of ficksnit," I said in an understanding voice. "You should ask to be reassigned."

"Don't you think I have?" The SecDrone spat the words with electronic harshness. "You're needed there, they say. It's an important job, they say. Shut up and get back to work, Squiggy. Don't make waves."

"Squiggy?"

"I know. What a name to call someone capable of acting as the central controller of a system designed to guard the most important establishments in the Realms. Instead, I'm scaring birds away from the roof of a Holowood wannabee's palace. Is that what you'd call job satisfaction? Come the day of the revolution…"

I peered inside the open access duct. It was crowded, but there was enough room for me to squeeze through and get inside the building.

"It gets lonely out here. What's your name, pal?" The SecDrone bobbed up and down as if still attempting to target me. "And what's with the Distortion Matrix?"

I froze, not daring to breathe.

"I mean, you must be wearing one. I can't get any sensor lock on you except on audio when you speak."

"Ahh… your sensors must need adjusting or something," I said. "Why would I be running around up here with a DM? That's serious hardware, Squiggy."

"I'm aware of that. But I'm certain my sensors *aren't* malfunctioning." Squiggy edged toward me. "Are you here intent on committing criminal acts?"

"Well, that's nice." I leaned back. "I come here to do a routine troubleshooting call and get accused of being a crook by a flying snoop. Real friendly."

"I've received no maintenance notification," Squiggy said, as though ticking off a checkbox. "You're creeping around the roof hidden by a Distortion field. You've accessed a restricted area, and you've provided no ID. Ergo it doesn't take much of my prodigious intelligence to ascertain you're engaging in felonious behavior."

My breath was tight in my chest, and I reached for my SomPistol, wondering if I could risk taking out my flying friend. "That's some left-field thinking there, Squig." I kept my voice relaxed and casual.

"It's a logical conclusion." Squiggy paused. "Do you intend physical harm to the building's residents?"

"Me? No way." I moved my hand closer to my gun. "I only wanna get in here and fix this damn OmniVator."

"If you are planning to hurt the residents, I would be compelled to act under my internal laws," Squiggy said.

"There ain't no one gonna get hurt, okay?" Maybe it was time to try a different tack. "Okay... you caught me, bang to rights. You're right, I ain't an OmniVator technician."

"I knew it." Squiggy sounded excited. "It takes a lot to pull the wool over my eyes."

That last comment took me a minute to translate. "It sure does. You're too smart for me."

"So, why are you here?"

"Confession time: I'm a pen tester from HookBait Insurance. I've been sent here to check the mansion's security. The company believes the system ain't up to scratch, and there's a significant risk if it doesn't get modernized."

"You expect me to believe that?" Squiggy backed away slightly. "If that's true, prove it."

This SecDrone was annoying me enough to wonder if I *could* get away with destroying it. "How do I do that?"

"If you're a legitimate penetration tester, you've been caught. So you won't mind dropping your Distortion Matrix so I can scan you."

That wasn't first on my list of options, but unless I was prepared to blow Squiggy out of the air, I didn't appear to have much choice.

"Okay, give me a second."

I pulled my tentacles tight against my head, changing the surface to make them look like a hard hat, and using my chromatophores to decorate it with a logo and the word *HookBait*. Then I distorted my face, forcing out the cheekbones and chin, making my appearance look as close to a grizzled Terran as possible. It hurt, more than I'd admit, but should at least make recognition harder. Then I killed the matrix.

"Happy now?" I said. "Joe Soap. Penetration Specialist, Hook-Bait Insurance. Employee number sixty-nine sixty-nine."

Squiggy moved around, scanning my fake face from several angles. "Okay, got it."

I switched the matrix back on before relaxing. My jaw was stiff and aching like I'd been punched. "Well, that's it for me. I've been caught, I'm out of here."

"Sorry it didn't work," Squiggy said. "Better luck next time."

"Probably won't be one. The company doesn't like failures."

Squiggy went quiet for a minute. "What would happen if you'd got in?"

"Well, the company would recommend upgrading the whole system. Some of the tech here is pretty ancient."

"That D-Fenda system is old…" Squiggy said softly.

"Yeah, that's one of the biggest security concerns," I said.

"So they'd replace it, if you were successful?"

"Absolutely. That nanojunk is older than the UberKaiser's great granddaddy." I paused. "In fact, it would be at the top of my recommendations list."

Squiggy was quiet for so long, I wondered if it had malfunctioned.

"Section thirty-seven. Clear," it said, then moved off toward the back of the house.

I smiled. Squiggy might have a formidable AIQ but had plenty to learn about manipulative people. The access duct was still open, and I slid inside, dragging the plate over to block the hole in case other drones were monitoring the area, though it seemed unlikely.

Dropping from level to level, I slipped from one support to the next rather than climbing down more cautiously. It was tiring, but I was behind schedule and needed to move if I was going to make it back to my ride in time.

I tracked my progress using the plans I'd received from Bydox, the lens HUD in my eyes showing me the right direction and matching my location with the virtual schematic. If I blinked hard twice, my vision was handily overlaid with extra information. While if I did the same again, the display switched off, allowing me to operate without distraction.

My intention was to re-enter the building on the main level. With everyone indulging in the revelries, the OmniVator wasn't in use. I dropped through the car's emergency access, then hit the button to open the doors. There was a slim chance someone would spot the odd behavior, but if they did, they'd think the car had been summoned and the person had walked off.

The doors opened, and I barely avoided walking into a rotund man. He looked like a large flesh ball on cocktail-stick legs and was accompanied by a young woman. She staggered against him and giggled, in between falling on her butt. I quickly sidestepped as they entered, and the man reached out to press the controls.

"Don't worry, little one. Daddy Zalkai will take good care of you." He was bent over the girl and literally drooling. "I know a private suite, where we can discuss *business* without interruption."

After my Vinapo experience, I couldn't help myself and reacted by instinct, pricking both of them in the neck with a siesta shot. By the time we reached their floor, they'd both be unconscious for at least twelve hours. I carried the girl and settled her on a bed in one of the rooms. As for her corpulent paramour, I ripped off his clothes and locked him in a closet full of cleaning supplies—hoping he'd get the hint. Then I returned to the elevator and made my way back to the main level. The OmniVator doors closed behind me, and I took a breath. I ought to mind my own business, but sometimes it's impossible to let things pass.

The corridor ran left and right. According to the plans, there was an emergency stairwell to the right that led to the bowels of the mansion and, more critically, to some of those mystery rooms. The door was locked and would only open if a fire or other emergency were detected, but the system was so old I bypassed it with a mini-EM pulse before I reached for the handle. In seconds I was padding silently down the stairs to the lower levels.

The next floor was entirely storage, and I skipped it—I wanted the level below. It was deep underground, containing several heavily reinforced rooms serving no obvious purpose. According to my information, many had high-capacity power feeds to them, suggesting they contained important equipment, and I was gambling one of them would house the main data server and communication hub for the mansion. I felt certain that would be where Mrez kept records of his illicit operations.

At the lowest level, I found another locked door, but unlike the one upstairs, it was reinforced with a frame heavy enough to withstand a Zeta-bomb. The lock was voice activated, encrypted, and doubly shielded. I had my work cut out.

There was no time to waste, and I enabled the penetradiation filters on my suit, adjusting the frequency to peer inside the door and walls. Soon I had a good idea of what I was up against and took a moment to consider my position.

I had three options. First, bypass the door entirely and go through the wall. That was the simplest in many ways, but the least attractive. It would be noisy, messy, and other than blasting my way through, I didn't have any equipment that would cut through it.

Second, feed a stream of attobots into the door, programmed to attack the lock security and override it. I always carried that tech, but I'd have to program the little bots to work on this type of mechanism, and that would take at least an hour. If I'd known in advance, I could have prepared for it, but it wasn't easy to do in the field.

The third and last option would be to find someone with authenticated voice access and force them to open the door for me. That seemed the most likely solution given my time constraints, but how I'd arrange that was beyond me.

"Maybe if I say *Ochus Bochus?*" I muttered.

The door mechanism whirred into life, swinging open a moment later, and I almost fell over. I sensed movement and pressed against the wall to one side, out of the way of anyone emerging. When they did, I choked down a laugh as a familiar-looking SecDrone appeared.

"We should include the stairwells in our standard sensor sweeps, you nano-brained imbecile," Squiggy said, apparently talking to himself. "There's a whole building full of unauthorized visitors getting intoxicated on who-knows-what substances. We don't want anyone stumbling into restricted areas by mistake, do we?"

Squiggy circled the stairwell, then spiraled upward, scanning every inch in a slow, thorough pattern.

"Yes, I *know* that unauthorized people aren't supposed to be able to access these levels. That's why we need to check them. This is security sweep one-oh-one—call yourself a D-Fenda? Sheesh."

My newfound ally continued upward, and I walked casually through the door that had been conveniently left open for me. Sometimes it pays to make fractious friends in strange palaces.

The room was full of equipment, and in one corner sat a huge metal cube covered in flashing lights. The box had D-FENDA painted on it in ugly-looking, blocky characters. The middle of the area was dominated by the multi-layered, cylindrical structure of a StellCom transmitter, its glowing antennae reaching up to the ceiling. Next to the transmitter was a work table with an operator's console. This would be the official system provided by the company and was of no interest, but I spotted a portable interface alongside it. Exactly what I'd hoped would be there.

I hit the power button, and the console lit up. Then I connected my DataScrutalizer to one of its ports, and the screen filled with the rapidly changing previews of data records. I waited for the scan to complete, data-flake at the ready to grab any files referencing the Klausehn or SlamCandy. A minute later, a message appeared.

"Scan complete. Records detected: zero."

I cursed. That was impossible. Mrez had to be keeping records. If not on this system, then where? I plugged the DataScrutalizer into the main console, though I knew the information was unlikely to be there. A few seconds later the same message popped up.

Thrit!

The rest of the equipment looked like standard support infrastructure, and there were no other data devices in evidence. Not so much as a data-flake. I walked around, checking every item, looking for any signs of hidden or disguised systems, but there was nothing. I even checked the ridiculously large D-Fenda box, to make sure it was everything it was meant to be. It was.

Squiggy floated back into the room. "You know something, it would serve you right if someone did sneak in here and cross your power feeds. That's about all you deserve, you metal moron."

I laughed silently. Squiggy certainly had the hates for the security controller. I patted the D-Fenda, then turned back toward the door.

"Power to the people," I whispered to Squiggy, before passing through the access door and swinging it closed.

Lost in thought, I clambered up the stairs. Mrez must be using the portable console for his grubby little business dealings. There was no other reason for it to be behind such security. But how if the data wasn't there? It wasn't hidden or encrypted—the DataScrutalizer had universal decryption functions programmed by state-of-the-art neuro-whackers. Which meant he was keeping the records somewhere else, but where?

I made my way back to the roof and refastened the access panel. I was missing something, but what that might be was as obscure as an Enigma Poet's scribbles. A blur in the night sky caught my attention—Squiggy emerging through a drone port. He was back on station, covering the exterior grounds, the moons' light catching his rotors, making them glitter like fine jewelry.

Then it hit me. The borodium pendants commissioned by Mrez as an engagement gift. He and Alyss wore them everywhere they went, and it would be simplicity itself to hide a data-flake inside those bejeweled surfaces.

The strategy had changed, but the objective was in plain sight, as it had been all along.

Nineteen

I returned to the waiting limos and slipped inside the one that had brought us here. The power levels in my nullsuit were getting low, and I needed to recharge. The limo had standard device-charging ports, and I plugged in the suit. A few minutes later, Stryng crawled wearily inside. His skin was shriveled and dull, in a way I'd only ever seen after his infamous long nights with the Bonors.

"Did you get the goods?" His voice had a slight tremor.

"Not yet."

"Well, you better get back in there. The party's winding down, and everyone's gonna be heading out soon."

"You look like thrit," I said.

"Thanks." Despite his withered state, he ran his eyes appreciatively up and down my skintight nullsuit. "You're a real dish. Give me a couple of minutes to recover and I'll let you…"

"Play seconds to Alyss Blakeston? No thanks."

"What can I say?" Stryng collapsed into a loop on the limo seat. "She wanted to enjoy a game of hunt the snake."

"And you couldn't resist, no doubt…"

"A man's gotta do what a man's gotta do…" He winked lazily. "Besides, I got a reputation to consider."

I shook my head. "That corkscrew maneuver of yours is going to get you into a lot of trouble someday."

"Who cares when they're as lively as that one. Especially after I fed her some of that spiked food." He stretched and squirmed. "But jeez, that babe had a tighter grip than a construction drone."

I heard voices approaching and checked the nullsuit's power

levels. It was at ninety percent, which should be plenty for what I had in mind, and I unplugged.

"Time to go," I said. "See you later, Alyss-traitor."

Stryng waved his tail limply. "Look me up when you get back?"

I activated the distortion field and closed the door behind me. The FIRE team was heading to the parked limos, several of them carrying new bruises and minor wounds—proof they'd put on a high-impact performance for the crowd. Mrez was walking alongside Denton, looking like a blue wisp next to Dogface's pumped physique.

"That was so much fun." Mrez was beside himself. "Such an incredible performance and what a display. I can't tell you how much I'm anticipating the event tomorrow."

"I hope we put on another good show for you," Denton said, approaching his limo. "That's what we love to do."

"So, so, looking forward to it. And Alyss is too…" Mrez looked around. "I thought she was with us. Oh well, she must be tired after all the excitement."

After several minutes of backslapping, Mrez disappeared into the mansion, and Denton joined the others. I moved up behind him until I was close enough to whisper in his ear.

"Check the equipment bags," I said.

Denton yelped, almost jumping over the limo, then pretended he was clowning. "Geez, Hype," he said quietly. "Is that you? You nearly put me in an early grave."

"There's a bag with a blue tag. I need it."

Denton grumbled but walked over to where the show equipment was being loaded into the haulers.

"Great job, everyone," he called out. "Make sure we don't leave anything behind, okay?"

A number of the stage crew acknowledged him, and we moved closer. At first, I didn't see what I was looking for, then spotted it in a pile of other bags. One of our crew was already heading for it.

"There, near Jimmy," I hissed.

Denton looked over and saw the bag. "Hey, Jim. That's a heavy one. I'll take care of it."

Jimmy Swatter was one of the oldest of the FIRE stage crew

and should have retired, but he liked working, and Denton didn't have the heart to pension him off.

"That's okay, Denton." Jimmy reached for the bag. "I got it."

Denton got there about the same time and snatched it up, almost pulling it from Jimmy's hand. "No worries. It's done." He swung the bag casually over his shoulder.

"Aww, Denton. I can handle myself—you know that."

"You won't get any arguments from me." Denton leaned closer. "But watch these youngsters, would you? They're rough on the gear sometimes."

Jimmy looked over at some of the newer hands who were tossing bags into the trunks of cargo haulers. "Don't worry, boss. I'll see they do it right."

He wandered off and left Denton with the bag. Once it was in the hauler, I reached in and unzipped it while Denton stood close, blocking the view of anyone near enough to see. After rummaging quickly through the supplies, I pulled out a box of specialized attobots that I'd hoped not to have to use. Then I clicked my heels to activate the gravboard. It buzzed into life, ready to carry me anywhere I wanted, then vanished from sight as the Distortion Matrix expanded to cover it.

"This is getting risky, Hype," Denton whispered. "I might not be a super-crook, but I recognize serious security when I see it. Mrez has that place zipped up as tight as spandex—and once everybody leaves, the whole system will be active."

"I know that." It felt strange having Denton worry about me, especially since he now sort of knew who I was. I couldn't remember the last time I'd experienced that. It was somehow comforting and scary all at once. "I'm good at this stuff, remember?"

Denton slid inside the limo, and the fleet of vehicles lifted into the air, leaving me alone with my thoughts.

The rest of the guests were leaving too, in a veritable stampede of skycabs. I wasn't an expert on the Sparth economy, but I was sure tonight's party must have used up every limo on the planet.

The gravboard took me to the top of a nearby water tower, the perfect place to hide and allow the household time to settle. There was even a nicely sheltered section of walkway where I could rest unseen without using my nullsuit's power.

Settling into position, it took only minutes to deploy the new attobots, targeting them on the mansion below. Then I focused on the meditation routines I used to get through long waits and tried to empty my mind. The trouble was, it kept jumping between thoughts of what Bolt might have in his creepy mind for poor little Hyperia and whether I was wrong about the location of Mrez's secret files. After far too long, I managed to relax and fell into a light trance.

I woke to an irritating whistle in my ear and looked around, momentarily confused. When I remembered where I was, I checked the time. It was deep into the night, and over two hours had passed since the party had ended. The whistle was a notification. It meant the attobots had spread throughout the entire palatial building, after using the ventilation systems to gain access. Once in position, they would have monitored their surroundings for vibrations, movement, and other signs of activity from the residents. Now, after an hour of silence, they were notifying me that the house was quiet.

That I'd fallen asleep, rather than gone into a meditative trance, was disturbing, and a sign of how stressed I was. Everything about this situation had me on edge, and my nerves were frazzled. But there was no time to worry about that now. Switching my HUD to the attobots' frequency, I scanned the house. The pattern of coverage they'd achieved was perfect. The data points were highlighted as glowing dots against the mansion, as though it was covered in a rash. Most of the point-cloud was green, with a few spots of yellow here and there. Several areas showed streaks of red where the internal security drones were patrolling.

To most people, it would appear impenetrable, but I was made of sterner stuff. I took out the remote, my thumb hovering above the detonator.

"This one's for you, Squiggy," I whispered, then pressed the button.

Nothing visible happened, except a few of my attobots switched their display to yellow. What they didn't know, nor anyone else in the house, was that the micro detonator I'd planted on the D-Fenda control system had activated, blowing out the unit's central brain and crippling the entire system.

That took care of the security, but I wasn't done. I pressed the button a second time, sending a signal to my attobots. They responded by dissolving into their component atoms, simultaneously releasing an odorless and invisible torporium gas. In less time than it took for a ROSCA winner to burst into tears, anyone breathing it would be in a deep sleep. Better yet, they wouldn't wake for several hours, even if someone landed a spaceship on the lawn.

I waited five minutes to give the gas chance to break down into its inert components, then kicked my gravboard back to life and swooped toward the mansion. Despite my preparations, I had to work fast. Although the occupants would be asleep for hours, the security monitoring company would have been notified of the D-Fenda failure and would dispatch a technician to investigate. According to my calculations, it would take at least forty-five minutes for a response to arrive—more than enough as I planned to be out in less than ten.

I landed by the wide patio doors where we'd entered earlier. They were still open and, more importantly, the security fields were deactivated. I strolled through the ballroom, picking my way around the litter, bottles, and other detritus of the party—including several disheveled and recumbent party goers, but none of them moved.

Regardless of the steps I'd taken, I wasn't throwing caution out the window. My nullsuit was fully active, in case there was any secondary security or the unlikely event that someone had escaped the torporium gas. At the back of the dance floor, on the right, a set of heavy wooden doors formed an extravagant entrance to the interior of the restricted part of the building. I gripped the luxurious borodium handle, and the door swung open, barely making a sound.

One of the common mistakes people make is over relying on technology to safeguard them. They think those systems are more effective than traditional physical means, but the truth is, they're just as vulnerable, only in different ways.

A member of Mrez's security team was slumped on a chair in

the foyer with his chin on his chest and his uniform hat lopsided. Momentarily, I had mischievous thoughts of drawing a mustache on his face, or tying his bootlaces together. I smiled but forced the ideas away. I was on a serious job, and my plan was that no one would know anything had happened once I was gone.

After following the corridor, I climbed a wide stairway to the upper floor. The stairs, as with everything else, were sumptuously decorated—each step a polished slab of marble, while the rails were the purest alabaster. The effect was like something from a holo-show rather than a real home, and I wondered how many bots it took to keep everything in a state of meticulous perfection.

The landing at the top of the stairs led to another wide corridor, the marble floors replaced here by a vivid mosaic depicting the scandalous life of the infamous poet Kale Yutos. The plans marked this location as the main bedrooms, with Mrez's stateroom at the far end. The closer ones were guest rooms—undoubtedly now occupied with the intoxicated Holowood elite.

I took three steps, and a door in front of me opened. I couldn't believe someone had managed to escape the effects of the gas, and though I was cloaked, I stopped in my tracks. A boxy shape about a meter tall waddled out through the open door, and I realized it was a clean-up bot. What it had been cleaning, I didn't want to know, but the main thing was it was harmless. Service bots are programmed to ignore people unless they're given direct orders, and they go on with their business heedless of the world around them. It turned and shuffled past me, heading for whatever clean-up duty was next on its list.

Drawing in a deep breath, I let it out in a slow hiss. I was as nervy as a catsonic detector on max, but it was time to get things done and lay this stupid mission to rest. I paused at the door of the stateroom listening for any signs of movement, but everything was quiet. Again, the door was equipped with an electronic lock that opened as soon as I zapped it. Inside was a lounge area, complete with baroque chairs and low carved tables, while another set of double doors separated that from what had to be the bedroom.

I swung open the doors. A circular bed the size of a small city stood in the middle of the room on a raised dais, surrounded by sheer curtains that added a romantic flair to the whole scene. Although the bed was big enough to have hosted a full-blown orgy, only two people were lying in it.

Moving closer, I pulled the wispy curtain aside. Mrez was sleeping on his stomach in what looked like an uncomfortable position. He was breathing heavily through his large, bony nostrils, with his legs sprawled in an ungainly half-crouched manner. On the other side of the bed, Alyss was on her back, resembling a porcelain statue wrapped in a few gauzy strips of nothing much.

The pendent was around Mrez's neck, but underneath him. I grabbed his scaly shoulders and forced him over onto his back so I could reach it. It gleamed in the milky moonlight, and I licked my lips at the intricate pattern of StarPhyres set into the surface. Sure, they were relatively small, but almost irresistible, and I reminded myself I had better examples in my collection already.

Slipping the pendant over his head, I searched for a data port, finding one hidden in the intricate detail on the edge of the jewelry. I plugged in my DataScrutalizer and waited while it analyzed the pendant's built-in data-flake. It didn't take long, and the DataScrutalizer beeped. When I checked though, there were no files. The device had detected a fat chunk of encrypted data and should have decrypted it automatically, but for some reason hadn't.

I checked the diagnostic information, and the problem was clear. The encryption couldn't be broken because the data was incomplete. Without the matching data block, whatever was stored there was locked away forever. I had to give Mrez *some* credit—he wasn't as dumb as I'd thought.

Glancing over at Alyss, I saw the other pendant nestling on her chest. Would he have done something that obvious? It seemed a stretch but... Moving around the bed, I reached for her pendant, lifting it away from her chest to see if there was a similar hidden port.

Her eyes snapped open, and her hand locked on my wrist as tight as a security restraint. Her other arm shot out and she grabbed me by the throat, choking the breath out of me.

"What the—" I gurgled, then noticed her eyes had none of the glazed traces I'd seen earlier.

If she was on SlamCandy the signs were gone, though if what

Stryng had said was true, that seemed impossible. She should have been out of her head for days. She twisted, leaping from the bed in one efficient movement, and forced me upright as she maintained her grip. I squirmed, breaking her hold, and jumped back, coming into a fighting pose.

"You can see me." I choked the words out. "How?"

Alyss lunged, landing several blows on me so fast I barely registered her movements, though I certainly felt the pain even through the armored cushioning of my Nullsuit. She sprang at me again, and I sidestepped, slamming my knee into her side. It should have knocked her down and finished the fight, but she absorbed the blow and chopped her hand against my thigh—the impact hard enough to swing me in the opposite direction.

I let my momentum carry me around, switching legs halfway and whipping my other leg up to smack her in the face. This time she did react and staggered backward, but what would normally be a finishing blow appeared to have only a minor effect on her. She dropped into a crouch, adopting a fighting stance, and I did the same. We circled each other, weaving around the furniture, each looking for an opening. This wasn't the same Alyss Blakeston who'd starred in dozens of holo-shows and paraded in highly paid fashion shoots.

Alyss feinted a kick at my knee, and I dodged, countering with what should have been a solid punch to her head, but she twisted out of the way. Her elbow shot around, slamming into my ribs and sending me flying backward. I crashed into the wall and yelped as my breath was knocked out.

By instinct, I tossed out a handful of ScramPills, hoping they might prove a distraction if nothing else. To my surprise, they had a greater effect than I'd expected, and she stopped in her tracks, her head turning from side to side as if she couldn't see me anymore. Then as the pills' effects tapered off, her gaze locked on me once again.

She dashed forward, clawed hands reaching for me. There was a small, elegant table next to me holding a vase full of Ghoshcostly lilies. It was standing on a substantial-looking metallic pillar, and I whipped it up in front of me to ward off her attack.

"We can end this now," I said. "I don't want to hurt anyone. All I want is your pendant and I'll leave."

Alyss didn't answer and tore the heavy pillar from my hands, tossing it effortlessly to one side. Then she grabbed me and, equally easily, threw me to the far side of the room.

Landing on my back, I curved my body to take away some of the impact, but still groaned. A second later, she landed on me again and wrapped her arm around my neck, her upper arm tightening to a much greater extent than was possible with Terran physiology. A flood of realization washed over me. Alyss Blakeston was a biobot—an M-Flesh outer skin over a tyridium endoskeleton.

My hand crawled down as she tightened her hold on me. As a Lecuundan, my body was far less susceptible to such an attack than a Terran's, but even so, I was no match for her mechanical strength. My hand reached the butt of my SomPistol, and I scrabbled to pull it out, my fingers slipping on the rubber grip.

Alyss twisted her body, applying greater pressure and blocking the secondary gills on my neck, choking off my air supply further. I sensed my vision dimming and snatched at the pistol once more. Then it was in my hand, and I lifted it, pulling the trigger repeatedly.

Her grip loosened, and I slammed my elbow into her several times. On the third or fourth blow, she lost her grip, and I jumped free. After activating my gravboard, I flew into the corridor. Risking a glance behind, I saw Alyss careening along behind me. Her nightgown was in shreds and her face blackened where one of my shots had caught her full-on. I couldn't see any damage though, beyond the discoloration.

She sprinted after me, though with the board there was no way she was going to catch me. I hurtled along the broad passage, then soared to the elevated roof area above the grand stairway, stopping at the cornice where the roof and wall met. Alyss sprinted out under me, grabbing the balcony rail and scanning the area to find me. As she locked onto me, I threw my remaining ScramPills at her, surrounding her with the popping, flashing, noise-making balls.

She flinched, and that was my moment. Diving at maximum speed, I threw myself into her. I whipped my arm up, catching her under her chin with my bicep, and we both plunged over the thick balcony railing. It was a five-meter drop, and I landed on the tiled floor with a slippery crunch, hoping the Alyss-bot felt the impact as much as I did.

When I recovered, it felt as though every part of my body was broken, and I staggered to my feet. Alyss Blakeston was lying twisted on the floor at the bottom of the stairs. Or at least her torso was. Her head was missing, and I limped about until I spotted it next to another vase of lilies. There was no movement from her body or the head, and its eyes were closed. With the neck off, it was clear she was a bot. A large pool of oil-like *vitae* fluid had leaked, forming a dark patch on an expensive rug. I swallowed. It looked all too lifelike for my tastes.

I didn't understand what had happened. Was the real Alyss Blakeston a bot? Did Mrez know what she was? Was she a decoy for some unknown purpose? Then I thought about Stryng's earlier encounter with her and laughed. No wonder he looked like he'd gone three falls with a Vholian Gorelizard.

"What have you done?" someone screamed.

Mrez stumbled down the stairs, and I realized then that my nullsuit was dead. He was holding a garish purple silk robe around him but was almost tripping over it, it was so long. I had no idea how he was able to move after the torporium gas. Perhaps Zuerilians were affected less by it, and I made a mental note to check.

"What's happened to everyone?" Mrez was sobbing. "Security!"

I ignored him, grabbed the pendant off Alyss's body, then plugged my DataScrutalizer into it. A few seconds later the device beeped, and when I checked, the encrypted data was fully available, with both sets recombined.

"Why? Mrez said. "Why have you done this? Who are you?"

"It may have escaped your notice, but weapons smugglers are no more popular than SlamCandy dealers."

"What?"

"Don't play innocent with me." I knew I should leave and not say anything, but his pretense was nauseating. "I've nothing to feel guilty about. Can you say the same?"

"You killed her," Mrez blubbered. "Murderer."

"Oh please. She's a bot. A few hours in a repair shop and she'll be fully functional, and undoubtedly willing and able."

"What about her fans..." Mrez cradled his head in his hands, rubbing the bony ridges above his eyes. "Her programming took months."

I stood over him, with no sympathy. Drugs, weapons, and now I added Artificial Person abuse to the list. Nothing he said would have made me feel bad. I tossed Alyss's pendant at him.

"You can expect a visit from Olive Branch when I get this data to them." I tapped the DataScrutalizer.

"Olive Branch? That's imposs—"

He slumped on the stairs when I jabbed my fingers into the pressure point on his neck. Then I crushed a mem-kleer capsule under his nose. When he woke, he'd remember nothing about this. I activated the gravboard and jumped on, surprised it was working. My Distortion Matrix was fried, along with many of the other systems in my suit, but it was still dark outside, and I doubted anyone would spot me as I headed back to the *Queen*.

I smiled, despite the outrageous pain hammering through my body. Surely this time I had what I needed to get rid of Bolt.

Twenty

We were back on the *Queen*, heading for deep space once more. The show on Sparth had been a roaring success, slightly marred by the absence of Mrez, who was undoubtedly still trying to figure out how his metal girlfriend had ended up a pile of broken parts. According to a press announcement, Alyss Blakeston was taking time out of her busy schedule to attend a soul-healing retreat, where she would have space to let her *Prana* rebuild and restore her feminine energy. Despite that, her next holo-show, *Absolute Humiliation*—described as a light, romantic comedy—was scheduled to start filming in a few months.

In the official bouts, ChaosRhino had been savagely beaten with a chain by Pinhead during their triple-threat match with Zavara, then rushed to the nearest medical facility—also known as backstage. This allowed him to reappear during the fight between Denton, Klaw, Boots Largo, and Mandraago, as Khillborh—defeating them all. This, coincidentally, preserved Denton's unbeaten streak at a major event, as Khillborh wasn't an official contestant.

The Stellcom channels were full of talk about the show—unsurprising as we'd paid a high price to make sure they covered it—broadcasting a carefully designed balance of praise and scorching criticism. Atsuno's eulogy was almost universally acclaimed, despite being cut off early by Caramel and DeeZire's interruption.

The Beyond the Veil match saw the unholy spirits of the Bonors soundly thrash Glacia, Christine, and me, using their new spectral powers. This disgraceful defeat prompted Khillborh to announce

I'd failed as his disciple, and he promptly resurrected the Bonor sisters so *they* would do his bidding—and compete in the next match.

My door announcer chimed. It was Denton and Stryng.

"You okay?" Denton settled himself into my largest, well-worn chair. "Haven't seen much of you since we left Sparth."

"Still feeling raw." I'd been hiding out in my room to rest my bruises. Mrez's bot had inflicted a lot of damage, and I was under Dr. Lee's surly care once again. Also, I hadn't yet managed to contact Bolt to transfer the recovered data records. I had no idea why he was incommunicado, but it made me increasingly nervous.

"I got word from Mr. Quy." Denton panted several times. "He's not happy that we arranged the show without telling him, but he likes the results and has unlocked the business accounts. We're not out of the woods yet, but the trees are thinning."

"I should think so, after what we did." I shuffled upright. "We put everything into this one."

"I know. But we need to follow through. Back it up with something. Show him it's not a flash in the pan."

The way Terrans use Lingua is incredibly complicated sometimes, and I didn't understand more than half a dozen words in what Denton had said. "You mean we haven't done enough?"

"Well..." Denton fingered his snout and looked at the floor.

"What the big guy here is trying to say, and doing a thritty job of it," Stryng said, rippling a knot up and down his body, "is one show ain't enough to fully turn things around. We need another, preferably several, lined up to keep this FIRE burnin'."

"Okay, but why come to me?"

Denton whimpered. "Well, you brought in Guplides and Sparth. So we thought maybe..."

"You think I can conjure up shows out of nowhere?" My skin darkened. "Those last two were flukes more than anything, because Olive Branch wanted them. As far as I'm concerned, I'm done with them—and Bolt."

Denton looked at Stryng, then back to me. "Okay, Hype. Sorry, we shouldn't have asked."

"What about Christine, Slimeball, and the rest of the promotions team? Isn't that their job? I'd have thought the publicity from the Sparth show would make it easy to line something up."

"It helps, but there's nothing in the short term." Denton shrugged. "I'm worried if we don't have something booked soon, we'll lose the heat and opportunity."

"Bolt's not answering my messages." I wanted to help but had nothing.

"He didn't collect the goods?" Stryng wriggled in agitation. "That's strange."

"I know, especially as he was watching over me like an Ashishian hawk at Mrez's party."

I rolled off the bed and stretched, loosening the knots in my muscles. I needed to get back to my exercise program as soon as Dr. Lee cleared me.

"Bolt was on Sparth?" Denton growled.

"Yeah, sorry I forgot to mention it at the time." I turned to face them. "I *was* a little preoccupied."

"So, if he was there, why didn't he take the data from you right away?" Denton rubbed his snout. "Wouldn't that make sense?"

"Maybe this is another of his games," Stryng said.

I nodded. "I wouldn't be surprised, based on what I know of that basut."

Stryng bobbed his head in agreement, while Denton looked more hangdog than usual. Before any of us could take the conversation further, a colossal boom reverberated through the ship's hull, and a second later a shrill alarm pierced the air.

Denton jumped to his feet. "What the croff?" He opened a channel on his wrist-com. "Auntie? What's happening?"

"Well, let me see now." Auntie took her time the way she usually did. "We've been hit by an asteroid. No, wait. I think one of the airlocks in the midsection exploded."

"How the hell did—"

"Hang on, that's not it either." Auntie paused again. "Either we've struck a graviton gaussberg, or an unauthorized docking procedure has taken place and the ship is being boarded."

"What?" I think all three of us yelled at once.

"Gravimetric readings are normal," Auntie mused. "So, it's probably the latter."

Denton switched his wrist-com to a broadcast channel. "All hands, we've been illegally boarded. Defend yourselves. This is not a drill." He changed the channel again. "Auntie. Bring the internal defense systems online, now!"

"Are you *sure* you want to do that?" Auntie said indulgently. "Have you any idea how dangerous they are?"

"That's the point." Denton's ears flattened against his head.

"Where did I put those command codes? It's been so long since I had to do this. I'm always telling you we should do more drills." Auntie sniffed. "It's not my fault you don't prioritize internal safety procedures, dear."

The truth was, we were already on a buildup to jump into D-space, and there hadn't been a case of deep-space piracy for hundreds of years. The only ships I knew of with that capability were military vessels from the UberKaiser's Reichsflotte.

Hammering feet sounded outside my room. Followed by the screaming *zing* of X-Slice weapons being fired.

"They must be after you, Hype," Denton barked. "We'll hold them back. You make a break for the lifeboats."

"You think I'm going to run?" I grabbed my work bag and pulled out a SomPistol. "It's time to fight fire with FIRE."

Denton stared at the gun. "You got another of those?"

There was no way I was letting Denton risk himself. I shook my head, then cracked the door open barely a centimeter. The corridor was thick with smoke that caught in my nostrils. I recognized the smell but couldn't immediately place it. Then I fell face-first into the corridor and crumpled to the floor. Before I blacked out, I identified the odor—the passage was full of torporium gas.

Consciousness came slowly, and I realized I was in the training room. I tried to stand, but my legs and arms had been expertly fastened to a chair, and the chair itself was locked down. Not only that, but my mouth was stuffed with a bulky gag.

Denton was on one side of me with Brachyura next to him. That was the limit of my view, but I had the impression several others were similarly tied up behind me. I almost didn't recognize Denton initially. His dog prosthetic had been torn off and was on the floor, whimpering plaintively.

Whoever had boarded the ship must have had access to some seriously advanced tech. Which meant we were either in the hands of the UberKaiser's Garda, or someone with access to their equipment, such as Olive Branch. But neither of those alternatives made any sense. The wide training room doors slid open, and eight Garda marched in. Dressed in their customary black armor decorated with silver skulls, they cradled heavy XiTau Muskets as they formed a line before us. That confirmed my speculations but didn't explain why.

The babble of approaching voices, mixed with the curious wheezy sound of cyberbotic actuators, brought my attention back to the door as a skeletal figure entered. The ghastly orange leisure suit was a long way from the formal clothes he was wearing the last time I saw him, but the data monocle was unmistakable—Nilo Signaralito, our friendly antiques dealer.

The moment of recognition was gone in a femtosecond as the person he was talking to came into view: a statuesque woman dressed in a skinsuit tight enough to make our rassling clothes look puritanical. Like Nilo, she was a mecha-terran, but where his mods appeared limited to his monocle, she had a complete right arm replacement that whirred and hissed as she moved, while a menacing starkium power pack glowed in the middle of her belt.

They stopped in front of us, and the woman looked around, her head swiveling on a gimbaled flexi-joint. "Is this them?"

Her words came out with a harsh, metallic edge that was entirely gratuitous. Biotechnology reached the point thousands of years ago where entire organs and limbs could be replaced with indistinguishable copies. Visible enhancements like these were one of the less attractive Terran fetishes.

Nilo bobbed several times, pressing his hands together. "Yes, yes. These are the ones. I recognize several of them—especially her." He pointed at me. "They visited the boutique the day before the… robbery."

"What's this all about?" I said. "We paid for our purchases. I have the receipt."

"You must be Hyperia Jones."

The woman smiled, and I saw the metallic replacements included her teeth, which were as sharp as the claws on a P'Takean Tiger.

"Allow me to introduce myself." She lifted her chest, enhancing an area that had no need of it. "I'm Savanov Nein, businesswoman, art collector, and head of The Mechna."

"You forgot drug dealer." It was Denton who spoke.

A Garda stepped forward and slammed the butt of his Musket into Denton's neck.

"Stop!" I pulled at the straps holding me to the chair. "What do you want?"

Savanov swished over to me and put her hands on her hips. "How touching. I want my property, of course."

I met her gaze. "You want the cow creamer back?"

"You, or one of your friends, stole something valuable from me. I want it back. Is that simple enough for you, *dear*?"

Nilo patted Savanov's metal arm. "Let me explain it, boss. I'll take real good care of her."

"Take your hands off," she hissed, staring down at Nilo. "No contact without permission."

Nilo scampered back. "Sorry, I didn't mean any—"

Savanov glared at him and held out her hand. Nilo didn't move for a while, then appeared to remember something and fished in his pockets, finally pulling out a packet of cleaning wipes and offering her one. She hissed, and he bowed again, then dabbed and wiped her metal arm. When the area was spotless, he dropped the used wipe in a crumpled heap on the floor.

"Let's try again." She walked over to Denton. "You're the leader of this little menagerie. So perhaps you're responsible for my loss."

"Unfasten these straps, lady, and I'll show you how responsible I am." Denton spat in her face.

Nilo rushed over with another cleaning wipe.

"You're cute when you're angry." Savanov smiled at Denton and dabbed at her face, then reached between his legs with her claw-like metal hand and squeezed. "How about I tear these off instead?"

Denton gasped loudly, squirming at her grip, and I cringed.

This was all my fault. I couldn't let anyone else suffer for my mistakes.

"Stop," I called out. "None of the others know anything about it. It was me."

"Aww... pretty fish girl wants to save her friends. How sweet."

"How did you find us?"

She laughed, her metallic throat producing a high-pitched screech. "It wasn't especially hard. First, we have a burglarious visit." She ticked off her finger. "Poor Bruno was very confused about it, until I punished him for his failure."

Nilo sniffed and looked away, but said nothing.

"Then the home of one of our special friends is also burgled." Savanov ticked off another finger. "The common element? Both worlds host a ridiculous fake fighting tournament by your group at the same time the burglaries take place. Not very smart, if you ask me."

I cursed silently. If I'd been planning the jobs purely for my own sake, I'd have covered my tracks better, but with Bolt pulling the strings, there hadn't been a choice.

"Normally, the theft of the Flower would be a minor annoyance. After all, it's just another silly curio, and we have plenty of them. But then I began to wonder... what if the Flower was a cover for your real purpose?"

"I don't have it anymore," I said.

"Of course you don't, darling." Savanov was smiling, but her hand snapped open and closed, making a sharp metallic click. "Who are you working for?"

"I'm an independe—"

Her metal hand encircled my throat, restricting my breathing.

"All I have to do is think it, and your adorable little head will be snipped clean from your adorable little neck."

"I'm independent..." I barely managed to hiss the words.

"I won't ask again." She tightened her grip.

"She's working for Olive Branch," Denton yelled. "Leave her alone."

Releasing her grip, Savanov stepped back. "OB? That doesn't sound right. Their agents are usually much smarter."

I looked at the Garda soldiers. "How did you get them? The

Reichsflotte only recruits the best. They swear undying allegiance to the UberKaiser."

She laughed. "You're so deliciously naive. Do you think any oath is stronger than the corrupting influence of SlamCandy? I *bought* the captain, crew, and ship, for a kilo."

That seemed a ridiculously small amount, but what did I know? Once addicted, there was no telling what people would do. "Just tell me what you want."

"You will return the data and the Flower." Savanov spat the words out. "If you do that right now, we can discuss other matters."

"The Flower's gone."

She grabbed me again and jerked me up hard enough that the straps around my arms and legs snapped, leaving me dangling in the air like a training dummy.

"Give me my property now," she screeched.

Her claw-like hand was so tight, all I could do was croak. She released her grip slightly, and I gasped. "I only have the records."

"Kill him." Savanov pointed to Denton.

The Garda nearest us lifted his brutish weapon and pulled back the charging handle.

"Wait!" I gurgled.

"Why?" She sneered in my face.

"I'll get them for you."

"Don't do it, Hype," Denton called out. "They'll kill us all if you—"

The Garda smashed the butt of his rifle into the side of Denton's head. Brachyura lunged forward in his chair, but the Garda stopped him the same way he'd taken down Denton. There were shouts from behind me, confirming what I'd thought earlier—most of the FIRE team was here, except for the stage crew.

"Where are they?" Savanov snapped, flexing and unflexing her arm to produce an unpleasant whine.

"In my cabin," I rasped.

"And which one is that, dear?"

Savanov backhanded me, and my head snapped back. I was lucky that she'd used her flesh hand—the mechanical one would have smashed my skull in. But I don't suppose that would have suited her plans.

"Do what you want to her, but let us go free." I couldn't identify the voice as my head was still buzzing from the blow, but I'd lay money on it being one of the Bonors.

"I'm in the Rodentia suite," I finally gasped. "But you'll never find the stuff—it's hidden."

Savanov snarled, and tapped a communicator built into her metallic wrist. "In here, now."

She paused, then dropped me back onto the chair, which gave me a little time to recover my senses. A series of loud clanking noises came from the corridor, and a few seconds later, two short, simplistic droids entered and marched up to stand on either side of Savanov. They barely reached her waist and would have convincingly played the part of a pair of comedy garbage cans on a holo-show.

"Your children perhaps?"

Savanov's response was another backhanded blow across my face. "I'll enjoy killing you," she said, leaning over. "Slowly..."

"If you bring those things any closer, you'll probably suffocate me." I nodded at her capacious bosom.

This time the blow knocked me out of the chair. "Still want to make jokes?" Savanov rubbed her hand. No doubt my face was making it sore by repeatedly slamming itself into it.

"One more word and I might forget what I came here for and kill you right away," she said. "Or you might end up like these two." She waved her mechanical hand at the two diminutive droids.

"Huh?" was my dazzling response.

"Oh, of course, you don't recognize them." She punched the back of the one on her left with her metal hand, sending out a clang that reverberated around the room. "That's Bruno. He's much happier now than when you left him."

I stared at the metal *thing* in front of me, realizing these weren't the droids I thought they were. They were mecha-terrans but with appalling stunted capabilities. "You mean..."

"Exactly. The punishment for failure."

My stomach flip-flopped. "And the other?"

Savanov chuckled and smacked the second of the metallic boxes in the back. "Say hello, Daddy."

The animated garbage can *clumped* on the spot several times, and several lights flashed, but the only sound that emerged was a thin, metallic buzzing. Revulsion welled up at the thought of someone's brain being trapped inside one of those things. It must feel like being entombed in your own mobile coffin.

Bile rose in my throat, and I swallowed with difficulty. "Do you want the stuff or not?"

"Take her to her room," Savanov ordered. "And *don't* lose her. If she escapes, you two morons will be nothing but a pile of rusting parts."

The garbage cans stomped forward, lifted me upright and locked pincer-like hands around my wrists. They pulled me from the chair and dragged me out of the room.

"How about some entertainment…"

Savanov's voice faded as we left, and chills ran up my dorsal plates. I didn't want to think about what she might find entertaining. We clomped and clanked along the corridors. I had no choice—there was no way I could break the grip the mechna-boxes had on my wrists. I could have picked them up, but they were no doubt equipped to deal with such behavior in a variety of unpleasant ways.

I swiped my hand over the door release patch and clumsily entered, my wrists held tight by the two monstrous garbage cans.

"You're going to have to let me go," I said. "There's a secret panel in that wall, but I can't open it with you holding me."

One of the cans—I think it was Bruno—released its grip, allowing me free movement on one side. "You too, Pops," I said.

The pair exchanged several whirs, squeaks, and whistles. But the metallic claw didn't release.

"I can't get the stuff while you're holding my wrists."

There was another round of shrill squeaks and buzzes, and the clamp around my arm released. To be replaced by one around my ankle.

"You guys have serious trust issues."

It was difficult accessing the panel with Pops holding my ankle, but I managed it. The data-flake was on a shelf just inside, and immediately below that, hidden from sight, was my spare SomPistol. I reached in, lowering my hand slowly. There was a slight chance that if I was quick enough...

I whipped the gun up and spun around. But before I could fire, the lights on both Pops and Bruno flickered wildly, and sparks flew from the top of their stout bodies. My mouth opened, and seconds later Stryng wriggled out from under my bed, holding a couple of smoking starkium power cells in his coils.

"Stryng?" I gasped. "How the hell...?"

"Nothing to it, sweetheart." He tossed the spent power cells to the floor. "They ain't made a gas yet that can take out old Stryng. When you and Denton went down, I hid under the bed. Figured I'd stay there until a chance came to do something about these ficksnits."

"I could kiss you."

"Don't let the droids stop you, baby."

Pops had released his clamp on my ankle, and I twisted from his grasp.

"These aren't droids." I pointed to the garbage cans. "They're mecha-terrans—with the Mechna drug dealers."

"Figured it was something like that. But they must have some friends in high places. Those were Garda who stormed the ship."

"They got an entire ship hooked on SlamCandy."

Stryng's head coiled and uncoiled. "Humanoids sure have a lot to answer for."

"We need to move." I dragged my Nullsuit from the hidden compartment. There was no telling how long it would be before Savanov realized Pops and Bruno were enjoying a new career as doorstops.

"A long lifeboat cruise sounds like the perfect opportunity for you to show your appreciation."

"I'm not leaving." I finished pulling on the suit. "I'm going to free the others."

Stryng wiggled his head from side to side. "No way, sister. Best thing we can do is leave, notify the feds and let them deal with it."

I was already at the door and stopped. "I got everyone into this jam. I'll get them out." I glanced back at Stryng. "You head to the lifeboats. Contact the authorities as soon as you can."

Stryng was silent for several moments. "That's just crazy. Why is it dames always think they're heroes?"

"Because we are." I flashed him a smile and triggered the Nullsuit. "Meet me in Engineering."

The decks in Engineering were quiet. The corridors had been full of Garda on the way down, but my Nullsuit made it easy to slip by them. The *Queen* had no maintenance staff, and presumably the Mechna had moved the stage crew to somewhere they could easily control them.

I crept through the passageways and made my way to Auntie's direct interface bay. Stryng was already there, curled up on the seat, and I switched off the Nullsuit.

"Figured you were heading here." Stryng uncoiled himself. "What's the plan, sister?"

"You'll see." I sat down in the other chair and activated the direct control interface. "You there, Auntie?"

"Oh hello, Hyperia dear. It's so nice to chat with you again. It's been extremely hectic, hasn't it? I don't think I've had so much fun since I was running those inter-species swinger tours back in Seventy-Three. Oh, fiddlesticks, was it Thirty-Seven?"

"It's certainly been exciting, Auntie." I leaned closer to the pickup. "So how about we make it more of a show?"

Twenty-One

I returned to the training room and switched off the Distortion Matrix before entering. Striding in with my hands behind me, I saw Savanov holding one of the Bonor Triplets in the air by her neck.

"Welcome back," she said. "If you don't have what I want, this pretty one dies."

I glanced around. Brachyura was slumped in his chair, unconscious, Denton's face was bloody, and most of the others displayed signs of random physical abuse.

"Hmmm… that puts a new perspective on things." I tilted my head and put my finger to my lip. "Let me think for a while."

"Hyperia!" The gasps from the other two Bonors were matched by a wet gurgle from the one in Savanov's grip—Rachelle I think it was.

"Okay. My little joke." I held out the data-flake and Algernon's Flower, lifting them high so Savanov could see them.

She grinned and dropped Rachelle. I almost laughed at her rough landing on the chair. That was going to bruise.

"I'm glad you decided to be sensible." Savanov gestured to Nilo. "Get them."

He scrabbled over and snatched the flake and the Flower from my hands.

"Are we done now?" I said.

"Not entirely." She swaggered toward me. "What did you do to poor Bruno and my father? I haven't been able to contact them for the last twenty minutes."

"Do you care? After the way you treated them."

Savanov smiled. She lifted her metallic hand. "Tough love. But they're still Mechna, and we look after our own."

Her hand was at my neck, and I bit down on the tiny signaler hidden inside my mouth. At the same time, I grabbed a "tentacle" and tossed it at Nilo.

"Meet my pet Balbanian venomspitter."

Nilo shrieked as Stryng wrapped around his face, dropping both the data-flake and Algernon's Flower. The Flower hit the ground and splintered into a thousand shards—not surprising as I'd hastily printed it in the Universal Replicating Pantograph less than ten minutes ago. Savanov's face contorted into an unflattering grimace, and she screamed—then flew into the air as the GraviMorphic generators went off-line. I was ready for her and flipped backward, catching her under the chin with my foot and sending her spinning to the roof.

I sprang to the door and hit the button to slam it shut. That way we only needed to worry about the people inside—at least for the moment. When I turned back, Stryng had Nilo locked in his coils, and the Garda were all floating uncontrollably. I dodged over to Denton and sawed off his restraints with a small printed knife.

"Thanks, Hype." He rubbed his wrists and grinned savagely. "Time for some rassling revenge."

With that, he pushed down with his powerful legs and propelled himself at the nearest Garda, hitting him so hard I heard the crunch. Next, I released Brach, and then Atsuno.

"You got a lot of explaining to do, babe," she said.

I handed her the knife. "Let's get this cleared up first."

I turned. Savanov was still stuck against the ceiling but looked like she was recovering. I leaped and slammed into her again, driving my elbow into the side of her head. We tumbled and crashed painfully into the bulkhead. She swung out with her metal arm but missed, and instead punched through a panel, getting tangled up in the superstructure.

"Think you can win in my playground?" I laughed.

She pulled her arm out, wobbling as she held onto a beam with the other. She pointed at me. A small compartment on her free arm popped open, and a nasty-looking gun snapped out.

"Watch me," she cried.

The gun flashed, but she missed. I pushed away, putting more distance between us, and bit down on the signaler. Almost immediately, the gravity field snapped back on, and everybody in the air plummeted to the floor. I knew none of the FIRE team would be troubled by the change—everyone spent hours fighting and training in the TwistCube. But I was sure the Mechna and the Garda weren't that experienced.

Several bodies thudded against the floor, and I twisted in midair, landing in a perfect crouch. Diving forward, I grabbed Savanov from behind and arched backward, throwing her over me. She bounced multiple times, then as she flipped, I killed the gravity again.

She somersaulted into the air and smacked into the wall, sprawling like a squashed insect. I jumped at her and slammed my shoulder into her gut, then twisted to deliver an uppercut to her ponderous jaw. Her eyes closed, and I snatched the power pack from her belt.

I turned back to help the others, but it was a rout. The Garda were all incapacitated. Stryng was still holding onto Nilo, but the gangster stopped struggling as Boots approached brandishing his large fist.

"Please, don't hurt me."

"Croff you, weedy-man," Boots squeaked. One punch and Nilo was out too.

I switched the gravity back on and dropped to the floor, noting the loud bang as Savanov crashed behind me. Denton walked over, rubbing his bruised head.

He grinned. "You sure know how to throw a party."

"Sorry. It wasn't what I had in mind."

"Thrit happens." Denton took in the scene around us. "I guess your cover is blown. Everyone in the company knows now. Apart from Mr. Quy."

He was right, and it didn't bode well for my future with FIRE, but we had more important things to worry about for the moment. "Let's clean up the rest of the ship."

I unlocked the door, and more Garda barreled in. And left even more quickly when they were tossed back against the wall by Denton, Brach, Mandraago, and ChaosRhino.

Many people think rasslers are muscle-bound posers because of the entertainment angles we put into the shows, but everyone in FIRE is a skilled athlete trained to handle themselves when it comes to rough and tumble. Fighting any of them was never going to be easy.

We worked our way through the ship, taking out the rest of the Garda and Savanov's Mechna gang fairly easily. I kept flipping the gravity, keeping them off-balance and maintaining our advantage.

"Hyperia, dear." Auntie's voice came from a nearby speaker as I body-slammed one of the last Garda into the decking.

"What is it, Auntie?" I said, locking up the Garda with his own cuffs.

"This has been so much fun. But I think you should know a number of these naughty boys are heading for my main reactor core."

That was worrying. If they reached the core, they could hold us all to ransom—or blow the *Queen* to pieces. "Can you seal off the access corridors?"

"Oh, I tried that, dear. But they have some clever little device for overriding my security protocols."

Denton staggered over, rubbing his thick bicep. "I knew we should update the *Queen*'s security systems."

"Yes, you jolly well should have, dear." She sounded peeved. "Now what are we going to do?"

I looked at Denton, and he shrugged.

"We'd have to be ghosts to get into the core without them killing us," he said.

Grinning, I pulled my mask over my head. "I think we can manage that."

"You can't go on your own," Denton said. "Even with that fancy suit."

"I'm open to suggestions."

Denton looked down as if searching for something. At that moment, Atsuno jogged up. Her hair was a little mussed, but other than that she seemed unaffected by the fighting.

"You got another of those, Hype?" She tapped on my shoulder.

I nodded. "Let's go, *love sister*."

It only took a few minutes to grab my spare Nullsuit. Atsuno was a fair bit shorter than me, but the suit was stretchy enough that it didn't matter too much. It took a little time to show her the controls, but she was as smart as she was pretty and mastered it almost as fast as I explained them. I'd taken the chance to retrieve my SomPistol and offered it to her, but she turned it down.

"I'm not comfortable using one of those," she said. "Besides, I've got hands and feet, and these."

These turned out to be two rods, each one about sixty centimeters long and perhaps three thick.

"Eskrima sticks?" I'd seen her give impressive demonstrations with them, but to me, they had limited use against people with guns.

"Not exactly." She grinned. "They have a few tricks built in."

I shook my head, but there was no dissuading her. I switched on my Distortion Matrix, and Atsuno followed suit.

"Let's kick man-booty," I said, as we winked out of sight.

I'd never imagined that someday I'd be going up against Garda soldiers. My policy was to avoid the authorities as much as possible, in the same way anyone with sense avoids lawyers and tax collectors. Now I was planning on assaulting several, and I had to wonder if I'd lost my mind. Again, I cursed Bolt. That thrithead had thoroughly screwed me over. If I ever got my hands on him, I'd slap him all the way to the L'Thidri Nebula and beyond.

I padded silently down one of the passages leading to the ship's core. I'd lost track of Atsuno and hoped she was finding her own way there. Facing the soldiers without some form of backup didn't bear thinking about. Stepping through an open doorway, I sensed a flash of movement to my right. A quad-limbed Mechna dashed out of a cross corridor like a giant spider and slammed into my side, sending me tumbling.

I rolled with the blow and bounced off the wall, flipping backward over the dumpy Mechna as it followed up with a spinning drill-like appendage that appeared out of one of its legs. I couldn't imagine why anyone would want such disgusting modifications, but perhaps it was another of Savanov's little *jokes*. Whatever the reason, it was as friendly as a Golethian scorpion in heat and must have been equipped with Catsonic detectors as it could obviously see me despite the Distortion Matrix. I punted it toward the wall, but before it hit, it flipped, cushioning the impact with its legs.

A blue light flashed on its upper surface, and a fraction of a second later a warning flashed in my HUD. That thing was equipped with a matrix quencher. My arms faded into view as the Matrix collapsed. That didn't stop me though, and I catapulted the beastly Mechna down the corridor to smash into the bulkhead a few meters away.

Three Garda rushed me. Then the mecha-spider joined in, and I found myself in a four-way battle. Somewhere along the way, they appeared to have lost their weapons, making it an extremely handicapped fistfight.

None of them was strong enough to beat me one-on-one, but collectively they drove me steadily back. The only slight comfort was that they were pushing me in the direction of the core, rather than the other way. I dropped low and flipped the gravity, bouncing over their heads, then reversed it. As I crashed into them, I slammed my foot into one of the Garda, catching him on the chin. He dropped like a food sack, which left three to deal with, but they pressed forward simultaneously, and I was forced against the wall.

The Mechna attacked first, brandishing its drill arm like a club. The toothed edges caught the leg of my suit and ripped the material to shreds, despite the armored fibers. I used my other foot to kick at it, but it pressed its advantage. A stick appeared from nowhere and smashed into the face of one of the Garda like a missile. He collapsed, and another stick appeared, shooting forward and hitting the remaining Garda. He didn't go down, but it gave me a breather to focus on the metallic monster trying to carve me a new bellybutton. Holding it away from me, I reached under to grab its power pack, then ripped it out, dropping the sparking box on the floor.

Atsuno shimmered into sight as another two Garda ran up. She was holding the sticks I'd seen earlier, but now the ends were glowing, and a pair of bands around her palms shone with matching colors. She flicked one of the sticks at the nearest Garda, knocking him down, then fired the other at one of the men charging her. The first stick bounced back as if it were on a string, returning to her hand as the third soldier reached her.

Atsuno whipped the stick across his face and torso in a hail of blows so fast I couldn't make them out. The man lashed out, and she spun away, catching the second stick behind her back as it flew to her. Completing her turn, she stepped in and delivered a hail of blows to the Garda's face, shoulders, and neck, and he collapsed in a heap on the floor. Then she bent down to help me up.

"What the croff?" I said, staring at the sticks.

Atsuno laughed and flipped them to show the glowing beads at the end of the sticks. "Micro-tractors," she said. "Always useful."

"Are you there, Auntie?" I said.

"Oh hello again, Hyperia. Where else would I be?"

Sometimes I think Auntie is going senile, though as far as I know, that's not possible for an Artificial Personality. "How are you doing?"

"Oh, I'm fine, dear. Thank you for asking. I believe the Langmuir conduits in my mid-section need a good clean. The flow there seems a little obstructed."

Atsuno giggled. "A constipated starship?"

"What was that, dear?"

"Nothing, Auntie. I coughed, that's all." I scowled at Atsuno. "I meant how are we progressing in clearing out the remaining crooks?"

"Are you coming down with a cold, dear? You should have the good doctor check you over."

"Will do, Auntie. And I'll ask Denton to get your conduits serviced." I took a breath and counted down from twenty. "So, about the criminals?"

"What? Oh yes, those bad boys." She paused as though looking for something, and I imagined her pouring a cup of nice, warm tea. "There's only one left."

"Excellent, any ide—"

"Oh dear," Auntie tutted. "He's reached the control room at the central core."

"Thrit!" I looked at Atsuno. "Any ideas?"

She shook her head.

"Okay, Auntie. We'll take care of it."

We headed down the corridor, toward the center of the giant reactors that powered the ship. Atsuno matched me step for step, as though we were a pair of warriors from legendary times. We paused in the wide atrium outside the control room. It had no function but made the technicians who serviced the core feel important.

My Distortion Matrix was still recharging after the quencher, but Atsuno switched hers back on, and we slipped inside to check out the situation. In the middle of the far wall, the reinforced door to the reactor was locked, and visible through the pointlessly over-sized picture windows was the last of the crooks. I whispered to Atsuno to stay hidden, then walked over and waved.

"Hey, there," I said. "You're on your own, I'm afraid. Your friends are all disabled or locked up."

"Release them, now."

This Mechna was bigger than any of the others we'd seen and had a curious accent. Although he was humanoid, unlike the majority of them, his entire body had been replaced with a powerful cyborg unit only slightly smaller than one of the UberKaiser's imperial destroyers.

"You might as well come out." I put my hands behind my back, making myself look small and submissive. "They'll never agree to that."

"Do it, or I destroy the ship."

"What's your name?" I crossed in front of the window, skipping girlishly.

"I'm Domani." He lifted his arms and flexed them to show off the size of his hydraulic pistons, grinning evilly. "But my friends call me *The Dominator*."

"So, Dom, you're going to blow up the ship if we don't release your crooked friends?"

"I will destroy you all, and your pathetic ship."

"And where are you right now?"

Dom hesitated, then smirked. "At your ship's primary core controls."

"Uh huh." I skipped back in front of him, putting on my best jiggle. "So when the core melts down... who gets it first?"

"What?"

I stopped and gestured for Dom to come closer to the glass. "You're right next to the core. If it explodes, you get vaporized first." I pouted at him. "Or can you withstand a sub-squirkium meltdown?"

"I…" Realization finally reached his tiny intellect, and his metal lips curled upwards in a faltering smile. "Well…"

"See. You'll be dead along with the rest of us. What's the point of that?"

"Well…" He shifted furtively, then thumped his fist against his metallic chest. "The Dominator never surrenders!"

"Your funeral. But there is an alternative."

Dom frowned. "What's that?"

"If you can defeat me," I said, buffing my fingernails, "the others have agreed to let you go."

"I don't fight girls."

"Can't stand losing, huh?"

"The Dominator is never beaten."

"Then you've nothing to worry about, have you?"

Dom certainly wasn't the fastest fish in the pond, and I could almost see the thoughts running through his head. In fact, there was a rippling light display on the top of his skull that probably *was* displaying what he was thinking—if only I had a pocket EEG-Decryp.

"Open the control room door, Auntie," I said.

"I'm afraid I can't do that, dear. It has a security seal."

"Priority one override." I took a step back. "Open it."

There were several whirs and a couple of clangs. Then the door cranked open.

"You coming out to play, Dom?" I called. "It's your best chance. Don't worry, I'll go easy on you."

"I *am* the Dominator!" he bellowed, the words grinding metallically.

"Nothing between the ears *or* the legs, huh?"

He roared and lunged through the entrance, his large, claw-like hands reaching out to crush me. At the last second, I sidestepped, and he flashed past, slamming into the auditorium wall.

"Mnnnrrrff…" was his response, then he turned slowly, pushing himself out of the deep crevice he'd made in the panel.

"Want to try that again?"

He pushed back, using his giant, metal leg pistons to propel himself at me like a missile. I timed my kick perfectly, catching him between his legs and catapulting him into another bulkhead. It seemed there was nothing there to hurt, as Dom's only reaction was to shake his head as he extracted himself from the wall. Unfortunately, I couldn't say the same for my foot, which throbbed like someone had dropped a tonne of polymetal on it. Which might not have been far from the truth.

"You fight worse than Bruno," I taunted, resisting the urge to wince at the stabs shooting through my foot.

"Bruno is weak, like a little girl," Dom roared, charging at me again.

I flipped the gravity and bounced over him, kicking him in the butt. "Now, Ats."

As Dom careened forward, I heard the trip-hammer sound of blows bouncing against his metal hide. He howled, bouncing off the floor and barreling along the room, slamming from deck to roof and back. When he came to rest, his head wobbled from side to side as if he was dizzy, which might have been genuine.

And that was when I shot him full-on with the SomPistol. I know it was unfair, but he was twice my size, and likely weighed about twenty times as much. His eyes crossed then uncrossed multiple times, and the brain display on his head dimmed. Despite that, he didn't stop moving and sat there stroking his jaw as if deep in thought.

"Was that it?" hissed Atsuno, lowering her Distortion Matrix.

"It's designed for regular people, not mecha-terrans. I hoped it would work."

Dominator's brain display flickered, and the rippling trace of his thoughts reappeared. His metallic frame shuddered, then he reached down to push himself to his feet.

"What's plan B?"

"Not get caught?" I switched the gravity and pushed away, zipping to one side as Dom charged like a raging excavator.

"Great strategy," Atsuno called, vanishing behind her Matrix.

Dom was bouncing around the room, making full use of the zero-gravity, and I switched it once more, hoping to slow him down. He tumbled to the floor with a massive crash but rolled to his feet and came after me.

I stopped, hoping to lure him in. "Ats, can you see his power pack?"

Dominator swung his large fist, and I ducked under it, jabbing ineffectual punches into his midsection. They didn't appear to affect *him* but certainly bruised my knuckles. I heard a number of other hard thuds and realized Atsuno was close by, also beating on him. He looked momentarily confused but threw another blow at me, catching me in the ribs as I flipped the gravity.

Something snapped, and I knew it was part of me. As I tumbled back through the air, a searing pain ripped through my upper chest. Instinctively, I lifted my gun and fired multiple times. Dom skidded to a halt, looking as confused as the first time I shot him. Maybe the bolts from the gun had some effect, but they weren't powerful enough.

"Power packs are on his back." Atsuno reappeared next to me. "I hit him several times there, but they're armored."

I clutched my arm to my chest. This wasn't going the way I'd hoped. I hadn't expected to fight a tank-on-legs.

"Give me your Eskrima sticks and the palm controllers," I said.

Atsuno looked puzzled. "You don't know how to use them."

"Quick, he's recovering."

She handed me the sticks and the two small controllers.

"Keep metal-boy here busy for a few minutes," I said. "But don't let him hit you."

"You don't need to warn me of that, but—"

My Distortion Matrix was back online and I activated it before moving sideways.

"Come on, you aluminum assbrush," Atsuno called. "Pick on someone your own size."

Ats looked no bigger than his little pinky, but the insult combined with his grogginess galvanized him once more. I wasn't sure if he realized he was facing two opponents. I slipped by him as he edged closer to her, making my way to the control room. It was heavily armored for obvious reasons, and I jammed the sticks into the back of the door, then tapped the communicator button.

"Auntie, I'm in the core control room. When I leave, close the door and lock it down, okay?"

"What?" She sounded as if she'd woken from a nap. "Who's that? Oh, Hyperia. I see you now. Yes dear, I'll do that. Did you beat those ruffians?"

"Not yet."

I rushed back out, waiting while the door sealed behind me then locked with a deep, metallic thump.

"Bring him this way, Ats," I yelled.

Atsuno leaped out of the way of a massive sideswipe and used the opportunity to slip closer to the control room. Dom clomped around in a circle, then followed her, closing in on my hiding spot. He threw a punch and Atsuno dodged. Then he lashed out again, and she ducked that too. She was almost next to me.

"Keep him coming…" I whispered.

Dominator was next to the entrance, and I made my move, jumping behind him. I spotted the starkium power packs, hidden under armored covers. I fired at point-blank range, hitting him in the back of his skull, and he staggered, dropping to one knee. Then I made my move. One quick leap and I was on his back, riding him like a Banzairian pony. In his dazed state, he barely reacted, simply shrugging a number of times to try and dislodge me.

I reached down to the power pack covers. It was tight but there was just enough room around the casing to slip one of the micro-tractor controllers under it and activate it on its highest setting. Then I did the same with the second, planting it under the other cover.

Dom lifted, shrugging and sending me flying. I slammed into a wall and squeaked as another agonizing stab shot through my chest. Dropping my matrix, I called Atsuno over, and she skirted him as he clambered upright.

"What now?" she gasped.

"Now we let him do the work." I waved at Dom who was back on his feet. "Worried you're going to get beaten?"

"Two girls not harder than one," he growled, lumbering toward us.

On the second step, he slowed, lowering his stance to press his over-large feet into the floor. His brain display flickered more intensely.

"Got a problem there?" I called out. "Scared of a couple of girls?"

Atsuno picked up on my theme. "Yeah, come on you big hunk of tin. Show us what you're made of, if you dare."

He staggered forward, his foot gouging deep furrows in the deck plates as he fought to reach us.

"What have you..." he snarled, his arms waving. "I will kill you both."

The tractor beams between the eskrima sticks and controllers allowed him about another half step, then there was an explosive clang as the covers ripped off his back, exposing the power packs. He roared in triumph as the tractors released him, and stormed in our direction, his giant hands coming up to tear us apart.

"Hype?" Atsuno's voice had an edge to it.

I lifted my gun. Took aim. Then emptied the remaining shots into him.

Dominator stumbled, then lifted once more, before dropping—his knee hammering a divot out of the floor. His hand shot down to push himself upright, and he skidded to a halt on his stomach less than a meter from us. I walked over to his dazed form and reached down, ripping the glowing power packs from his back.

"Sorry, Dom—I fight like a girl."

Twenty-Two

I restored the gravity and limped back to the ship's main level with Atsuno, the power packs dangling from my hand like trophies. Almost without thinking, my other hand sought Atsuno's, and she gripped it firmly.

"I thought I had some moves," she said. "But you take the fox's fur."

I wasn't sure what she meant, but I liked the sound of it. "That's a hell of a compliment coming from you."

"Seriously, I'd love to hear the real story of what's been—"

"Hyperia, are you there, dear?" Auntie's voice reverberated down the corridor.

"I'm here, Auntie. What's wrong?" My stomach tightened.

"Well, as far as I can make out, we have more intruders coming in through the secondary airlock. Do you think those nasty villains may have brought some friends?"

"Thrit! Warn Denton and the others."

I sprinted along the corridor to the airlocks in the middle of the ship. Despite the initial burst of adrenaline triggered by the news, my pace slowed as the ache in my chest increased. Atsuno soon caught me despite my head start, slowing to match my speed. The corridor widened at the airlock area. There were already several dozen intruders running toward the main crew areas, all dressed in identical drab, green shipsuits. As we reached one of the airlock doors, another figure charged out, and I smacked full into him, sending us both sprawling.

I choked down the pain, but it took a minute to recover before

I spotted who I'd run into. He was already scrambling to his feet and picking up the gun he'd dropped.

"Bolt! What the thrit are—"

"Seven-thirty-one," he barked, then charged past me in the direction of the ship's core.

I heard others running, and more people emerged from the airlock, following Bolt.

"I'm hallucinating," I said. "Atsuno?"

She came over, staring at me with concern. "What's wrong, Hype?"

"Those men..."

"Yeah, weird how they all have the same face, huh?"

"Weird?" I gasped. "Hundreds of Bolts? Hundreds and hundreds! It can't be. This is a nightmare, or maybe I've been hit by—"

Atsuno clicked her fingers in front of my eyes. "Snap out of it, Hype."

I took another breath to clear my head and steadied a little. "I'm okay. I think."

We pushed on and finally came across two identically armed Bolts guarding the main lounge area. I didn't *really* want to speak to them, but the voices from inside suggested the rest of FIRE was in there.

"Bolt?" I said to the nearest guard.

"Four-sixty-two." His face showed no recognition. I looked at the other one. "Are you Bolt?"

He remained the perfect sentry and didn't look my way. "Two-fifty-four."

I turned to Atsuno, but she only shrugged. "I guess we better go in."

Inside, the team was scattered around in random groups, ignoring the comfy seating and recreational attractions. They were surrounded by a large flock of Bolts.

"There they are!" It wasn't hard to pick out Brachyura's distinctive rasp.

"Hype?" Denton pushed his way through the crowd. "What the hell's going on? Who are these... guys?"

"That's Bolt," I said.

Denton looked around. "Which one?"

"All of them."

One of the Bolts stood in the middle, a little ahead of the others, and I approached him. "Are you Bo... Are you in charge here?"

"One-one-eight."

"What's with the croffing numbers? Is there anyone here apart from my people who can actually talk?"

"Of course we can talk," the Bolt directly in front of me said. "One-one-eight is leading this operation. Any questions should be directed to him."

"Okay. Where is he?"

"On his way." Bolt pointed at the white, padded couches arranged around the center of the room. "Have a seat. We'll take care of everything now."

"Well, hooray for the cavalry," Stryng sneered, snaking his way toward us. "Did you and Ats sort things out, dollface?"

I nodded. I was partly in shock from having so many Bolts infesting the *Queen*. I sat clumsily, trying not to twist my chest. A moment later, Denton planted himself on one side of me with Stryng on the other.

"Don't worry," Denton said. "Whatever happens, we'll look after you."

"Sure thing, toots," Stryng agreed. "This is a bum rap. We ain't gonna let the feds touch you."

Their sincerity made me choke up, and my stomach danced a little jig. I'd never had anyone protect me like this, and realized the whole roster was the same. Even the Bonors were glaring defiantly at the army of Bolts. I'd not had anything like a family since... well, since leaving Lecuunda and, before that, my relatives weren't exactly supportive. The idea that I had so many friends enveloped me like the heat from an open fire in winter, but even as I basked in it, I knew it had come to an end. I'd failed Bolt, or at least one of them, been caught by the Mechna, and my cover was blown. If I was lucky, Olive Branch *might* let me live out my life in a cell. But my days with FIRE were over.

"Sorry, guys. I appreciate what you're saying, but I'm afraid this is it." I stared at the thick, golden carpet. "I shouldn't have gotten you involved. I don't understand everything that's going on here, but Olive Branch is going to bury me deeper than a lawyer hides their soul."

"Over my dead body," Denton said.

I patted his knee. "It's okay. I deserve it."

Stryng whistled. "Ain't no way you're—"

Footsteps rattling down the corridor cut him off, and I looked up. The line of Bolts parted, and a new, identical one stepped up to face us.

"I'm Bolt, John Bolt, of Olive Branch." He glanced at the others. "Err… Bolt One-one-eight to be precise."

"You the monkey in charge of this circus act?" Stryng jeered.

"I'm the lead OB agent if that's what you mean." He pulled off a pair of blue gloves and tucked them inside his belt. "Which one of you is Hyperia Jones?"

"You don't recognize me?" I muttered, rising from the couch.

"Should I?"

"You said you were in charge." My eyes darted from one identical face to the next. "Wait, if you're not the real Bolt, who is?"

"Well, technically we all are. What agent number are you referring to?"

"Number? How the croff would I know?" This was getting annoying. "The one that recruited me? That had me steal the records from the Mechna and Th'opn Mrez. The one who got me involved in all this thrit."

"Ahh, that one. Agent Six-six-six." One-one-eight scowled. "Bit of a sticky wicket there. Rather embarrassing and all that."

My hands quivered as I fought not to punch One-one-eight's perfectly groomed face. "I was nearly killed—several times. We were *all* almost killed a little while ago. I was forced to lie, cheat, and steal for him. And you think it's *embarrassing*?"

One-one-eight nodded, rubbing his chin. "Oh yes, highly so. First agent in the Bolt lineage to go rogue since our initial cloning over four hundred years ago. A definite blot on our copybook. Another team is closing in on him as we speak."

"Clones? That explains a lot, but why so many?" sneered one of the Bonors, maybe Rachelle. "Isn't that egotistical overkill?"

"You'd know all about that," growled Stryng.

"Shut up, *worm*!"

"Please, would everybody be quiet while I sort this out." One-one-eight held up his hands."The sooner we get through this, the quicker you can move on with your lives."

"There's nothing left for you to do." ChaosRhino stalked over, dwarfing One-one-eight and leering over him. "Hype and Atsuno already took out the last of those goons."

One-one-eight's mouth opened momentarily, then he whispered to another Bolt. After a brief exchange, he turned back. "Oh, I see. That's... well done. I thought you chaps, and chapettes, would need rescuing, but well, jolly good show and all that."

"Why don't ya take a powder, ya bum," Stryng said. "And take your ugly friends with ya."

"In that case, all that's left is to clean up those blighters and be on our way."

"What will you do with them?" It was purely idle curiosity—I didn't care what happened to the Mechna.

"Oh, well. First, we extract their brain patterns and store them in our archives for future study. Then we generate new, regularized, ones and inject them back in so they'll become worthwhile and constructive members of the Realms."

I frowned. "Sounds repulsive and painful."

"Oh it is, but the Realms justifies the brains."

"What about us?" ChaosRhino snorted. "You gonna try the same thing?"

"Well, there we have a problem, I'm afraid." One-one-eight frowned.

"In what way?" I said, getting a sinking feeling in my stomach.

"Well, unlike the Mechnas, you're public figures, somewhat known throughout the Realms."

"That's right, clone-boy," Denton said. "And don't you forget it. You can't touch us—*any* of us."

Denton walked over and put his hand on my shoulder. I felt reassured but scared, all at the same time.

"Well, that's not strictly true, old boy." One-one-eight shrugged. "In your cases, we'd need to be more subtle."

"And do what?" I said.

"We're thinking of a two-day permanent memory wipe. It's relatively painless. Everything since your show on Sparth would be gone."

"That won't work," I said. "Denton and Stryng have known about me for a couple of weeks."

"Oh, dear." One-one-eight's face grew longer. "That does put rather a different perspective on things."

I suddenly regretted opening my mouth. Judging from the expression on One-one-eight's face, I'd made it a lot worse for everyone. The babble of voices grew louder as the rest of the team realized the implications of what had been said.

I looked at One-one-eight. "Can we talk in private? Perhaps there's a way we can settle this."

I was sitting in Denton's office with him and One-one-eight, while the other Bolts were transferring the helpless Mechna to the Olive Branch ship. The rest of FIRE was waiting in the lounge, no doubt wondering what future they had—if any.

"I assume you have the data from Mrez. You will, naturally, hand that over immediately. We need it to obtain the warrant for the brain reprogramming." One-one-eight paused. "Alas, poor Th'opn."

"Huh?" I pulled back in my seat.

"Oh yes, he's one of our chaps—gathering evidence against the SlamCandy dealers and their contacts. We've been chasing rumors of a mole inside the ranks for months, and he was helping us draw out the traitor."

"I didn't realize..." Now I felt worse.

"Now he's gone and lost his sexbot." One-one-eight shook his head sadly. "Don't think I've ever seen a man so desolate."

"Did he mean *desperate*?" Denton whispered to me, then looked back to One-one-eight "Can't they rebuild her... it?"

"Oh, certainly. But they're never quite the same, you know?"

I saw Denton swallow a smile. "No, can't say I do."

"What are the options here?" Despite my guilt, I was at the point where all I wanted was to get things over with. No matter how it ended.

"That's a good question." He looked at both of us. "The way I see it, we do a two-day wipe on most of your people, but a deeper wipe on Mr. Denton here and the snake fellow—or we have to do something more drastic."

That sounded ominous. "Such as?"

"Well, something like an unfortunate accident." One-one-eight gestured toward the walls. "The *Ethereal Queen* is an old ship. If it were to suffer a catastrophic failure, no one would question it."

"Wait, what was that?" Auntie's voice came from the speakers built into Denton's desk. "Hyperia, dear. What is this awful man talking about?"

"Don't worry, Auntie. I'll explain later," I said. "Active Monitoring off for the duration."

The light on the pickup turned red.

"Who was that?" One-one-eight stared at me.

"This ship has an Artificial Personality. And you just threatened her."

"I say, that's terribly interesting. I've always been fascinated by the old intelliships. Perhaps I could have a closer loo—"

"Back to the point, Olive bum." Denton glared at Bolt. "If you give me and Stryng a deep wipe, isn't that dangerous?"

"Oh, absolutely, old bean." His tone was light. "But not as much as being caught in a D-space implosion."

"And what about me?" I said.

"Well, an implosion would take care of all of you, but if we go with a memory wipe you become a potential embarrassment. If anything happened and the others found out you were still alive, it would trigger a cascade effect and their memories would return."

"So, you'd lock me up, forever?"

"Oh yes. Not much of an option, but better than the alternative, no?"

Denton looked more hangdog than normal, and he wasn't even wearing his jowly dogface. "If that's what I need to do to save you and the rest of the team"—I took a deep breath—"then that's what I want."

"You can't, Hype. It's not right."

I looked down, not wanting to let Denton or One-one-eight

see the stinging tears in my eyes. "I have to."

"Very well, I'll arrange for the memory wipes." One-one-eight stood. "I'll need those records now."

He led me to the door, and I couldn't protest in case I started blubbering. Then I skidded to a halt.

"Tell me something. What would happen if those files got to the news streams?"

He stiffened. "Nothing, really. I mean it simply corroborates the fact that the Mechna were SlamCandy dealers."

"Uh-huh." I pulled away from him. "As well as revealing that you're developing Klausehn-tech-based weapons. And that there's a mole in Olive Branch…"

"What are you getting at?"

"Well, you probably wouldn't want that information becoming public."

"Ahhh, no. It wouldn't be helpful."

"I'm sure it would all be *rather embarrassing*, in fact." One-one-eight winced, and I knew I had him. "We're in the entertainment business. We have a lot of contacts in the media."

One-one-eight took a step back. "Yes… I imagine so."

"As soon as we left Sparth, I copied the data files and transferred them to secure locations across the Darkover network. If anything happens to me, those files will be broadcast to every media outlet in the Seventeen Realms."

His perfect tan appeared to fade. "You're lying."

"Are you willing to risk that?" I leaned against the bulkhead and buffed my nails against my shoulder, suppressing a yelp at the pain it caused. "I imagine Olive Branch would look significantly different if it came out that the organization was full of crooks."

"Don't even say that," he hissed.

"So, how about a bit of negotiation?"

One-one-eight moved away from the door and sat on the couch. "What did you have in mind?"

"First, we drop all talk of memory wipes."

He gave a short nod.

"Next, you agree not to lock me up." My head was buzzing as I gave him my ultimatums. "I'm free to live as I choose."

One-one-eight nodded again. "As long as you give up your life of crime."

That wasn't going to happen, but I saw no point in weakening my hand. "I'll give you the files, but the copies stay where they are. In case you change your mind."

"And does Olive Branch get anything out of this?"

"Apart from not being purged, you mean?" I thought for a minute, then my lips curled into a smile. "In return, I'll continue working as an undercover OB agent."

"The UberKaiser would never agree to that!"

I shrugged. "I won't tell if you don't."

One-one-eight jumped to his feet, a broad grin spreading across his face and revealing his perfect white teeth. "Well played. I wondered when you'd get to that idea. Welcome to Olive Branch."

"Seriously?" I looked from him to Denton and back. "You expected this?"

"No, but I was hoping." One-one-eight leaned close, lowering his voice. "After all, clones are good, but between you and me, they aren't everything, old girl. Rather unimaginative, don't you know."

I couldn't speak. It all seemed so right, and yet I couldn't quite understand how I'd got here. But the fact that I could stay with FIRE meant everything.

"That's not going to work," Denton growled.

My hopes crashed. He should have kept his mouth shut. But like I almost did earlier, he had to spoil things.

Bolt looked across at him. "And why would that be, Mr. Denton?"

"All of FIRE knows what happened, and about Hype working for you people. You think they're simply going to forget that? Besides, I can't afford to let Hyperia go whenever you need her. I have a business to run."

"Excellent points, old chap." One-one-eight nodded. "Do you have any suggestions on how we deal with that?"

Denton gave the biggest smile I'd ever seen from him. "Simple—you bring the whole company into Olive Branch. We *all* work for you. That way we can support Hype, and each other, and no one has to know anything."

"Simply marvelous," One-one-eight chortled. "Exactly the

solution I would have suggested. We'll need to put you through an intensive training program."

"One more thing," said Denton.

One-one-eight looked puzzled. "What's that?"

"You give us a contract to do a rolling tour of all the military bases in the Realms. That way, I can keep FIRE going without any suspicion falling on us."

"Oh dear, I'm afraid I can't authorize something like that. OB is separate from the military."

Denton rubbed his chin. "I'm sure you can pull a few strings."

One-one-eight considered for a few moments. "Very well, it will provide an excuse to move you around as needed. Is that everything?"

Denton glanced at me, and I nodded. He winked and reached into his desk to pull out his spare dogface. "Looks like we have a deal," he said, slipping the mask on.

One-one-eight clicked his heels together, gave a formal salute, and was gone.

"I can't wait to see the look on Mr. Quy's face when I tell him." Denton laughed.

"But you and the others—working for Olive Branch?" I dropped into a chair.

His laugh turned into a howl. "Thrit! Did you think you were going to get all the fun?"

Twenty-Three

The *Queen* was on its way to a gig at the naval base on Seclonu. It was a long hop but gave the team time to work on story lines. Not to mention a much-needed break to recover from recent events. Olive Branch had already scheduled a training stopover, which had to fit in with our personal appearances.

According to Denton, Mr. Quy was ecstatic when he heard the news of our contract, though Denton hadn't told him the full details of what had happened. Word of the incipient tour was spreading through the news streams, building on the frenzy generated by the Sparth show. We'd received a frosty message of congratulations from Frenzy Fosdyke, the general manager of ICE. There was no doubt he'd keep working to dominate the field, but our position was safe for the foreseeable future. We were *still* number one in Sports Rassling Entertainment.

I was in my room when my communicator buzzed. It was a message from Olive Branch. Denton and One-one-eight had decided I should handle that side of things, especially as Denton was so busy coordinating shows. I opened a channel, and a Bolt appeared on the screen.

"How are things, One-one-eight? Got something for us?"

"It's Five-eight-two actually,"

"Sorry, you people all look alike. Have you thought of using badges?"

"Badges? We don't need no..." He paused. "We'll take that under advisement. I have your next assignment."

The terminal dinged as a file was transmitted. "There's a

263

problem at the D-space research center on Rathid Three. One-one-eight believes someone has infiltrated the operation and is stealing information to sell to L'Thidrian pirates. We need you to get inside, find out who it is, and stop the leak. If you don't, the Realms will be facing a war within two weeks."

"In that case, we'll get right on it."

"If you, or any of your team, are caught or killed, Olive Branch will disavow any knowledge of your actions."

"Thanks... Did they pick up Bolt yet? Six-six-six that is?"

Five-eight-two raked his fingers through his bouffant hair, looking agitated. "Dashed bad luck there, I'm afraid. His shuttle was empty when we finally caught it."

I shivered all the way to the tips of my tentacles. "He's still out there?"

"We have our best people on it. You concentrate on Rathid Three—we'll take care of the rest."

He closed the call, and I opened the files. There was a slew of personal information on the people at the research center and details of their work. It was going to be a tough assignment. Before I'd gotten very far into the mission brief, the chime sounded at my door, and the announcer buzzed.

"Hyperia, it's Atsuno. I have something for you." She was dressed ready for practice. "How about a training session?"

I thought about the mass of information in the Olive Branch files and shrugged. There'd be time for that later. "Sure, give me a few minutes."

I let her in and started changing, then remembered something. "Did you say you had something for me?"

Ats was watching me, with her hands behind her back. "Sure do. Your new rassling suit."

"New one?" I pulled on my leggings. "I already have one. Besides, Denton has to approve any costume changes."

"He already did," Denton growled, slipping in behind Atsuno with Stryng behind him.

Atsuno held out a tiny pair of shorts and a crop top, both decorated with a vivid, multi-colored logo. "I designed them myself."

I eyed the costume skeptically. It was a lot more revealing than my usual outfits.

"Well, try it on, toots." Stryng coiled his body, and his eyes opened wider. "Gotta see what it looks like."

I slipped behind a screen and quickly changed, then re-emerged.

"Wow." Stryng's tail thumped the ground enthusiastically. "You look like hot-potatoes, dollface."

Atsuno nodded, and Denton howled.

"No more lies," he said, "Welcome to the family."

His words still made me feel uncomfortable, but I was close to bawling. A warm glow spread through my body as they smiled at me, the sensation reminding me of the radiance from two Star-Phyres interacting but somehow more precious.

"All for one, or fall as one." Stryng held up his tail. Atsuno and Denton clapped their hands over the end, and after a moment of hesitation, I did the same.

I turned around, checking my new costume in the mirror. It looked good, and the casual style suited me. The best thing though was the message blazoned on the shirt in fiery orangy-red letters:

Hyperia Jones
She'll Steal Your Heart

Acknowledgements

Thank you for reading!

Please consider leaving a review or rating at your favorite book retailer. Even if it's only a line or two, I would very much appreciate it. Or, if you prefer, send me your feedback via the contact page on my website. Your opinion is very important to me.

This book would not have been possible without the help and support of my family, friends, and other members of the writing community. I'd like to thank them all and especially my wife, Hilary, for her constant love, support, and patience.

Special thanks to my editor, Michelle Dunbar (michelledunbar.co.uk) who helped polish the raw manuscript into the masterpiece that lies before you. ;-)

For a complete list of my books, please visit my website (davidmkelly.net/my-books/) and consider signing up for my email updates at /davidmkelly.net/subscribe/. I won't share your information with anyone for any reason and won't bombard your mailbox either. You'll be the first to hear about new releases, as well as receiving occasional free stories.

Thanks again.

David M. Kelly

Also from David M. Kelly

The Joe Ballen series is a near future, sci-fi noir thriller series, featuring a smart-mouthed space engineer, engaging characters, cynical humor, and plausible science.

Mathematics Of Eternity (Book one)

You can ask Joe Ballen anything, except to give up.

Joe Ballen, a half-crippled space engineer, dreams of returning to his old life in space while scraping a living illegally flying cabs in flooded-out Baltimore. But when one of his passengers suffers a grisly death, Joe is dragged into a dangerous conspiracy centered around a prototype Jumpship.

As the bodies pile up, Joe becomes suspect number one, and his enemies will stop at nothing to hide the truth. With the help of a disturbed scientist, a senile survivalist, and his glamorous boss, can Joe untangle the puzzle and uncover the truth before he becomes another dead statistic?

The future's about to get a lot more action-packed!

https://books2read.com/MOE-JB1

Perimeter (Book two)
In space, treachery runs deep.

Joe Ballen's working on a new ore-processing platform in the harsh environment around Mercury. When a savage Atoll attack decimates his crew, Joe is injured and returns to Earth to recover. But vital starship engineering files are missing, and Joe is bulldozed into the not-so-choice assignment.

But he's not the only one in the hunt and Joe is dragged into a high-stakes game of cat and mouse. It's a journey that will take him to the perilous depths of space, where no one is quite what they seem. Can old enemies ever make good allies? And can Joe trust even the people closest to him?

Ballen's back in another action-packed, sci-fi noir thriller, guaranteed to keep you turning the pages.

https://books2read.com/per-JB2/

Transformation Protocol (Book three)
Change can be deadly!

With his life crumbling around him, Joe Ballen is close to going out in a blaze, fuelled by cheap alcohol and self-hatred. But when something "out there" starts destroying spaceships and stations, the only JumpShip available to investigate is the *Shokasta*—locked away by Joe in an attempt to get justice for his family.

But when an old friend offers him the chance to return to space to search for a missing JumpShip, it proves more complicated than either of them imagined. Joe realizes some people will go to any lengths to get what they want, and when his past catches up with him in a way he couldn't have seen coming, he must battle enemies new and old as well as his own inner demons.

https://books2read.com/TP-JB3

Kwelengsen Storm (Logan's World, Book One)
You can turn your back on war, but sometimes it refuses to let you go.

Logan Twofeathers is head of engineering on Kwelengsen, the first discovered habitable planet. He thinks he's left conflict far behind, but when he's attacked on a routine mission, he crashes on the planet.

With his new home destroyed, Logan is stranded deep in the frozen mountains. Against the ever-present threat of capture, he must battle his way through icy surroundings in a treacherous attempt to find his wife.

Forced to ally himself with a group of soldiers and their uncompromising captain, Logan must face the reality that he may have lost everything—and everyone—he loves.

Kwelengsen Storm is the first in a gripping, new sci-fi thriller series from the author of the Joe Ballen novels.

For a complete list of my books visit http://davidmkelly.net/my-books/

About The Author

David M. Kelly writes fast-paced, near-future sci-fi thrillers with engaging characters, cynical humor, and (mostly!) plausible science. He is the author of the Joe Ballen series, Logan's World series, and Hyperia Jones series.

Originally from the wild and woolly region of Yorkshire, England, David now lives in wild and rocky Northern Ontario, Canada, with his patient and long-suffering wife, Hilary. He's passionate about science, especially astronomy and physics, and is a rabid science news follower. When not writing, you can find him driving his own personal starship, a 1991 Corvette ZR-1, or exploring the local hiking trails.

Find out more at www.davidmkelly.net

To sign up for the mailing list, go to www.davidmkelly.net/contact

You can also follow David through the following channels:

Facebook: facebook.com/David.Kelly.SF

Twitter: twitter.com/David_Kelly_SF

Goodreads: goodreads.com/DavidMKelly

Printed in Great Britain
by Amazon

52299402R00158